"I feel like I've just been kicked in the head by a horse, and I'm still expected to make life decisions for my kid."

Automatically, Asher's gaze shot to Harper, who was still chewing on her toy, but he couldn't help but to look back at Luna again. Was it possible that she was his child instead? No. Harper was *his*. He was certain of it.

When he glanced up again, he caught Willow studying Harper, her brows drawn together. He knew the questions in her eyes were mirroring his own. Their gazes connected for a few seconds, and then they both looked away.

He could have kissed Luna, who picked that moment for another round of giggles. Until she lifted both arms. To him. He swallowed, his gaze flitting to Willow. Her frown made it clear what she thought about that.

"Looks like you've won my daughter over."

But not you.

* * *

Book Five of The Coltons of Mustang Valley

* * *

If you're on Twitter, tell us what you think of Harlequin Romantic Suspense! #harlequinromsuspense

Dear Reader,

I am excited to share Asher and Willow's story with you. I loved having the chance to bring these two characters from very different backgrounds together while exploring the damage that long-held grudges can have on our hearts. I was privileged to collaborate with eleven fine authors in this continuity series, along with our talented editor, Carly Silver. Their ingenuity and patience have helped me to build a better story.

Moving into Mustang Valley and enveloping myself in the world of Payne Colton and his family have been a delight. I can't wait to see how all the pieces come together while getting to know new characters and savoring their romances along the way. I hope you're enjoying the ride as much as I am.

If you loved *In Colton's Custody*, you might also like my earlier titles for the Harlequin Romantic Suspense line, *Shielded by the Lawman* (Feb. 2019) and *Her Dark Web Defender* (Nov. 2019).

I like staying in contact with readers, no matter how you choose to connect. Sign up for my newsletter at www.dananussio.com; join me in the Coffee, Cupcakes and Contemporaries reader group (www.Facebook.com/groups/1426474880768003); or connect on Facebook (www.Facebook.com/DanaNussio) or Twitter (www.Twitter.com/DanaNussio1). You can even drop me a line on *real paper* at PO Box 5, Novi, MI 48376-0005.

Happy reading!

Dana Nussio

IN COLTON'S CUSTODY

Dana Nussio

HARLEQUIN
ROMANTIC
SUSPENSE

Special thanks and acknowledgment are given to
Dana Nussio for her contribution to
The Coltons of Mustang Valley miniseries.

Recycling programs
for this product may
not exist in your area.

ISBN-13: 978-1-335-62644-8

In Colton's Custody

Copyright © 2020 by Harlequin Books S.A.

This edition published by arrangement with Harlequin Books S.A.

For questions and comments about the quality of this book, please contact us at CustomerService@Harlequin.com.

Harlequin Enterprises ULC
22 Adelaide St. West, 40th Floor
Toronto, Ontario M5H 4E3, Canada
www.Harlequin.com

Printed in U.S.A.

Dana Nussio began telling "people stories" around the same time she started talking. She's continued both activities, nonstop, ever since. She left a career as an award-winning newspaper reporter to raise three daughters, but the stories followed her home as she discovered the joy of writing fiction. Now an award-winning author and member of Romance Writers of America's Honor Roll of bestselling authors, she loves telling emotional stories filled with honorable but flawed characters.

Books by Dana Nussio

Harlequin Romantic Suspense

The Coltons of Mustang Valley

In Colton's Custody

True Blue

Shielded by the Lawman
Her Dark Web Defender

Harlequin Superromance

True Blue

Strength Under Fire
Falling for the Cop

Visit the Author Profile page at
Harlequin.com for more titles.

To my hero of thirty years, Randy, who does all the cooking, endures my deadline mania and makes it possible for me to live my dream of writing stories all day. I love you. To our daughters, Marissa, Caterina and Alexa, who learned to fend for themselves during said deadlines and have grown into strong women who are courageously following their own dreams. And to Isabelle Drake, Veronica to my Betty, the academic who instructs me on how life imitates comic books and the friend who reminds me to live the real thing outside the pages.

Chapter 1

Asher Colton latched the barn door and strode toward the corral, his favorite boots scraping the dusty earth in a comfortable rhythm. That the man he'd known for only two days matched him in both pace and in the number of scuffs on his boots made Asher grin. Those were small similarities, and they didn't know anything for sure yet, so he schooled his features as he sneaked another glance at the guy next to him.

Unfortunately, Jace Smith caught him peeking, so Asher stared out over the open fields and banks of trees that made up Rattlesnake Ridge Ranch. With its rich red, Arizona soil stretching to the base of Mustang Valley Mountains and kissing the sky where the heights dipped, the Triple R was the only place Asher had ever been truly content.

Well, until recently.

Now the land he oversaw at least gave him an excuse

to look away from the newcomer and prepare himself for whatever question he would pose next.

Instead of asking one, Jace cupped both hands over his headful of dark hair. "That sun is already a killer out here, even this early in the morning."

The side of Asher's mouth lifted. The guy might have seven more years of life experience than Asher's thirty-three, but when it came to ranch education, their guest was as much a newborn as their spring calves were.

"What did you expect? It's May in Mustang Valley. Highs are always in the mideighties this time of year. It's not that different from anywhere in southeastern Arizona, is it?"

"Guess I spend too much time in the air-conditioning."

"Ya think? Anyway, I told you to wear a hat."

Asher adjusted his own and wiped sweat from his forehead as he'd already done a dozen times that morning. Unlike their guest, who'd been staying at the mansion the past few days, as ranch foreman, Asher had already been at work for hours.

"Yeah. Need to get me one," Jace said, as he pulled out a pair of sunglasses and slipped them on.

"Would be a good idea."

It was hard to believe anyone living in that part of the state wouldn't already own a decent cowboy hat, especially someone who might be, well, a *relative*. He pointed farther up the panel fence with cedar posts and caps.

"Come on. I promised to show you the new additions."

"Has it been a big season?"

"Great so far. We're getting several hundred calves a day."

"Are those good numbers?"

"Really good. Our operation runs over twenty thousand cows and another ten thousand heifers. Both Angus and Hereford. In case you don't know, cows are females that have had at least one calf, and heifers are females that haven't calved yet."

"I know that. I'm not that much of a city slicker."

"Good to know." Asher doubted Jace was telling the truth but didn't call him on his fib. It wasn't the guy's fault he'd been raised in the city. Or, possibly, by the wrong mother.

A few months earlier, Asher's whole family had been rocked by the revelation that his oldest brother, Colton Oil CEO Ace, had been switched at birth. Since then, his dad had been shot, a crime in which Ace was a suspect, and was in a coma; the family had worked to track down the "real" Ace. Jace's arrival at the ranch two days earlier had been a surprise, but if the information Jace had received was true, then they might have solved their mystery.

"This place is amazing. I'm lucky just to have seen it." Jace looked up and down the fencerow. "If not for the earthquake last month, I might never have found the courage to find out *for sure* if I'm one of the babies someone switched at that hospital."

"Tragedies definitely shake us up and spur us to action." Asher was talking about his own family, but the other man was too caught up in his story to notice. "Oh. Pardon the pun. You know, *spurs*."

Jace smiled over at him before returning to his story. "If I'd spoken to Luella anytime in the past decade, I could have asked her some questions about what that nurse had said, but I doubt she would have told me the truth. She never did about anything else."

Asher purposely didn't look at Jace then, giving him time to collect his composure. It was a kindness that men gave to each other.

"It's too bad you had such a difficult relationship with your…well, the woman who raised you."

That Jace always referred to Luella Smith by her first name was telling. Some mother she must have been.

Asher had kept it to himself that his two brothers were still tracking Luella, the woman who had apparently switched her healthy son for a sickly baby, Ace, but Jace's connection to her gave his story credibility.

"Bet that keeps you busy."

Caught lost in his thoughts, Asher blinked. Jace gestured toward the field. He was clearly trying to change the subject, a ploy Asher should have been familiar with since he used it whenever anyone brought up his ex-girlfriend, Nora.

"We're busy, all right. No sleep for ranchers or ranch hands during calving season. Poor Harper. Half of her nighttime diaper changes have come from the housekeepers and the kitchen staff lately."

Twice as many in the daytime, too, now that his most recent nanny had hightailed it out of town. His shoulders drooped over the slim pickings he would face in yet another candidate search. How was he supposed to prove that as a single dad, he could be a better parent than his father ever had been, when he couldn't keep consistent childcare for his six-month-old daughter?

"Cute kid, by the way."

"Thanks." Asher couldn't help grinning at that. It was hard not to like a guy who complimented his baby.

"Strange, isn't it?"

"What?" Asher slid a glance his way. "Not sleeping or changing diapers. I get a lot of practice at both."

"I bet you do, but that's not what I meant. It's just this whole situation. I still can't get used to it. I keep looking for any physical resemblance between us."

"Find any?"

"With you? Not so much."

"That would be less likely. Either way." Asher rushed to add the second part.

Why did he keep getting ahead of himself? They had no proof yet. He owed it to his family to remain skeptical until they did. Ace deserved at least that much.

Anyway, Jace was right. Asher looked no more like the guy than he did his adopted brother, Rafe. Jace bore no resemblance to Asher's full siblings, blond twins Marlowe and Callum. On the other hand, with all that dark hair and those blue eyes, Jace fit right in with Asher's half brother, Grayson, and half sister, Ainsley, the other two children of Payne's first marriage. Everyone at the mansion had noticed.

"Guess we'll know for sure soon enough."

Asher startled as the other man seemed to have read his thoughts. "S'pose so."

He gave the dirt an extra kick and ground his molars. They might as well have been talking about the weather rather than the life-altering reality that Jace might be the real Ace.

Just thinking it made him feel disloyal to the man he knew as Ace. If only they could turn the clock back four months, to the time before that mysterious email had dropkicked his family's world and the structure of Colton Oil. Before they'd learned about the baby switch. He longed for those days of blissful ignorance.

"How do you think Ace is doing?" Jace asked.

Not as well as you. Somehow, Asher managed not to say that out loud, though Jace's questions from the past two days were starting to annoy him. "As well as can be expected for a guy whose life has been flipped on its head."

"I get that."

Asher shrugged. Jace clearly could relate to receiving news that had changed his life, but it was probably easier for someone to discover that a silver spoon might be slipped in his mouth than to have one yanked out, along with a few teeth.

"It's just that Ace is the only one of your siblings I haven't met yet," Jace continued. "I totally understand why the others are keeping their distance until after the DNA test. I appreciate that they at least dropped by and introduced themselves."

"Six of seven isn't too bad for just two days."

His siblings were curious. No one could blame them for that when they might have been meeting Payne Colton's *real* firstborn with his late first wife, Tessa, for the first time.

"But Ace's situation is a little different," Jace continued.

"He's been busy, too."

If lying low back at his loft condo in the city's industrial zone—or at the Dales Inn in town—counted for *busy* anyway. In Ace's defense, he had to stay put while the media trucks lingered at the hospital and just outside the ranch's main gate.

"Is he still considered a suspect in your dad's attempted murder?"

Asher bit back the temptation to tell Jace to mind his own damn business. Depending on the results of the test they'd scheduled, Colton family matters just might *be* his business.

"He's been questioned and told not to leave town. Now you know everything I do."

"What about Payne? Any updates on him?"

"Nothing beyond what Ainsley told you two nights ago."

"That's what I figured."

If Jace noticed the edge to Asher's voice, he didn't show

it. Anyway, there was no more to say. His dad was still in a coma, and there was no guarantee when, or even *if,* he would ever awaken.

"He'll wake up."

Asher stiffened, the other man rightly guessing his thoughts again.

"Hope so."

"When did you say Ainsley would pick me up for the test?"

"About twelve thirty. Appointment's at one." Not soon enough for Asher. At least then it would be her turn to play Twenty Questions with Jace.

"I knew that. I'm just nervous, I guess."

Asher shifted his feet. The Coltons weren't the only ones whose lives were in flux. Still, that didn't make him want to talk about it. Or think about it. Good thing they'd finally reached the near side of the calving pasture, where several cows were nibbling grass and nursing their young.

"These are some of our newest arrivals."

He leaned forward to rest his forearms on the six-inch-wide fence cap, and the other man followed his example.

"Wow, the calves are amazing."

That was something they could agree on. If nothing else on the Triple R made sense to Asher lately, this land and the cattle were things he understood.

"See that calf closest to the fence?" He pointed to an animal with distinctive markings on its head and legs. It was pulling voraciously on its mother's teat. "He just showed up last night. Thought he was never going to get up on his legs."

"Looks like he made it."

"Yeah." His lips lifted. After a rocky start, the little guy was doing just fine. Asher had secretly been calling the calf "Lucky Boy," but he couldn't let it get out that the foreman was nicknaming new arrivals.

"What was wrong with him?" Jace asked.

"A healthy calf usually stands up and nurses in the first two hours. Those from difficult births, like him, sometimes take longer. It's critical that calves nurse within the first four hours to benefit from the antibodies in colostrum. If they don't, we're forced to tube feed them."

Jace made a sad face as he watched the animal several seconds longer.

"Poor little guy. What did you end up doing?"

"Just as we started to intervene to give him his best chance for survival, he popped up on his feet and went to his mom for breakfast."

"Sounds like a lucky calf to be born on the Triple R. Are you calling him Lucky?"

"We don't give them nicknames."

"That's not a rule, is it?"

Asher shifted his head so Jace wouldn't see his grin. He still didn't want to get ahead of himself, but he had a good feeling about Jace. It would be nice to have at least one sibling who cared about animals as much as he did. His cell buzzed in his back pocket, interrupting his thoughts. He pulled out the phone and checked the number to make sure it wasn't Neda, one of the housekeepers, calling about Harper. Usually, he let business calls go to voice mail and answered them when he returned to his office at the back of the barn, but he froze at the words on the caller ID. *Mustang Valley General Hospital?* Had his dad's condition changed? Or worse? Maybe Payne Colton wasn't the kind of dad people wrote greeting cards about, but that didn't mean Asher wanted him to…

"Sorry. I should take this."

He stepped away and turned his back before tapping

the button to answer the call. "Rattlesnake Ridge Ranch. May I help you?"

"Have I reached *Asher* Colton?" a female voice asked.

"This is Asher." He squeezed the phone tighter and pressed it against his ear.

"My name is Anne Sewall. I am the administrator at Mustang Valley General Hospital."

"Has something happened with my father?" he blurted before he could stop himself.

His heart thudding, he clamped his free arm to his side and waited for the worst news he could imagine.

"Oh. No." The woman made a strange sound into the phone. "You'll have to call the nurse's station on the floor for specifics on your father's condition. I'm sorry for causing you distress."

"Then why *are* you calling?"

It was a testament to his superior restraint that he didn't include *the hell* in his question. What had she thought he would assume? It wasn't a secret in town that his dad was a patient at Mustang Valley General.

"There's another, unrelated matter that we need to discuss. I was hoping that you could bring your infant daughter to my office today and—"

"What are you talking about? And what do you want with Harper? Was there something the pediatrician missed in her six-month checkup?"

"No." Her nervous chuckle filtered through the connection. "It's not that. Again, I apologize, Mr. Colton. I realize that this is unusual. But if you'll just meet me in my office, I'll explain the whole situation."

"I would rather that you explain it right now." His mother had always called him stubborn, and he was proving her right, but he couldn't help it. This woman had already frightened him *twice*, and he wasn't about to let her go for a hat trick.

"That would be highly irregular." She cleared her throat again. "This is a delicate matter. We don't customarily divulge this type of information over the phone."

"Well, I would say that it's not *usual* to phone a community member out of the blue and, in the space of two minutes, give him concerns about both his father and his child." He didn't care if he was the one jumping to those conclusions. She should have explained herself better.

"Fine." She sighed. "Obviously, this information would be more appropriate if given in person."

"Noted. So?"

"I'm sorry to inform you that there's a possibility that your daughter, Harper Grace Colton, and another infant, also born on November 2, might have been accidentally switched in Mustang Valley General's nursery."

"Again?"

He didn't care if his question came out as a yelp. Was this a joke? In what realm of possibility could there be two Colton babies—albeit forty years apart—who'd been switched at birth?

"How could you let this happen?"

"Now, we don't know anything for certain, Mr. Colton. That is why we're asking you and the other party to bring your infants in immediately for DNA tests."

She prattled on about how sorry the hospital board was for this possible mix-up, but he wasn't listening. All he could think about was his sweet little Harper, with her crop of light brown hair, those dimples like his and eyes as brown as Nora's. How could there be a chance that she wasn't his? Or Nora's, if a mother who abandoned her baby could even count as one.

Harper was his. She looked just like him. Everyone said

so. He shook his head to dismiss the unfathomable possibility that they weren't even related.

"What kind of bumbling hospital are you guys running?"

"We deeply regret this possible mistake. Thankfully, we'll be able to clear up the questions with a DNA test. It won't hurt the infants. Just a cheek swab."

She spoke about it as if it was only an inconvenience, like an online retailer mixing up two customers' packages. As if the results of those tests wouldn't have the power to destroy not one but *two* families.

"I'll be there as soon as I can."

With that, he clicked off the call. He didn't care if his tone was rude.

"Everything all right?"

Asher's shoulder blades squeezed together. He'd forgotten that he wasn't alone. He glanced at Jace. Concern etched in lines between the man's brows. Jace's shoulders were back, his arms pressed to his sides, as if he was preparing himself for bad news. The kind that could devastate a guy who thought he'd just found his father.

"It's not about Dad," Asher said automatically, not even bothering to include *my*. It was the decent thing not to worry the guy unnecessarily about Payne, like the hospital administrator had done to him.

Jace's shoulders dropped forward. "Thought I'd never get the chance to meet him. If we find out he and Tessa really are my parents, then I already missed the chance to know one of them."

Asher nodded, staring at the ground. He couldn't imagine what it would be like for a guy to track down his possible biological parents, only to learn that one of them had passed away years before. He couldn't think about that just then, either. One crisis at a time.

"Look, there's something I need to take care of. Can you hang around the ranch until my sister picks you up? Our cook, Dulcie, will make you whatever you like for lunch if you stop by the main house kitchen."

"I know my way around. I've met Dulcie, too."

"Oh. Right." He wasn't thinking clearly.

"Don't worry about me. I can find something to occupy my time." Jace pulled his phone from his pocket. "Maybe I'll even catch up with my friends back home. They probably think I've vanished by now."

"Probably. Okay. Thanks."

Asher started toward the house.

"And Asher?"

He looked back once more.

"Whatever it is? I'm sure it will be okay."

He nodded, unable to trust his voice. Though he could have told their guest where he was going and why, he wasn't ready to share it. Even if Jace might have understood the trauma of a switched-at-birth situation better than anyone. And even if they could have carpooled to Mustang Valley General since Jace was headed to the same lab. Heck, with Dad still there, they should have applied for a Colton bulk discount on their medical bills.

Asher continued up the path past the rows of white barns and outbuildings. He had to force himself not to run to the house and his own wing on the third floor, where Harper would be just waking up from her morning nap. Once inside his living quarters, he sprinted all the way to the nursery, unbuttoning his sweaty plaid shirt as he went. He would grab something clean on his way out the door.

In her room, Harper was already sitting up in her crib and making cute sounds for the video monitor that Dulcie watched from the kitchen. Wisps of the baby's barely there hair stood up, punk-rocker style.

"Where's my Harper girl?"

She squealed, her wide, toothless grin stretching even farther.

His possible big brother had said everything would be all right. But Jace couldn't promise that. Just like no one could guarantee that Payne Colton would awaken from his coma and demand an accounting of the first-quarter books at Colton Oil. Depending on the outcome of today's DNA test, Asher's life and that of his sweet baby girl might never be okay again.

Chapter 2

Willow Merrill startled at the sound of the blaring horn while driving her mini SUV past one of the few stoplights along Mustang Boulevard, also called "Mustang Valley Boulevard" on some old maps. Okay, that light had been pink. Well, more fuchsia.

"Sorry."

She waved at the other driver, who scowled back at her through the open window. At least it hadn't been one of her day-care clients. She needed to calm down and pay attention to her driving if she wanted them to arrive at the hospital without heading straight to the ER.

At least she didn't have to worry that the honk had frightened her six-month-old baby. Luna's squeals coming from the rear-facing infant car seat in the back told Willow her daughter was just fine.

"What are you laughing about back there?"

The baby cackled as she did at all her mother's jokes.

Great. Her kid was going to be a thrill seeker, a luxury Willow had never known.

Her kid. Willow swallowed. How had she forgotten, even for a few seconds, why they were headed to the hospital in the first place? This couldn't be happening. The woman on the phone had to be wrong. One more thing in a week that had started out bad and had gone downhill from there. Her gaze flicked to the notebook in the passenger seat. She'd written all the details from the call on it before giving her own instructions to her staff and racing out with Luna in her arms.

There had to be a mistake. How could there be a chance that precious Luna wasn't her child? The infant's tawny skin was as dark as hers, and the child's capful of brown hair had already begun to curl. If only basic resemblance could guarantee that they were mother and daughter. Nearly a third of Arizona's population was of Latino heritage like her, so babies with Luna's hair and skin coloring were hardly rare in Mustang Valley.

An ache formed in Willow's chest, squeezing and twisting. Heat gathered behind her eyes. No, she wouldn't cry. Luna needed her to be strong. She needed her mother. And nothing could convince her that Luna wasn't the baby she'd once cradled inside her own body and had met at her first breath. She'd promised *this child* a life filled with the type of security Willow had only dreamed of. Could she have made that vow to the wrong infant?

Managing to avoid more near misses on her trip along the town's main drag, she pulled into the hospital campus and parked at the five-story building's main entrance.

She buckled Luna in the stroller the child loathed and rolled it through the automatic doors. Following the signs, she headed down a long corridor and stopped in front of the administrative offices.

A woman in a light pink pantsuit pounced on her the moment she pushed Luna inside.

"You must be Mrs. Merrill." The woman pumped Willow's hand, a flush climbing her own pale neck, her blond bob bouncing. "I'm Anne Sewall, but please call me Anne. I appreciate your coming over so quickly."

"It's Willow. And thanks for giving me the information over the phone."

The older woman's glasses shifted as she wrinkled her nose. "I didn't have a choice, since the other party had insisted that I release the details that way."

Other party. That was the only descriptor Willow had for someone who might be about to steal away her child. She wasn't ready to wrap her thoughts around the possibility that another mother might be raising an infant biologically connected to her.

"Will your husband be joining us this morning?"

Willow shook her head. "No. He was my ex-husband. I mean, well, both he and his new wife are deceased."

The last development was recent enough that this was the first time Willow had been forced to explain it to anyone beyond close friends. The part about Xavier leaving her for another woman, though, was well-traveled history.

"I'm sorry, Mrs. Merrill."

"Thank you." She would have preferred to say, "don't be," but she couldn't tell a stranger that.

Anne wrung her hands and then crouched in front of the stroller where Luna was already fussing and wiggling against the harness safety restraint.

"You must be Miss Luna Mariana Merrill. You're a beauty."

The baby scrunched her face, so to avoid what would surely be a good wail, Willow unsnapped the buckle and lifted the child into her arms.

"She takes compliments better once she's out of that contraption."

The administrator struggled to her feet and pointed to a place next to the wall. "Why don't you park the stroller right there and take a seat inside my office? I'm sure the others will arrive shortly."

An image of a happily married couple and child, a family worthy of a Thomas Kinkade painting, invaded Willow's thoughts as she pulled the diaper bag from the stroller handle. Would a judge see that intact family unit as a better choice for *both* babies if this awful premise turned out to be fact? She shook her head to push away the thought, but nothing could calm her insides.

Just as she stepped inside Anne's office, a beep signaled that the reception-area door had been opened.

Anne held up her index finger. "I'll be right back."

From somewhere outside the room, the administrator's muffled voice melded with a baritone one. Willow dragged one of the visitors' chairs as far as she could from the other, sat and settled Luna on her lap.

Needing something to do with her hands, she straightened her baby's mint-green top and smoothed her fingers over the striped leggings. Then she gripped one of the open sides of her chambray shirt that she'd thrown on over her clothes and tried to cover her bare legs. If only she'd had time to change out of her work clothes.

"We'll be fine, sweetie. Just fine." She only hoped what she'd told her daughter was true.

She straightened as heavy footfalls grew closer to the office.

"Right in here."

Anne's voice preceded her into the room. A man followed her inside, carrying an infant whose photo could have been given as Luna's direct opposite. The baby had ivory skin and light brown hair, and she was dressed in a fancy floral sundress and matching headband.

She didn't resemble Willow, either, if having brown eyes didn't count. Though the babies were supposed to be the same age, this one appeared smaller than Luna, but that might have had to do with the man carrying her. The one who crowded the doorway with those broad shoulders and muscular arms, emphasized by his fitted black T-shirt.

Anne gestured toward the guest chair and then crossed behind her desk and sat.

"Come in and have a seat so that we can begin."

The man didn't budge, though, as his light green eyes focused on Willow. Something about him struck her as familiar, but then he looked like a cowboy, and ranch hands were almost as common as cattle in the area. He had tousled brown hair, long on top and trimmed close at his neck. His bronzed skin was probably the result of too much outdoor labor and not enough sunscreen rather than any genetic bent. Those thigh-hugging jeans and the boots that had missed a shine or a dozen didn't fit, either.

Well, the jeans did.

At the sound of someone clearing her throat, Willow blinked several times, her neck and cheeks burning. What was she doing? Had she been staring at the guy who might have come there to take her child? Sure, he'd been looking back, but probably only at Luna, as he searched for any resemblance to signal that she was his. Well, she wasn't. Willow's arms immediately tightened around her baby, who squirmed and whined.

Anne gestured to them. "Willow Merrill, I'd like you to meet—"

The cowboy took one step inside the room and waved to interrupt her. "Please, allow me. I'm Asher. This is Harper."

Though his expression had been stoic until then, it transformed, twin dimples and all, the moment he pressed his cheek to the top of his child's head. Something Willow chose not to define squeezed inside her chest. She and this *Asher* weren't on the same side in this situation, and she needed to remember that.

"And that young lady is Luna."

As Anne completed the introductions, she shifted in her seat and gestured toward the guest chair again. This time Asher sidled over and settled with Harper on his knee. The infants peeked at each other, taking turns hiding their faces.

"Pleased to meet you, Luna." Asher cleared his throat. "And Willow."

"You, too," she said, though she was anything but pleased. He probably thought he was being cute by speaking to her daughter first. She wasn't impressed.

Anne folded her hands together and nodded at Willow.

"I'm so glad you were able to get away from the day-care center to come in this morning. Tender Years, right?" She waited for Willow's nod before turning to Asher. "And I know how busy you must be on the ranch at this time of year, so I appreciate your both coming in so quickly."

He nodded, shoving his hand back through his hair in what was probably a habit. Neither stated the obvious that they'd had no choice but to accept that invitation.

"I thought it would be easier to share the information on the possible switch with all of you at the same time, but you both must agree to discussing these matters publicly, in accordance with HIPAA medical information laws."

"Fine by me," Asher said.

"Me, too." She was still hanging on the words *possible switch*. That still meant it might not be true.

Anne glanced over at the open door. "You didn't say, Asher. Will Harper's mother be joining us?"

Her *mother*? His wife? Willow shot a glance at the empty doorway. As if it wasn't bad enough that she'd been checking out the guy who should have been her adversary, she'd never considered that there would be a *she*.

"Long gone," he blurted and then cleared his throat. "I mean, my former partner is deceased."

Those two things didn't mean close to the same thing, but that was none of her business. Even if she couldn't get over how coincidental it was that both babies had already lost a parent at such a tender age, she couldn't worry about that just then.

Willow cleared her throat. "I'm sorry to hear that."

"Please accept my condolences," Anne said.

Asher nodded, his gaze sliding to Willow. "Luna's dad?"

"Same."

"Oh. Sorry."

He didn't remark on the fact that they'd both experienced a loss, so she didn't bring it up, either. Since there was more to her story than she'd revealed, she figured he'd skipped a few chapters, as well.

Her daughter saved her from having to say more by wiggling in her lap and starting to fuss. Unlike the infant Asher held, Luna wasn't a fan of sitting still and watching grown-ups talk. Willow hoped the pacifier from her bag would at least comfort her for a while.

Anne planted her elbows on her desk and clasped her hands together, drawing their attention back to her.

"Okay, here's why I called you in today. We've received an anonymous call from the concerned friend of a hospital volunteer. That volunteer was worried that she accidentally switched two newborn female infants on November 2. She couldn't stop thinking about it, but she was too afraid to speak up. Her friend reported it instead."

"Did you say 'anonymous'?" Willow blurted. Could it have been related to an unsigned letter she'd received the week before at the day-care center?

"How could that have happened?"

Willow blinked as the man seated next to her posed the question she should have been asking. That threatening note back at the office probably had nothing to do with this matter, and it certainly wasn't as critical.

"And why was a volunteer even in there?" she asked. "Why would someone not even on staff have the opportunity to make a mistake like that?"

Anne opened her mouth to answer, but Asher didn't give her the chance.

"Doesn't this hospital have safeguards to prevent that? At least by now?"

His last comment made no sense to Willow, but she nodded anyway.

She pointed to her bare wrist. "Yeah, those bracelets that the nurse assistant checks every time she rolls a bassinet into a patient's room should have prevented something like this."

Anne cleared her throat, her gaze sliding to Asher before she addressed them both. "No, volunteers shouldn't have been involved in those critical moments. And, yes, there were safeguards in place. But there were extenuating circumstances on that November day when both of your infants were born."

"What were those?"

Asher's voice was tight, as if he was trying to control his frustration.

"First, we were understaffed that night. Flu season hit

early. Second, it was a full moon, so all the birthing rooms were occupied."

Willow leaned forward, startling her daughter, who'd just nodded off. "You're going to blame this on a 'full moon'? Isn't that an old wives' tale anyway?"

"Ask any labor and delivery nurse, and he or she will tell you it's not." Anne smiled and then shook her head. "But, no, I'm not going to blame the situation on anything. I just wanted you to know how something like this could have happened this time."

Willow nodded and gestured with a circular motion for her to continue.

"There were five infants born on that night shift, all between 2100 and 0000. That's between nine and midnight. The nurses, volunteers and even the on-call obstetrician were quickly moving back and forth among the rooms."

Asher straightened and shifted his contented infant higher on his thigh. "If there were five babies, why are *we* the only ones sitting here?"

Anne held her hands wide. "The caller said the possible switch was between two female infants. The other three born that night were males."

Willow blinked several times, a memory popping into her thoughts. "It's also because Luna went into distress and had to be delivered with forceps, isn't it? She was rushed from the room right after delivery to be examined."

"Harper had the cord around her neck," Asher said. "So, same situation. Rushed from the birthing room. It's still no excuse. Never was."

"You're right," Anne said. "But at least we can see how a volunteer could have been called into service and how a rushed mistake could have been made when snapping on the bracelets, right?"

Willow shrugged, and Asher did the same.

When neither spoke, Anne continued with her explanation.

"We're going to clear up these questions quickly. We'll be conducting legally admissible maternity and paternity DNA tests, free of charge. The tests will compare twenty of your genetic markers to those of both infants and determine the probability that either of you could be a parent of either child."

The woman's words sounded more like a lecture in Willow's college biology class than any real-life situation involving her and Luna.

"Why do the tests need to be legally admissible?" Willow asked, but she had already come up with her own answer before Anne lowered her head and stared at her hands. If the hospital had made the mistake, the board would expect a lawsuit. They would be getting one.

Asher's arms tightened around his daughter, finally causing her to squirm. Willow leaned forward and studied the infant. Harper didn't look like her. She also appeared to have a calm nature. No one would ever have described Willow that way. She was intense and always moving, more like Luna.

"This is crazy!" Asher popped to his feet, startling Harper, who whimpered. "This is my child. You might think there's been a switch, but you're wrong."

Anne stood and stepped around the end of her desk. "Please take a seat, Mr. Colton. We will figure this—"

"You're a *Colton*?"

Willow leaped up as well, and Luna let out a wail, her pacifier dropping. Willow was surprised that she managed to catch it. After all, the administrator had just invoked the name of the family she hated most in the world.

She bounced and swayed to calm her child before speaking again in a lower voice. "You're Asher... *Colton*?"

"Yeah. So? I already introduced myself."

"Not quite," Anne noted. "You didn't say your last name."

No wonder he'd looked familiar to Willow earlier. She'd probably *seen* him before, holding court with the rest of his family, considered Mustang Valley's royalty. Maybe spinning around town in one of their luxury cars.

"Please sit. You're upsetting your daughters."

They'd been staring warily at each other, but at Anne's words they glanced at their own children and lowered into their seats again.

Willow's gaze lifted to Asher again. From his innocent expression, she would have thought he'd never received a look of loathing in his life. Given his last name, she doubted that.

"So, yes, I'm a Colton, if that matters. It didn't save me from having to be involved in a mess like this again, did it?"

Willow stared back at him. *If that matters?* Hell yes, it did. Then something else he'd said struck her. *Again.* Mustang Valley was a small town. Even before it had hit the news, she'd heard about his family's infant-switch scandal. That didn't mean she had to pity them.

The Coltons might have once been able to take everything from her mother, but she wouldn't allow their Richie Rich spawn to take her only child. Even if he was Luna's biological father.

She sneaked another peek at the infant in Asher's lap. If Luna could be his, Harper could be *hers*. Could she bear living in the same town as the child she'd carried for nine months without having the chance to know or love her? On the other hand, could she give up the baby she'd nursed, diapered and loved for six months?

"I can't do this," she said.

"Well, then, let's get this over with."

Asher's words crushed hers, contradicting them in both loyalty and intent.

Didn't it matter to him which infant he took home? Was his daughter as interchangeable as one of the cows on the Triple R?

"We can go to the lab right now," he continued.

Anne gripped her hands together. "Unfortunately, we can't do the test today."

"But you asked us to bring our children in immediately."

Asher's voice lifted an octave, but, somehow, he remained in his seat this time.

"Yes, I said that, but when I called the lab, I discovered that they were booked all day. I scheduled you both for ten tomorrow morning."

Willow drew her brows together. "How can that be possible? This is a hospital."

"All emergency lab work will be handled immediately," Anne said. "But *elective* lab work requires an appointment."

"You don't call possibly switched infants an emergency?" Why was Willow making Asher's argument for him? She wasn't in a rush to find out answers that could crush them, but she couldn't help herself. "Or maybe a potential *lawsuit*?"

Asher tilted his head, studying the administrator.

"Is that a *usual* practice in the lab, or were those new rules announced today?"

At his odd question, Willow peeked over at him again. She was reminded again of headlines like "Colton Oil CEO Ousted" and "Colton Patriarch Shot: Son Questioned," in the weekly *Mustang Valley Times* and on the local news.

"Let me guess. Some other testing is taking priority over two six-month-olds."

Anne straightened. "I don't have any details regarding the backup at the lab, and, even if I did, I wouldn't be able to discuss them because of privacy laws."

The administrator didn't make eye contact with Willow, but she peeked at Asher before she lowered her gaze to her hands. That tell was the only confirmation Willow needed.

Why didn't someone just say that it had to do with the Coltons? Something bigger than even a possible mix-up of Payne Colton's grandchild. Since the family company had paid for updates to make the hospital a state-of-the-art facility fifteen years before, they probably thought of it as one of their properties, just like they ran Colton Oil. Just like they *owned* Mustang Valley itself.

"Fine. Tomorrow at ten." Asher gathered his daughter and marched out of the office.

"Fine," Willow echoed, before collecting her diaper bag, propping Luna on her hip and stomping out after him.

He was probably just angry that the news and the delay had disrupted his schedule and his charmed life. She had more to be upset about than he did. As if it wasn't bad enough dealing with the awful possibility that Luna might not be hers and trying to explain her inappropriate reaction to a man who'd turned out to be a Colton, now she would be forced to face him again the next day.

So, it continued. Everything bad in her life started out with the Coltons and only went downhill from there.

Chapter 3

"I didn't think you'd ever call," the woman whined into the phone the moment she answered.

His sigh came through the line, just as she caught sight of her profile in the mirror. Neck skin taut. Face flawless, she decided, as she brushed her fingertips along her own jawline. Still beautiful. She'd deserved better than she'd been given.

"Are you listening to me?"

"What? Oh. What did you say?"

"I said I told you I would call as soon as it was done. And I did."

"Yes, you did." She pushed her shoulders back and faced the mirror straight on. The last thing she needed was for there to be frustration in the ranks. Not when she was so close to getting the revenge that she'd craved so deeply it felt embedded in her soul.

"You always keep your promises...for us. And I appreciate each one."

He harrumphed. "That's better."

The man filled her in on the newest development that had required creativity outside her specific instructions. She wouldn't stomp on the guy's ideas when he was helping her to get what she wanted.

"Why does it matter?" he asked in the cajoling tone that had long since begun to annoy her.

"What are you talking about?"

"*Him.* Why does he still matter?"

Because he did. Why couldn't the guy get it through his marble-sized brain? Wasn't it bad enough that she'd been forced to see a reminder of all she'd lost right downtown that morning? She smoothed her hands over her floral-print skirt and matching summer sweater set.

"Like I said before, I need to put this behind me, put *him* behind me, so I can think about only you." She paused to turn on the syrupy charm. "That's what you want, isn't it? It's what I want."

She nearly choked on her own saccharine tone, but when he didn't respond immediately, she knew he was still on board. For now. She gave him his next instructions, made some promises that she would keep when hell was covered with ice cubes and then clicked off the phone with barely a goodbye.

Despite too many delays, her plan was finally coming along. Someone in Mustang Valley was going down. Soon. Once that happened, she could kick her assistant to the curb, as well.

Asher strapped Harper in her stroller, slid off the silly headband that one of the new housekeepers had insisted went with that dress and popped her favorite car-keys-style teething toy in her chubby hands. Then, taking a deep breath, he wheeled her down the hall to the entrance.

"Let's get you out of here so you can have a fresh diaper."

He could pretend that escaping that office was for his daughter's sake, but he was the one who had to get out before he said something that could make things worse. As if that was even possible. No, they'd hit the rock bottom of horrible the moment he'd received the news that his child might not be his.

Now the DNA test to prove or disprove that premise would be delayed so that the hospital lab could fawn over his family and confirm whether Jace was the real Ace.

He pushed the button for the hospital's wheelchair-accessible door and waited for it to swing open before pushing the stroller through. "You okay, little darlin'?"

He could have kicked himself for his outburst in the administration office that made Harper tear up, but she seemed to have no lasting effects. Instead, she happily chewed on her keys, still the same sunshine she'd been every day of her life, no matter who provided day care for her.

She pulled the toy away from her lips and began another round of her "da-da-da-da" song that she'd begun recently, though she hadn't added any more words to her collection yet. A lump of emotion collected in his throat. Her tune got him every time.

As he reached the curb of the circular drive where cars lined to pick up patients, he paused. Willow Merrill hadn't caught up with him, but why did he care? She wanted nothing to do with him, and that feeling was mutual. What was her problem anyway? From the moment she'd learned his last name, she'd looked furious.

What had his family done this time? Had one of his

brothers dated her and dumped her in the past? Asher might have had his share of dating escapades, before Nora, but he was innocent when it came to Willow Merrill. He'd never met her before. He was certain of it.

There was no way he would have forgotten those intense eyes, the color of the seasoned terra-cotta pots at the main house, not to mention that mass of deep brown curls. Luna had twisted her fingers in it a few times while they'd sat in that office. He hated that he'd been jealous of that baby and her lucky hands.

Asher blinked away the image and the unwelcome tingles that came with it. What was he thinking? He didn't date anymore. He wanted only one female in his life, and this one needed him to provide regular bottles, fun nighttime baths and dry diapers in addition to the lavish attention she deserved.

He wouldn't let Harper down by losing focus on what was important. He was her dad. First. Always. And if he were considering some private comfort, it wouldn't be with someone who could take away his child.

"Were you waiting for me?"

Asher jerked his head to find the woman he had *not* just been thinking about pushing her stroller up behind him.

"No. Just trying to catch my breath." At least the second part was true. If he had been waiting for her, it was only because he'd learned she owned a day-care center. There couldn't be any other reason.

"I get that."

Willow appeared to be taking a few fortifying breaths herself as she stared out into the parking lot. She was tall, he couldn't help noticing. Barely shorter than his six feet in height, even in slip-on tennis shoes. Her legs were also impossibly long beneath the cuffs of her jean shorts. He hadn't missed those legs before, but he doubted any straight man under ninety would have. And those older than that, only because they wouldn't get a good look at them. *Willowy*. Strange how she seemed to fit her name, as if her parents had done an excellent job of predicting the statuesque woman their daughter would become.

In the stroller next to her, Luna flailed her arms and struggled against her harness straps as if to remind him she was there.

"You hate being trapped in there, don't you, Miss Luna?" He smiled down at her. "Couldn't blame her if she hates this whole day. I know I do."

Willow's posture drooped then, her head tilting forward, as if the weight of the information they'd learned that morning had parked on her shoulders. Her hands shifted from the stroller handle to the base of her neck, where she bunched those riotous curls.

She must have misjudged the ramp on the pavement, though, as the stroller pitched forward. A shriek escaping her throat, she lunged for it, but Asher caught the runaway cart first, while keeping one hand on Harper's stroller.

"Whoa there, NASCAR Nellie. Trying to make a break for it?"

"Thanks for the catch," she said as she reclaimed the handle, "but she probably isn't in the mood for jokes after that meeting. She's been working up to a good cry from the moment we got here. And you can see how much she hates her stroller."

Asher would have asked Willow if she was talking about her daughter or herself when she'd spoken of the impending tears, if Luna hadn't picked the moment to prove her wrong by throwing her head back and giggling.

"Does she always sound like that when she's crying? If so, I need to come up with more one-liners."

Willow gave him a mean look but then shrugged. "Further proof that I don't know anything today."

"Me, neither. I feel like I've just been kicked in the head by a horse, and I'm still expected to make life decisions for my kid."

Automatically, his gaze shot to Harper, who was still chewing on her toy, but he couldn't help but to look back at Luna again. Was it possible that she was his child instead? No. Harper was *his*. He was certain of it.

When he glanced up again, he caught Willow studying Harper, her brows drawn together. He knew the questions in her eyes were mirroring his own. Their gazes connected for a few seconds, and then they both looked away.

He could have kissed Luna, who picked that moment for another round of giggles. Until she lifted both arms. To *him*. He swallowed, his gaze flitting to the child's mother. Her frown made it clear what she thought about that.

"Looks like you've won my daughter over."

But not you. He shrugged. "You already said she hates the stroller. She's just thinking I'm the patsy who'll help her escape."

She scoffed, but he figured that was the best answer he could expect to get from her.

He gestured toward the hospital door. "Everything in there was, well, crazy. The news. The delay on testing. All of it. I don't know about you, but I'm going out of my mind."

Though her gaze narrowed, she nodded. "Yeah, me, too."

"Do you think we could go somewhere and just, you know, talk about it? I could use someone to talk to right now, and if you're half as freaked out as I am, maybe you could, too."

She didn't say yes, but she hadn't automatically refused, either, so he licked his suddenly dry lips and tried again.

"We have some brand-new calves on the ranch. Maybe we could take the girls out to one of the barns to see—"

"Pigs will fly before I step foot on the Triple R."

"Okay." He stretched the word out. "That's a long time."

"Look. Sorry. I don't mean to be rude, but…" She shook her head and pushed her stroller forward. "I'll just see you tomorrow—"

"I know the ranch can be, well, *big*. How about we talk at your place, then?"

She stopped but didn't look back at him. "Not going to happen."

"It's not like that. I mean… Well, how about somewhere *neutral*? Like Bubba's Diner."

"I couldn't eat."

"Then what about Java Jane's? Just coffee. Half an hour. Tops."

She was still shaking her head. He'd never begged a woman to stay with him before, except Nora, and she'd left anyway. Those two situations were nothing alike, but that didn't explain why it had become so critical to him that Willow would say yes.

Was it more than that she owned a childcare facility and he needed to find a new nanny for his daughter? Or even how she'd reacted when she'd found out about his family? Could it have been because she was the only one who might understand the fear and misgivings inside him that threatened to eat their way out?

For what felt like hours, she didn't answer, but finally she looked back at him.

"Just thirty minutes?"

"Absolutely."

"I'll meet you there." This time she headed down the walk.

He'd won. He should just keep his mouth shut and wait for a better time to ask, but the words escaped all on their own.

"And when we get there you can tell me why you automatically hate me because I'm a Colton."

Chapter 4

Willow yanked open the door to Java Jane's, propped it with the stroller wheel, pushed the door wider and angled the contraption inside. She pulled off her sunglasses and waited a few seconds for her eyes to adjust to the muted industrial lighting in the building with its black-painted ceiling, bare brick interior walls, long counters with high-back stools and a spattering a tables and chairs.

Asher stood up from the table in the corner and hurried over to her.

"Sorry. I would have gotten that door for you."

"I could handle it perfectly well by myself, thank you."

"I see that."

He flattened his lips into a line as if attempting to suppress a smile. He failed.

"I figured you'd decided not to come."

"I almost didn't."

She'd also parked down the street with the air-conditioning

running long enough to blow through a quarter tank of fuel, but she wasn't about to tell him that.

"You weren't needed at *the ranch*?"

"I could step out for an hour or two. What about you at the center?"

"I checked in. The staff said it's been an uneventful day. After I left anyway." In fact, Candace Hill, her longtime employee and friend, had told her to take her time getting coffee after the harrowing morning she'd spent.

"Hello, darlin'."

Willow blinked, and her arm jerked back, but Asher missed all of it, already crouching in front of Luna's stroller. Her daughter beamed and lifted her arms for him to pick her up. The traitor. She would have to teach her to be more cautious around handsome men. If the test results gave her that chance to educate Luna about anything.

"We're over here."

Instead of lifting the child, he guided them to the table where Harper sat, holding a toy in her hands and guiding it to her mouth. A second high chair had been arranged near the first, and he'd pushed the next table over to allow for stroller parking.

"Thought you said you didn't expect me to come."

He shrugged, then pointed to the seats for the infants. "I thought Luna might prefer to sit in one of those."

Good guess. She continued to frown instead of saying so.

"I hoped you would come," he admitted finally. "Though I had time to change Harper and get her settled before you finally showed up."

Neither said more as she shifted her squirming daughter from one piece of equipment to the other and lowered into a seat with the babies between them. She reached in her bag and handed Luna a teething ring, which her child quickly dropped on the floor.

"You've already learned the Parent Pickup Game, Miss Luna?" Asher chuckled.

"Oh, yes. She's an expert at uh-oh." She grinned. "Luna knows that Mommy will pick it up for her."

Willow did just that, but she stuffed the ring in her diaper bag instead of handing it back to her daughter. She pulled Luna's pacifier out and helped the infant guide it to her mouth, clipping its leash to her shirt, just in case. The baby sucked hungrily on it, hinting that she would need to be fed soon.

"Let me get you something to drink."

Asher reached for his wallet, but Willow removed hers from the diaper bag. She handed him a five-dollar bill and an extra single for a tip.

"Coffee. Black. But if you'll get both drinks, I'll watch Harper for you."

"Anything for Luna?"

"Double-sided tape for her hands?"

He grinned over her joke. "I'll see what they have."

Harper's gaze followed her father as he crossed to the shop's counter, but she didn't cry out. Clearly, she was used to being left in another's care.

Asher returned a few minutes later carrying a lidded paper cup and a large plastic one containing some frou-frou drink with chocolate and whipped cream.

At her lifted brow, he shrugged.

"I can get black coffee at home. Even great coffee. Our cook always makes sure there's a fresh pot. But this?"

She shook her head and then stood to accept her drink from him, away from the babies so they wouldn't risk spilling on them. When his calloused fingers accidentally brushed hers, she pretended not to notice. Instead, she took a drink right away. It burned all the way down. She closed her eyes but managed not to squeal.

"By the way, that's really hot."

"Thanks for the warning." After setting the cup on the table, out of the reach of either baby, she pressed her sore tongue to the roof of her mouth.

"I still can't believe you showed up. I figured I'd scared you off by throwing out that question."

"It was only reason I did come." Unless curiosity counted, which it didn't. "At least one Colton needs to hear what I have to say."

Asher set his drink in the middle of the table, next to Willow's, settled back in his chair and crossed his arms.

"Then hit me with it. There are plenty of reasons someone in Mustang Valley might not be in the Colton fan club. Probably dozens."

Her expression must have given away her surprise because he laughed.

"No powerful business ever became that way without its leaders stepping on some toes, necks and even a few heads in the process."

Though Asher didn't mention that someone must have had something significant enough against Payne Colton to want him dead, his silence suggested that he was thinking about his dad.

"This 'stepping' happened closer to home."

"Which of my brothers is responsible?" He held his hand across his rib cage in a mini bow. "Whatever he did, I apologize on his behalf."

"It was your dad."

"Oh, God. You're not his—you're not my…?"

"Your sister? Hardly." She couldn't bring herself to say *father's lover*, which probably was what he'd meant at first. Her chuckle couldn't have sounded more awkward. "Now that would have complicated all those genetic markers that Anne was talking about earlier."

"I don't even want to think about that."

Neither did she, especially after she'd been checking Asher out when he'd first arrived. "It's plenty screwed up already." He lifted his cup off the table, popped it open and took a drink from the top, getting whipped cream on his lip. With the back of his hand, he wiped it away. "Then what did my dad do?"

Though he'd seemed to give voice to her thoughts, Willow blinked over the second part of what he'd said. From what she'd heard about the Coltons, right or wrong, they always circled their wagons whenever one of them was under attack.

"My mom worked as a maid at the Triple R. For years."

He leaned his elbows on the table and rested his chin in the vee he'd formed between his hands. "I probably should apologize just for that part. It can't be easy cleaning up after some of the animals I live with. What's your mom's name?"

"Kelly Johnson."

"Johnson. *Johnson?*"

He appeared to be searching his memory for the name, but his gaze narrowed with a different question. One she was familiar with.

"My mom was Scottish. She never married my father, who was Latino. I got my coloring from him, but I don't know many specifics about him, other than he was a ranch hand on the Triple R and blew out of town right after she told him she was pregnant."

Asher squinted. "I still don't recognize your mom's name or remember hearing this story."

"How old are you?"

"Thirty-three. Why does that matter?"

"Because it happened two years before you were born."

Besides clearing up why she'd been unable to remember him from the short time she'd attended Mustang Valley High, it also made her two years older than he was.

"That makes sense."

He must have been trying to recall *her* from high school. That had to be his reason for staring at her that way.

"Well? Your mom?"

He only wanted her to share her story. She should have been focused on that, as well. If she didn't tell it soon, she wouldn't get the chance, with as antsy as Luna was becoming in her high chair.

"Payne's first wife, Tessa, hired my mom. After Tessa died, Mom worked for his second wife, Selina, who was vicious but for some reason liked her. She even gave her a big raise."

"Your mom must have been great. I've heard horror stories about Selina from back then."

"After those two divorced, she continued to work on the ranch once Genevieve came into the picture."

Asher held both hands up in a plea for her to stop. "Please don't tell me that my mom was part of this, too."

She shrugged at that. "Sorry. Genevieve usually treated the staff with respect, but Payne stepped in."

"What did he do?"

"This one night while your family was out, Mom did something stupid. She'd just found out she was pregnant, and the guy had abandoned her. So, to cheer herself up, she tried on one of your mom's fancy dresses and some of her jewelry."

She sat back and crossed her arms, waiting for his judgmental comment. When he nodded instead, she licked her lips and continued.

"Just once, she wanted to know what it was like to look

and feel like a princess. To imagine she lived a different life. Like the royal Coltons."

"We're not like that."

He looked away and reached for the slobbery toy Luna was about to drop and centered it between her hands again. "Sorry. Go on."

"Unfortunately, your family came home early. Mom didn't have time to take off the dress or the jewelry. Payne accused her of planning to steal all of it and fired her on the spot."

Asher shook his head, his brows furrowing.

"Didn't she just explain it all to him?"

"She tried, but he wouldn't listen. Though Genevieve defended her, too, she might as well not have bothered with the weak appeal she gave. My mother left the ranch jobless, homeless and pregnant."

"Did she tell them the last part? They didn't send her packing after that, did they?"

The obvious compassion in his eyes surprised her. A Colton who cared what had happened to a staff member and her unborn child?

She shook her head, both in answer to his question and in her attempt to make sense of what he'd said. "She had too much pride to tell them about the pregnancy."

He blew out a breath. "What they did was bad enough already. I'm sorry—"

"Mom told me that story so many times," she rushed on, interrupting his apology. She finally had the chance to share it with someone else, and now that she'd told him all he needed to know, she couldn't stop herself from saying more.

"It was her cautionary tale to remind me that I should create security for myself. She was always chasing it for us. Different cities. Different schools. She even married some guy for a few years, looking for a better life. That didn't work out.

"So, she used to preach about the important things. An education. A home. Maybe a business. Things that no one could ever take away."

Finally, Willow stopped herself, blinking. She'd agreed to have coffee with Asher because she finally had the chance to call out one of the Coltons about the injustice to her mother, but no way had she initially planned to share so much.

He nodded, his incisive gaze making her squirm.

"You said 'was' and 'used to.' Is your mom...?"

"Yeah. A kidney condition. Four years ago."

"She never got to see her granddaughter?"

At least he didn't make a comment about the baby they *thought* was her mom's grandchild. That would have been too much to handle.

"I'm sorry about your mom. And I'm sorry for what my parents did to her. And you. I'm glad that my mother tried to stand up for yours, even if she was bad at it." He shook his head. "But Dad... What can I say? He jumps to conclusions, and then he doesn't want to admit he could ever be wrong, so..."

"He makes enemies," she finished for him. She took a long sip of her coffee, which was already getting cold. "Thanks for the apology. I shouldn't have snapped at you when you mentioned going to the ranch. Or when Anne revealed your last name. All that happened a long time ago. It's just that I'm so freaked out after everything this morning."

"Believe me, I get it." He slurped the last of his sweet drink through the straw. "But you kind of sound like one of those *enemies* you mentioned, so I wouldn't tell your story to anyone else for a while. You'll end up repeating it as a potential suspect to my future sister-in-law, Junior Detective Kerry Wilder."

"Is she the one investigating your dad's attempted murder?"

He nodded, but he looked around as if he was suddenly concerned that they might be overheard. "I shouldn't even joke about suspects."

"Your brother's been questioned, right?"

This time, he didn't answer.

"You're probably not supposed to talk about it at all."

"Not if we can help it. Why do *you* know so much about it?"

"I read. Maybe it's not the *New York Times*, but I get something that resembles news from the *Mustang Valley Times* and the *Bronco Star*. I even sometimes get the chance to sit down and watch WXVY-TV."

"The Valley," they chorused, repeating the local TV news station's tagline.

"Do *you* think I should be questioned?"

She didn't even know why she asked it. An hour ago, she was disgusted to find out she was dealing with another Colton. Why did she suddenly care what he thought about her?

"No. I don't."

She needed to look away, but she could no more make herself do that than she could force everyone with the last name "Colton" to move out of Mustang Valley. This was crazy. He'd only admitted that he didn't believe she was an attempted murderer, not that he thought she was beautiful or sexy, yet her body hummed with a certain *something*. She would rather plan a dinner party for his whole family than to define it.

Her high-strung baby saved the day by crying out. This time, at least, she appreciated the outburst.

"Sorry. I need to feed her."

"Yeah, Harper's getting hungry, too."

How he could tell, Willow wasn't sure. Harper had barely made more than a whimper. Even working all day with several infants, she'd never been around one who was so *polite*. Now, her Luna made her needs known to everyone.

As he pulled a small cooler from his diaper bag and withdrew a prepared bottle of formula, Willow lifted her wiggling child from the chair and laid her across her lap. She threw a receiving blanket over her shoulder for modesty, bunched up the T-shirt under her chambray shirt and unclipped her nursing bra. Luna latched onto her breast immediately like the experienced infant she was, her tiny body finally relaxing.

"I wonder where the microwave—"

When he stopped, Willow looked up and met his stare. He stood, frozen in place, the baby bottle lifted as if he was about to do a formula demonstration. That her cheeks burned only annoyed her more.

"Oh. Right." He lowered his arm and averted his gaze.

In her insular world at the day-care center, she never had to deal with people preferring for nursing mothers to hide in dressing rooms or filthy restroom stalls just to feed their infants. Was Asher, part of the monied Coltons, one of those?

Harper let out a little whine that must have been a full-blown fit for her, so Asher bent and handed her a pacifier to tide her over until he could warm her bottle.

His gaze lifted as he straightened again, but the expression he wore wasn't the judgmental one she would have expected. If anything, he looked sad.

"If Luna's my child, she'll never forgive me for taking her from her mother, the only parent she's ever known."

Chapter 5

Asher cradled Harper and fed her a bottle, though she'd mastered the skill of holding one on her own a few days before. He didn't want to consider that he might be hiding behind a six-month-old rather than to explain what he'd said to Willow. As if he could interpret his intense reaction to seeing the deep connection between the nursing mother and her child. He'd already retreated to the coffee creamer bar with its tiny microwave oven to avoid her questions.

He brushed back Harper's silky hair. How could he explain that even in the nursery, where he'd packed every piece of equipment a baby could ever need or want, he still worried he was failing to give his child everything she deserved? Like a mother to love and comfort her as Willow had been doing for Luna.

"She must have been hungry."

Willow pointed to the eight-ounce bottle that was already half-empty.

"Guess so."

Asher propped Harper up and pulled the bottle away so she could burp; his daughter could do that for herself now, too. Willow deftly moved Luna from one breast to the other. It would have been a seamless switch if the baby hadn't grabbed the blanket and taken it with her, exposing a patch of her mother's bare skin in the process.

Probably just her rib cage, but nonetheless, Asher couldn't help but to gawk. What was wrong with him? He wasn't a prepubescent kid getting his first peek at internet porn. He was a *father*, for goodness' sake. And Willow was a mother, merely feeding her child. The least he could do was to see her as a Madonna figure and have the good sense to know that she was hands-off for him. She'd certainly had good reasons she might not want anything to do with him, or at least his family.

"Oops." Willow chuckled, her complexion reddening, as she readjusted the blanket and her daughter's squirming form. "She's getting too wiggly lately in public. Guess I'll have to start carrying backup bottles of frozen milk with the baby food I've been introducing."

"She's a lucky girl to have had her mother around to give her such a good start by breastfeeding."

Why did he keep saying stuff like that to Willow? Wasn't his dumb comment about him taking Luna away from the mother she'd bonded with bad enough? She was a stranger, yet he'd already admitted that he didn't suspect her for the attack on his father, though he hadn't ruled out his own siblings at first. He'd nearly told her he wasn't confident in his abilities as a single dad. He'd never admitted his insecurities to anyone, not even the twins, Marlowe and Callum. Now he was all but posting them for Willow on the coffee shop's chalkboard menu, between words like *cappuccino* and *macchiato*.

"You said that Harper's mother had *passed*. Was it during childbirth?"

He scoffed. "I know. It's wrong to speak ill of the dead, but Nora Wheeler's departure wasn't that noble. She took off a few days after I brought them home from the hospital."

"Wasn't the mansion up to her standards?" She raised a hand, as if to hold off his response. "Sorry. I couldn't resist."

He frowned but continued anyway. "Worse. Said she didn't want to be trapped in a small town with me. And she didn't want to be a mother."

"A little late for that."

Luna popped her head out from beneath the blanket, finished eating, but this time Willow caught the cloth. She rearranged her clothes and tucked the blanket in her diaper bag.

"I thought it was pretty late, too." He set Harper's empty bottle on the table and rested her against his chest so she could nap if she was ready.

"Were you surprised by her sudden change of heart?"

"Now that I think about it, not really. She was always a party girl. I hate to admit it, but I used to like that about her. I used to have my share of adventures, too."

"Adventures?"

The word must have left a foul taste in Willow's mouth from the way she repeated it.

"But when she got pregnant, I did the stand-up thing. I even proposed, though she said we should wait. I still thought we were both on board for the rest."

Asher didn't know what was worse, the annoyance he'd read in her expression earlier, or the pity that replaced it. He lowered his gaze and tried to ignore the discomfort in his gut. Like that familiar drop in a moving elevator, his stomach took its time to catch up on the ride.

"Do you know where she went, you know, *before*?"

"LA. But I got the best end of the bargain." He tickled Harper's ribs, and she giggled with that bubbly sound he wished he could bottle.

"How did she…?"

"Viral meningitis. Her mother told me she caught it at a rave or something."

He held his shoulder blades against the chair back and stared at his hands. Why had he shared so many details? He didn't want to talk about it. Not now. Not ever.

"That's terrible. I'm sorry." Then after a few seconds, she added, "Do you ever worry you won't be able to do all of this without her?"

"Hell no."

The words were out of his mouth before he could stop them. Even knowing that Willow was only responding to the feelings of inadequacy that he'd given off before didn't make him want to take that back.

"I *am* doing it without her. Every day."

"Yes, you seem to be—"

"Am I doing a perfect job?" He interrupted her, on a roll and unable to stop. "Absolutely not. But I'm…here."

Asher hoped she hadn't heard the slight break in his voice, but he doubted he'd gotten that lucky. He was relieved when she excused herself to take Luna into the ladies' room for a clean diaper. He'd planned to change the subject when she returned, but Willow spoke up again before he had the chance.

"Wow, we're a pair."

"What do you mean?"

"My ex dashed before he died, too. I was still pregnant when he filed for divorce to be with one of his women."

"*One* of them?"

"There were three that I knew of."

An ache settled in his chest. If Willow was aware of three, then that total was probably much higher.

"Legally, the divorce couldn't be finalized until after the birth, but he got married again before the ink on the papers dried. He never bothered to meet Luna."

"How did *it* happen?"

"He and his uh, wife, died in a car accident two months after Luna was born."

Willow tucked her chin and slid Luna's curls behind her ears, her movements jerky instead of fluid as they'd been earlier.

"What are the odds that both of us would have exes who left us and then died?" They weren't perfectly chosen words, but he couldn't help saying something to distract her from her sadness. He could relate to it more than he cared to admit.

The corners of her mouth tipped up again. "After this morning, neither of us should be betting on odds. Especially you. How could something like that happen in a family once, let alone *twice*?"

At least she hadn't named it out loud. Talking about the possible switch made it all too real.

"Guess you and I have a little in common, after all," he said finally.

Willow shrugged. Maybe she wasn't ready to go *that far*.

"Luna inherited your husband's estate, right? At least the guy could give his kid something."

"She doesn't need anything from him."

At the fierce look in her eyes, he grinned. "I'm sure she doesn't."

Still, he couldn't help wondering whether she was talking about Harper or herself.

"The way that Xavier blew through *our* money, there won't be anything left anyway, by the time the probate court is finished with it. He left no will. We didn't have anything to divvy up in the divorce, either."

He tilted his head, squinting. "Didn't you say you owned a day-care center? Tender Years? It's about a block off the main boulevard, right? I remember it. A big, blond, stucco place with an outdoor staircase to the second floor." At her nod, he continued. "And don't you own your home?"

"This might come as a surprise to a *Colton*, but not everyone is a homeowner."

Asher lifted his hands in surrender. "That's not what I… I mean—"

At her chuckle, he frowned.

"Couldn't resist again? Well, try."

"Fine. I own the building where the center is located. Well, the bank does. And, since Luna and I live in the upstairs apartment, I technically do own a house."

"How was that not an asset?" He considered it for a second. "Did you have it before you were married?"

"Xavier thought I was crazy for insisting on a prenup."

"Not so crazy, after all."

"And not homeless."

"Tender Years is pretty successful, right?"

Her gaze narrowed. "Why? Are you trying to buy my business? Or the building? Neither are for sale."

"Are you always this suspicious?"

"Can you blame me?"

"I guess not, but, no, I don't want to buy your business." His chuckle sounded flat to his own ears. "It's just that, well, I've had trouble finding a good nanny, and—"

"And you wanted to know if there's a slot available for

Harper? We've been full. We even have a wait list. Hold on. Was this the *real* reason you asked me to meet you?"

Willow Merrill was too smart for her own good.

"Well, it was *one* of the reasons."

"Figures. Of course, you need something from me."

She probably assumed that the Coltons took from everyone in their lives, and he hated giving her proof.

"But I don't need a slot. I just thought with you being in the business, you might know some qualified candidates for a private nanny position."

Willow didn't answer immediately and tapped her fingers on the table instead.

"Don't you think I would have hired them to work for me if I knew of any good candidates?"

"Possibly."

"And does this mean the Coltons are too good for a day-care *center*?"

This time he palmed his forehead. "I didn't say anything like that. It's just that my job isn't nine-to-five, so I need someone at the house. It's a convenience thing. And I get to see her more often. Besides, didn't you already say you have a waitlist?"

She leaned back into her chair and crossed her arms, but this time she didn't answer. One point for Asher, though he doubted he'd get many of those with Willow.

"Maybe it won't work out indefinitely, but I've got to find something for Harper. Soon. Could you add her to your list, just in case a spot becomes open?"

"I'll see what I can do."

"Thanks. I appreciate it."

"Anne Sewall said you're the foreman at the Triple R. That's not a usual position for a Colton family member, is it?"

He lifted and lowered his shoulder. "Maybe not, but

it's perfect for me. I'm much happier on horseback, out riding the fence line, or helping to pull a new calf than I ever would have been working in the Colton Oil office like some of my siblings."

She looked at him strangely, as if he'd surprised her.

"No desk job for you?"

"Oh, I have a desk and more paperwork than I'd like sometimes, but I also get to stare out over the fields toward the mountains at sunrise and sunset."

"Sounds nice."

"It is. I can't wait to share the land with my little girl."

He stood with Harper in his arms and crossed to the stroller. After clicking the level to recline the seat back, he laid the infant in it. Then he glanced at Willow, who'd pulled her sleeping baby closer in her arms. She kissed the top of her child's dark curls.

At once, his own words struck him, causing an ache to spread inside his chest. *My little girl.* Neither of them knew for certain that the children they'd been raising were even their own. He cleared his throat, but the lump that had formed there refused to dislodge.

She glanced up at him, her dark eyes appearing to read whatever he'd given away with his own. Then she seemed to mine them for something more. He needed to look away, to break the spell that caused his pulse to thud at his temple, but he found himself a willing captive. Hungry for a connection. With *her.*

A ringing phone pierced the moment, though, and caused Luna to startle awake. Immediately, she cried out.

Willow lunged for her cell and read the screen, rocking her child, who would have none of it. She wiggled and cried.

"It's the center. I have to take this."

Asher did the only thing he could think of to help. He

reached out his arms. Willow stared at his hands as if they were more enemy than rescuer. Then, with a frown, she held the baby out to him. Something told him this action was a bigger sacrifice for her than only a moment of needing quick parental backup.

"Come here, sweetie."

At first, he held Luna at arm's length, as she stopped crying and stared back at him with wide, cautious eyes. Willow kept looking back over her shoulder, her features pinched with worry, as she stepped outside to return the call that should have clicked over to voice mail.

Luna's gaze shifted to her mother and then back to him, as if trying to determine if she should be upset, so Asher slowly moved in a circle and kept turning. All babies were different, but this method worked with Harper, so he gave it a shot.

For a few seconds, Luna stared back at him, but when he smiled, her lips lifted, too.

"You know I'm a friend, don't you, Luna?"

He bent his elbows, drew her closer, finally settling her on his hip. The scent on her hair was the same one that had distracted him while they'd been in that tight hospital office. The perfume her mother wore. Like a field of wildflowers.

Luna had just rewarded his efforts with a happy squeal when Willow threw the door open again. She glanced from Asher to her daughter and shook her head, her movements robotic, agitated.

"We've got to go."

"What is it?"

Willow shook her head as she lifted Luna from his arms and then hurried over to buckle the baby in the stroller she hated. Why wouldn't Willow look at him? Was it about the call or that he'd made her daughter laugh? The infant was already crying out again as Willow pushed the stroller past him. Sobbing with her arms extended—to him.

"See you tomorrow?" he called after her as she reached the door.

She answered without looking back. "I'll be there."

"I would never try to take her, Willow," he blurted.

This time she paused. He'd made a promise he couldn't keep if he found out that Luna was his. He'd contradicted his earlier words, as well. But maybe he'd broken through to her.

"What is it?" he asked again. "Can I help?"

Her shoulders dropped forward. "The Arizona Department of Health Services inspector showed up at the center unannounced. Someone filed a complaint with the state."

"Why would anyone do something like that?"

"Someone wants to shut us down." She straightened again and reached out to push open the door. "And I have no idea who's planning it."

Chapter 6

Willow parked inside the only open space in the two-stall garage, the other side packed but meticulously organized with shelving units, storage bins and parking for the collection of ride-on toys. The tools of the day-care trade.

Would the inspector, who'd invaded her house, take all this away from them—the security she'd been so determined to build for herself and for her child? Would Willow be forced to break the promise she'd made to her own mother that she would always be independent?

"That can't be happening," she said as she opened the rear door of her SUV.

Luna looked back at her, already lifting her arms. She'd wondered earlier if the call about the switch could have been related to the threatening letter from the week before. Now she had to believe that all of this was connected. *You deserve everything you get, bitch. Tender Years will be history.* Some of the words from the letter that had been tucked in her front door repeated in her thoughts then. Was this what the writer had been talking about? Would whatever he or she had planned be something worse?

She couldn't think about that now. Not when the state official, who could damage her business, was still inside. She had just pulled Luna from her car seat when the door to the house crept open. Candace leaned her head out, her thick salt-and-pepper ponytail falling forward over her round, amber-skinned face.

"He's with Tori and Alicia in the crib room," she whispered.

Willow peeked at her watch, noting that it was naptime. "Being quiet, I hope."

"He's been okay, really. He's already been through the kitchen, the toddler room, the activity room and the backyard."

"Did he go into my apartment?" She winced as she pictured her unmade bed and the rinsed cereal bowl in the sink. It was the one place she didn't have to be fussy.

"No. I made it clear that is your private residence, and none of our charges is ever allowed past that locked door."

"What will we do if he finds something? What if we get written up?"

Candace shook her head, the ponytail swinging. "You know he won't. You're so focused on the rules that you could probably teach this stuff to anyone opening a new center."

"Rules keep the kids safe. That's also our job."

"Yeah, you always say that, too. I'll see you inside."

Candace closed the door, leaving Willow still holding Luna in the sweltering garage.

Willow's hurried breathing finally slowed for the first time since she'd received the call at the coffee shop. How could this all have happened on the same day? Wasn't the news about Luna enough?

If she hadn't been wasting time at Java Jane's, with a *Colton* no less, maybe she could have done something, at least been there when the inspector had arrived. She'd told Asher she'd agreed to meet him only so she could have the chance to tell her mother's story, but it was more than that, and she knew it. More than wanting another opportunity to see Harper since they could be related, Willow was curious about the single father who was caught up in that mess with her and Luna. She knew better. Look at what curiosity did to cats.

Anyway, what would she have done differently if she'd been the one to answer the door instead of Candace or one of the other staff members? Would she have refused to let the guy in? All that would have accomplished was to get the center shut down.

Even if that had to be the intent of whoever had filed the complaint.

Willow closed her eyes to hold the panic welling inside her at bay. She couldn't let Tender Years be shuttered. She'd worked too hard, sacrificed too much.

She took a deep breath that was neither fortifying nor calming and climbed the steps into the house. A pale, bespectacled man passed her just inside the doorway.

"You must be Mrs. Merrill. I'm Inspector Robert Bilkey of the Arizona Department of Health Services, Child Care Facilities Licensing." He lifted his badge so she could get a better look at his credentials and then smiled at her daughter. "Just a few more spaces, and I will be out of your way."

"Out of my way?"

Was that code for he'd found something awful and would be filing a report about it? Though she followed him into the garage, he didn't answer, already examining the see-through tubs of supplies. With a frown, she closed the door and continued into the house. It was the first time all day that Luna seemed at ease—except for those few minutes with Asher—and Willow was the one who wanted to cry.

She moved from room to room, examining their contents with a more critical eye than usual. Were there sponges, which health officials considered breeding grounds for bacteria, on the kitchen sink? Were all outlets carefully covered in the toddler room, which had once been the formal living room? Were the gates closing off the trash cans in the diaper-changing area properly sealed?

The sliding barn door marking the entrance to the formal dining room, which had been converted and lined with cribs, offered no clues about what the inspector had been looking for. Everything seemed to be in its proper place. If she'd made a tragic error, she had no idea what it was.

Tori hurried toward her with a toddler, Derrick, propped on her hip.

"Is the inspector gone yet?" she said in a stage whisper.

Willow reached up to brush the child's sweaty red hair and then gestured with a tilt of her head toward the garage.

"Think he found anything?" Tori asked.

This time, Willow shrugged. As with any other inspection from a governmental agency, what he found would depend on how hard he was searching.

Candace passed them in the hall, guiding three-year-old Hannah by the hand. "You never said what happened at the hospital. Did they already do the test?"

Willow shook her head. "I can't even think about that right now."

"Didn't you say something about a Colton?" Tori prompted anyway.

Madeline rounded the corner with two-month-old Isabella in her arms. "Yeah, what's the scoop?"

She couldn't blame her staff for being curious, after the way she'd bolted out of the center earlier. Anyway, they were friends and employees, a business model that had worked well for them until now. But everything was different today. She shook her head a second time. She wasn't ready to talk about it.

Candace released the little girl's hand and held out her arms to Luna.

"Here, angel. I bet you're ready for some lunch and your nap."

Like always, Luna moved easily into the day-care worker's arms. They all loved her like she was their own.

Willow was still searching for the words to give them a brief accounting of what had taken place at the hospital when the door to the garage opened again. The inspector stepped inside, the tablet he'd been typing on earlier tucked under his arm.

"Everything looks like it's in order here." He stepped toward the door.

"I don't understand, Mr. Bilkey," Willow called to his retreating back. After the panic he'd caused at her place of business, she couldn't let him leave without answering some of her questions.

"Why did this inspection happen in the first place?" she asked when he paused.

"As I told your staff when I arrived, there was a complaint against your center, filed with the state."

Who'd ever had a problem with Tender Years that hadn't been solved through a simple conversation? She searched her memories. None of her employees had left under uncomfortable circumstances. No children had been unenrolled because of a disagreement in the past few years, either. Sure, like at many day-care centers, she'd occasionally had trouble with parents who regularly picked up their children late. Had someone been upset enough about the extra charges—a clearly stated penalty in their contract—to try to hurt her business by contacting the state?

"But the complaint appears to be unfounded, so there shouldn't be any further follow-up at this time."

Was the guy serious? It seemed to be "unfounded," so the state agency didn't plan to ask more questions about it? Or about the person who'd submitted it?

"Is it possible to find out filing details?"

He was already shaking his head before the question was out of her mouth. "Sorry. But we don't release that information."

"You mean someone can suggest that a business has safety or quality issues, but the owner has no way to address the accuser?"

The inspector didn't appear to be listening as he slid his finger over his tablet and tapped through several screens. He pushed his glasses higher on his nose. "That's strange."

"What is?"

He lifted his gaze as if only then realizing he'd spoken aloud. Again, he shook his head.

"Come on. Give us something here. You know the report was bogus."

Finally, he shrugged. "It's just that the report appears to have been filed anonymously. It's not supposed to be possible to file a report without a claimant. I don't even know how it was processed."

Willow blinked several times, that *anonymous* character scoring points against her for the third time: first the threatening letter, then the call to the hospital about the possible baby switch and now the complaint with the state. All three things had to be connected, didn't they?

He licked his lips and shifted his weight from one foot to the other.

"Don't worry about it," she found herself saying. "You were just doing your job."

Clearly, someone else hadn't been doing hers or his, but she didn't say that. His embarrassment assuaged, he finally allowed her to usher him to the door.

As soon as she closed it, she collapsed against the wood. It was all too much. This morning she'd believed that the news they'd learned was the worst thing that could happen to them. Now, though, no matter the results of the DNA test, if whoever was targeting her business was successful, she would have no way to support her child and nowhere for them to live.

If they learned that the babies were switched, what judge would grant custody of either of those children to her?

"Everything's going perfectly," the woman said into the phone without bothering to say hello.

"Well, good morning to you, too," he said. "But let's not get ahead of ourselves."

Because she could picture him grinning like an idiot, she was glad this wasn't a video call. Still, she had to give him credit for his effort. Their plan was working out just as they'd hoped. She had to ensure that it stayed that way.

"All of the important players seem to be in on the deal," she said. "They're making this easy."

"I told you we could do this. I said it would be a piece of cake, too."

"Yes, sweetheart, you did." She would give him that, though, technically, the idea had been hers. They always were. Her friend might have had the desire to make it work, but she was better at execution.

"So, it's 'sweetheart' now?"

"Sure."

And it would continue to be if he didn't screw this up for her. For *them*. She'd waited too long to find the perfect plan and an adequate partner to execute it to let it fall apart like her past few attempts.

"Now get back to your job," she said. "It's almost time for me to do mine."

"Have fun and stay in touch."

"You know I will."

For effect, she made several kissy noises into the phone and hung up before he could reciprocate. She would stay in contact, all right. Every step of the way. Everyone else appeared to be finding good things in this life. It was about time for her, well, for *them*, to get their fair share.

Chapter 7

Asher pulled his pickup to the side of the road for the third time during the drive from town to the Triple R and allowed the latest emergency vehicle to pass. The first two had been unfamiliar police patrol cars, and the third was an ambulance. All were headed back toward town.

"What the heck is going on?" he asked the passenger buckled in the car seat in the back.

Harper's only answer was a whimper that stretched to a whine. He couldn't blame her. Instead of going back to the ranch and putting her down for her afternoon nap in her own bed, he'd driven around Mustang Valley several times, surveying some of the damage from the earthquake a month before. He'd even driven by a few sites where his brother Grayson, a first responder for his own agency, and Grayson's new fiancée, Savannah Oliver, were helping with relief efforts. Still, Asher hadn't wasted enough time, so he'd stopped at Mustang Park.

He'd burned through more of the diesel in his quad-cab pickup than he cared to admit, while he let her nap in the back, but at least Jace would already be at his hospital appointment by the time he returned to the ranch. He was in no shape to answer more of his potential brother's questions just yet.

"Sorry, kiddo. We'll be home real soon if we can stop having to pull off all the time."

As if responding to his comment, a strange-looking truck with a flashing light sped toward them. It wasn't uncommon for him to pass no cars on a trip to and from town. This made four. Even though the vehicle was three-quarters of a mile back, Asher remained on the shoulder until it passed. Under the emblem for the Arizona Department of Public Safety were the chilling words *Bomb Squad*. His stomach muscles clenched.

"Oh, God, no," he said what he hoped was under his breath.

He didn't want to upset Harper more than she already was, but he had to know if he was right. Without any proof, he was almost certain that those emergency vehicles were headed straight to Colton Oil headquarters.

After making a U-turn in the middle of the two-lane highway, he pulled behind the fast-moving vehicle and kept pace. He could afford a ticket, not the loss of his family members.

A half mile from the exact location he'd predicted, they came upon a police roadblock, a squad car with the familiar Mustang Valley Police Department insignia on the door, parked across the two lanes. Lit flares were on the road in front of it.

The bomb squad vehicle wove around the police car, tossing up gravel from the shoulder. If not for the precious cargo in his back seat, he would have followed it. Instead, he honored the posted officer's demand to stop.

He parked his car at the side of the road, unbuckled Harper from her seat and pulled on her hat and sunglasses. Then he approached Officer Lizzie Manfred.

"Hey, Lizzie. What's going on at the headquarters?"

"Oh, hi, Asher." She waved at his daughter. "Hey, Harper. Sorry. I can't let you guys through here. No one, other than emergency personnel, is allowed beyond this point."

"But my family—" His gaze shot in the direction the bomb squad truck had already disappeared.

She shook her head. "The whole Colton Oil staff has been evacuated, using local school buses. You can be reunited with your family members at the Affirmation Alliance Group Center."

"Why there?"

She shrugged. "They have the facilities, and they offered."

"Makes sense." The group had been helping the community a lot lately, particularly following the earthquake. It was great to see local organizations doing some good.

"Can you tell me what happened?"

"Sorry. Any official announcements need to come from Sergeant Colton."

"Spencer wouldn't mind if you shared details with me." He was a distant cousin, after all.

"I like my job. I plan to keep it."

"Fine. Thanks."

Asher returned to his truck and buckled Harper in. He forced himself not to speed as he drove to the Affirmation Alliance Group Center. Sure, he'd heard that his brother and sisters were fine, but he needed to see it for himself.

A yellow school bus remained in the center's lot when

he pulled in and parked. About a dozen people chatted in groups outside the building's front door, a fair, blonde woman he recognized as Affirmation Alliance founder Micheline Anderson milling among them. He could only hope that his family members were inside.

He carried Harper to the entrance. His sister, Marlowe, pushed open the door just as he reached the curb. Her face ruddy, her long, light blond hair falling forward over her face, Marlowe looked nothing like the unflappable Colton Oil CEO he knew. She cradled her rounded belly as if trying to protect her child.

"Marlowe," he called out as he rushed toward her.

His one arm closed around her, his wiggling daughter sandwiched between them. He pulled back but still rested his hand on Marlowe's arm.

"Are you okay? Is the baby okay?"

Despite her red face, she smiled. "I'm fine, big brother. *We're* fine."

"Well, you don't look so good. You should sit down." He guided her to a park bench farther down the walk. "Did you call Bowie?"

"I just got off the phone with him." She awkwardly lowered herself onto the wood and then gestured for him to join her. "A good fiancée wouldn't let him find out about this on the internet, would she? Speaking of which, how did you find out?"

"I saw all the police cars."

"You saw them from the ranch?"

"I was in town."

He stopped at that. His sister was already worked up enough. He could share his own story with the family later.

"So, what happened?"

Marlowe held her hands wide. "Someone called in a bomb threat to the main office line."

"To Dee Walton? What did she do?"

"Dee was the perfect admin hero."

She waved to the olive-skinned woman with short brown hair. Dee waved back.

"She followed Colton Oil emergency protocols and the Department of Homeland Security bomb threat procedures checklist," Marlowe continued. "She didn't hang up the phone and called from a different one. She copied down the number from the phone's display and even wrote down the caller's exact words."

"Who'd want to blow up Colton Oil?"

Asher's gaze met his sister's, her frown mirroring his. They both had a good idea, even if they didn't know the specific *who*. It had to be connected to the anonymous email that opened the can of worms about Ace not being a real Colton. It could even have been the same person who'd shot their father.

What about the tip regarding his and Willow's switched-at-birth situation? He blinked as his mind added that last matter to the list. Whether the switch could be connected in any way, nothing was *his and Willow's*. Only Harper's and his.

"Have you called Mom yet?"

Marlowe shook her head, her frown deepening. "Wish we could keep this from her altogether, but someone at her Garden Society meeting has probably already told her. She'll be calling anytime now."

"She actually went?"

"I talked her into it. She needed a break from sitting beside Dad's bed at the hospital."

"You think we had any chance of keeping a secret about a bomb threat in Mustang Valley, especially when Garden Society runs like an intercom system?"

At least his sister laughed at his joke instead of calling

him out on his failure to take his share of turns at his father's bedside. It wasn't just because he was too busy at the ranch, either. He hated seeing his powerful father lying there, fragile and helpless.

"What about Callum? Did you tell him?"

"Not yet, but he's probably already aware. Twin telepathy, you know."

He grinned. Marlowe was trying to joke, too, but the bomb threat had clearly shaken her. Like him, she had a child to protect. Automatically, his arms tightened around Harper.

Rafe strode their way then. Sporting dress slacks, a modern untucked dress shirt and a short blazer, he wouldn't have appeared different from any other day on his job as the Colton Oil chief financial officer if his dirty blond hair didn't look as if he'd combed it with a rake.

When Rafe stepped closer them, Asher stood, but their brother reached for Marlowe.

"You doing okay?"

"I'm fine," she said as she stood. "I'm thinking about making a sign that says that."

Rafe's lips lifted. "You do that. I'll even loan you my markers once we get back to the office."

As he glanced at Asher, Ainsley rushed over from the parking lot, Jace keeping pace next to her.

"Oh, good," Ainsley said. "You're out here."

Asher looked back and forth between her and Jace. He was still amazed by how much the two of them resembled each other, even if Ainsley didn't look like the composed Colton Oil corporate attorney she usually was at work. Her eyes were wide, she sounded winded and some of her chestnut-colored hair had fallen loose from the clip at the nape of her neck.

Ainsley hugged her sister and brothers, something she

rarely did with any of her siblings. Then she patted Harper's head.

"Wait." She stepped back and pointed from Asher to his daughter. "What are you two doing here?"

"He was in town," Marlowe answered for him.

Asher exchanged a look with Jace, but the other man didn't mention the suspicious call that had caused Asher to rush from the ranch earlier. Another reason to like him.

"Glad you're okay." Jace stepped forward, as if he intended to hug Marlowe, too, but stopped and shook her hand instead.

Asher scuffed his boot on the ground. Well, no one was perfect, and their relationship was still tentative.

"I was just taking Jace back to the ranch after the DNA test when Selina called," Ainsley said. "She's furious."

Marlowe rubbed her hand over a spot on her abdomen. "Not too happy about it myself. I had an important meeting with a potential account today. Now I'll probably lose the deal when they seek out options at Robertson Renewable Energy instead. It's getting too risky to deal with Colton Oil."

Or to *be* a Colton. No one spoke Asher's thought aloud, but they all had to be thinking it.

"You and Bowie trying to keep it in the family now?"

They all laughed at Ainsley's joke, added too late and referring to Marlowe's fiancé's position with Colton Oil's rival company, but the levity sounded forced.

"I had a meeting scheduled late this afternoon, too," Ainsley told them. "Guess I'll have to reschedule."

"What would Dad think if he saw all this?"

Marlowe crossed her arms as if she regretted her words. For several seconds, no one spoke. Just four siblings, possibly five, wrestling with the notion that they might never know what their father thought about that or anything else. Marlowe's ringing phone came as a welcome interruption.

She reached down on the bench for it and glanced at the screen. "It's Mom."

Asher exchanged a smile with Marlowe over her correct prediction as she answered.

"Hi, Mom." She stood and stepped away to continue the conversation. "Yes, I'm fine…"

Suddenly, Selina Barnes Colton shoved open the building's door and burst through, wearing sunglasses and a low-cut business-casual dress, a cell phone tucked between her shoulder and ear. As she marched toward them, her trademark long, dark honey-colored hair caught the breeze.

"Well, look at who got to miss out on all the chaos this afternoon." She slipped the sunglasses on her head.

Since it was clear she was speaking to Ainsley, Asher didn't bother answering her. He always tried to stay out of the path of the tornado that was Colton Oil's vice president and head of public relations. He couldn't imagine how Willow's mom had once won over the hard-to-impress executive. That he'd only met Kelly Johnson's fiercely independent daughter, and he was thinking about her there, in a crowd of displaced workers after a bomb threat, suggested that the women in her family knew how to make an impact.

"I had an errand to do," Ainsley said.

She didn't have to explain it since Selina was the Colton Oil board member who'd insisted that they should track down the *real* Ace Colton in the first place.

Asher waved his free hand to get his older sister's attention. "Any news about your 'errand'?"

Ainsley shook her head. "We won't know anything for a week. I even tried to *incentivize* faster results, but the lab technician said they've received a few rush jobs, and they won't be able to get to it sooner."

Asher shook his head. "The Colton name sure didn't help us out there."

What would Willow have said about that? Something, he was sure.

Selina frowned at them both by turns and then stepped over to their houseguest and held out her hand.

"You're Jace."

He nodded. "I am. And you're Ms. Barnes Colton."

"Call me Selina."

Jace glanced past her and gestured toward the crowd of Colton Oil workers. "I'm so sorry that this has happened to you all. It's awful."

They all nodded their thanks. Introductions out of the way, Selina drew Ainsley, Rafe and Asher out of earshot of any possible eavesdroppers and filled Ainsley in on the events she'd missed while she was out of the office.

"As if Colton Oil PR wasn't difficult enough already, this is a nightmare. How am I supposed to spin these stories? I'm still getting calls from media outlets asking for confirmation that Ace Colton was switched at birth."

"You haven't answered the question, right?" Asher asked.

She shook her head. "I'm continuing to give them the official company line that it's a private family matter."

Ainsley used her appeasing attorney smile.

"You're doing a wonderful job, Selina, even in these tough circumstances. Payne will be so proud of the work you've done when we get the chance to tell him about it."

Asher was impressed, both that Ainsley's voice didn't break when she referred to their dad and that Selina appeared to be softening, at least for a moment.

"Even so," Selina said, pursing her lips, "it's only right that the quote 'There's no such thing as bad publicity' is attributed to P. T. Barnum, of Barnum & Bailey Circus fame.

This is a circus, minus the big top. The quote's wrong, too. This publicity is downright destructive to our brand."

She pointed at Asher. "And you have to do something about all those reporters camped out by the gate at the ranch."

He nodded. They were getting annoying, calling out questions to him every time he pulled into or out of the property.

"I thought that the earthquake would be enough to send them packing or at least give them something else to report on, but they probably just called in reinforcements. I doubt a bomb threat is going to help the situation. We can't keep it out of the press."

He gestured to the media trucks already lining the road just off the Affirmation Alliance property. "Just like here, I can't do anything about reporters, as long as they stay off the Triple R or Colton Oil land."

"Well, your father would do something about it." Selina slammed on her enormous sunglasses and walked away. Rafe waved and strode toward some of the other employees.

Ainsley was chuckling when Asher shifted back to her. "She sure told you."

"Well, that 'official company line' of hers only confirmed that the story about Ace was true, anyway," he said. "All the papers and TV reports I've seen have reported it as fact. We might as well just address it."

"Oh, no. I want to stay off Selina's bad side, so I'm going to stick with the official statement." Ainsley grinned. "Say it after me, 'private family matter.'"

Marlowe shuffled back over to them, apparently having convinced their mother that she and her baby hadn't been blown up at work. Asher shivered at just the thought of that, a reaction he hoped the others missed. They were the ones who could have been killed that day. Not him.

Selina crossed back them. "When do you think we'll be getting back into the building?" she asked Marlowe. "I'm already getting calls for a statement, and I don't have my laptop to be able to draft a press release. It will need to be a good one."

Marlowe shook her head. "I didn't even shut down my computer or lock my office."

Asher glanced down at Harper, who was again nodding off on his shoulder. "Hey, everyone, I've got to get back to the ranch. Anyone need a ride anywhere?"

"And miss our chance to ride in a school bus for the second time today?" Marlowe said, earning laughs from the rest of them.

But as Asher stepped away, a Mustang Valley Police Department cruiser pulled to the curb without flashing lights or a siren. In his navy blue uniform, Sergeant Spencer Colton climbed out and walked straight toward them.

"Hey, Sergeant Colton," Asher said as the police officer passed him.

Spencer nodded and kept walking. He stopped in front of Marlowe. This was clearly official business.

"I need to update you on the situation at Colton Oil. Would you like for me to do this privately?"

Selina lifted a hand as if to assert that she deserved to hear the news as well, but Marlowe scanned the group, her gaze stopping on Jace.

"I'll be right over there." He pointed to a far bench and started that way.

Marlowe crossed her arms and faced the sergeant. "Okay. What do you have?"

"The bomb squad and the explosive-detection canines

have swept the whole complex, including the grounds, and there were no suspicious devices located."

"You're saying it was a false alarm?" she asked.

"You mean a hoax?" Selina said.

Spencer shook his head. "Whatever you call it, making a bomb threat, whether explosives are located or not, is a serious crime. If arrested, the suspect will face felony charges."

"But at least we have determined that there is no active threat, right?" Marlowe pointed out. "When will we be allowed to return to the building?"

The sergeant stared at her. Asher could understand his sister's need to minimize the situation, if only to calm her own rattled nerves, but their cousin appeared to be having none of it. Spencer crossed his arms just below his shiny badge.

"The building will reopen in an hour or so, but this investigation isn't over. We not only have to know who targeted your staff but why. We also need to find out if this threat is connected to the attack on your father."

He paused, as if to let that first part sink in, and then continued.

"Until we know the answers to all those questions, we have to assume that Colton Oil employees and family members as well might be in danger."

Chapter 8

Willow's throat tightened the next morning as she pushed Luna's stroller through the doorway into Mustang Valley General's crowded lab waiting area. She'd arrived thirty minutes before their scheduled appointment so she would beat Asher there. She needed to have the upper hand with him in at least some small way.

"Hey, Willow. Over here."

Asher sat in a chair in the corner, Harper on his knee. His diaper bag occupied the seat next to him.

You've got to be kidding. She stood in the doorway, the wheel propping it open. At least Luna wasn't fighting her stroller harness as much as usual. Willow should have known better than to think she could arrive earlier than a cowboy anywhere in the morning when they were equally familiar with sunrises in their jobs.

"Come on." He moved his hand in a circular motion. "We saved you a seat."

She strode toward him, having become the most interesting entertainment in a packed waiting room where a long stay was implied. In his uniform of jeans, boots and another dark T-shirt—this one navy—he seemed to pop out against the muted, pastel colors and seashell prints lining the walls. Did the man own any clothes that didn't fit him like they were made for his exact brawny dimensions?

What was she doing? She refused to notice how his sleeves strained when he pulled a cloth from his bag to dab at the baby's drool. Nor would she consider that she might need a tissue to wipe at her own.

Even if she was in the dating market, which she absolutely wasn't, and if he didn't happen to be a Colton who could take her child, which he *was*, Asher had all but admitted he was a ladies' man. He'd mentioned his "adventures." If her ex hadn't taught her to avoid men like that, she didn't know what would.

Harper, looking comfortable in a onesie dress, squealed as Willow and Luna reached them.

"Well, hello, sweetie." She reached out and brushed the infant's cheek.

"Guess I'm not the only early riser." Asher pulled the bag from the next seat and gestured for Willow to sit. "You know, I nearly had to throw down, twice, to keep this spot for you."

"Thanks for your sacrifice."

"Anytime."

She swallowed. He might not be so obliging to her once they received the test results.

Willow pulled Luna from her stroller and handed her the chilled teething ring she'd packed in the insulated section of her diaper bag.

"Is it always so crowded in here?"

"Probably backed up from yesterday's rescheduled tests."

"Because of the Coltons?"

"No." He stared at the appointment desk instead of at her, but finally he shrugged. "Well, not *entirely*."

"You can't help it if people fall all over themselves to please your family." She cleared her throat. "Now can we get this test over with?"

"No problem. I'll just march up to the desk and insist that because I'm a Colton, we should go to the front of the line. It worked like a dream for us yesterday."

He had a point. His name hadn't gotten him any special treatment at the hospital.

"I would just as soon forget yesterday happened altogether," he said.

"That's something we can agree on."

And agreeing with a Colton, on *anything*, was something she'd never expected to do.

"What happened with the state inspector?"

"How did you—"

She stopped herself as she remembered. What had she been thinking, blurting out that information to him the day before? As if the Coltons wouldn't already have an arsenal of the best lawyers and community support to use against her if their babies really had been switched, she'd given him more ammunition against her in court. Now they would be aware that her business had been in trouble with the state, as well.

"Oh. Right," she said. "It turned out to be nothing."

"If that's true, I'm glad. Because it didn't sound like 'nothing' when you got the call."

"Why don't we just say that yesterday was a lousy day and leave it at that?"

"Okay."

She expected an argument, or at least for those perceptive eyes to stare at her until she spilled her story. He did neither thing, bouncing his daughter on his knee instead.

"Our family had a rotten day, too," he said after a long time.

"Why? Was the caviar too salty? Or was the champagne flat?"

This time he rolled his eyes. "Does making fun of my family ever get old for you?"

She grinned. "Not yet. But, okay, I'll stop."

"If you haven't figured it out, I'm more a burger-and-a-frosty-mug type. But no, salty fish eggs weren't the worst things that happened yesterday."

"What was it?"

"I thought you followed the local news."

"I do, just not last night. Why? What did I miss? Did something happen with your dad?"

He blinked a few times and then shook his head.

Her next thought had her sitting straighter. "Did someone find out about our, uh, situation?"

She shivered as she asked it. The only thing that could be worse than news of the possible switch getting out would be if it ended up being true.

"Nothing like that. There was just a bomb threat at Colton Oil."

"A bomb threat?" she called out.

At that, he chuckled. "I thought there still might be a handful of locals who hadn't heard yet. Thanks for fixing that."

"Do you always make light of serious stuff?"

"Maybe."

"So, what happened?"

His voice just above a whisper, he gave her what had to be the bare-bones version of the story.

"That must have been terrifying for your whole family. You're lucky the police didn't find anything."

"Even without my dad and Ace working there, I still had a sister and a brother in that building when the threat came in. Marlowe's pregnant, too."

Willow swallowed. She'd wasted so much energy hating the Coltons without thinking of them as a family. With a different set of problems from hers, but a family just the same.

"My other sister would have been in her office, too, if she hadn't been on an errand." He glanced over at her. "In the hospital lab."

If Asher had made the comment a few minutes earlier, Willow might have chuckled, but she no longer found any humor in it.

He lowered his voice again. "She was there for a DNA test to determine if our guest at the ranch is my dad's first-born son. That baby really was switched at birth."

"You win."

Asher blinked several times. Was he as surprised as she was that he'd admitted so much?

"What do you mean?"

"Your day was worse than mine." She grinned. "I take it you weren't supposed to share some of those details with anyone."

"None of them. But apparently I'll say anything to hear *your* story."

She tilted her head toward one shoulder and then the other, considering. He'd made himself vulnerable, so it only seemed fair. "It's going to seem small by compari-son, but as I told you, there was a complaint filed against the center. Someone did it online. Anonymously."

"What was it about?"

"The surprise inspector wouldn't tell me, but he did say

he didn't know how it could have been processed since the system requires all complaints to be signed."

"Someone was determined to make it happen."

"That's what worries me."

"What do you mean?"

"It's not the first unusual thing that's happened at the center lately."

Asher had been staring down at Harper, but now he glanced her way. "What else?"

"On Sunday, I received a letter, where the writer said that Tender Years will be closed by the end of the month. It said I can say goodbye to Mustang Valley, as well."

"Sunday?"

"It wasn't mailed. I found it stuffed in my front door. Printed on plain white copy paper. It has to be related to the complaint, right?"

"You must have pissed someone off. Disgruntled former employee?"

When she shook her head, he squinted. "From 'Anonymous'? That guy is sure getting around lately."

His words were light, but his hand—the one that wasn't steadying his child—was fisted against his pant leg. Was he feeling protective of her and Luna? She wasn't sure what to think about that. She didn't need to be taken care of. By anyone, let alone a *Colton*. So, why was she tempted to like it just a little?

"Willow Merrill?" a medical technician called from the open door that led to the examination offices.

As she stood, she released the breath she'd been holding. Keeping Luna in her arms, she pushed the stroller toward the opening. She had to be off her game if she was even tempted to rely on Asher. He was on the opposite side of a potential lawsuit that could leave her childless. She needed to remember that.

The woman smiled at them and then lowered her gaze to the paperwork in her hands.

"Asher?"

He stood and strode across the room with Harper. When he reached them, the woman led the way down the hall.

"We'll be in examination room four," she said without looking back.

We? She'd expected them to be in separate rooms. Privacy laws and all that. Apparently, that wasn't the way this would work.

The woman indicated for them to take the two seats against the wall. No one would be sitting on the examination bed.

"I'm sorry we all have to be in here together, but you saw how backed up we are," the technician said. "Since we need samples from all of you for the legally admissible test, we'll do it here."

"Fine," Asher answered for all of them.

"Now, I'll need identification from you both before we begin. A driver's license will be fine."

Having been warned about the requirements for a court-admissible test, they both had their IDs ready. An assistant knocked, opened the door and handed the tech a tray with four plastic-packaged test kits on top. She took their licenses to make copies.

"I'll do each adult's test first and then the infant in your lap," the woman said as she opened the first. "It won't hurt. Just a buccal swab test, where I'll rub one of these around on the inside of your cheek, gathering samples of your DNA."

She held up a long one-ended cotton swab along with a tube it would go in when they were finished.

"Then I will walk the tests to the lab myself to preserve the chain of evidence."

After placing half of a double-barcode sticker on the paperwork and the other half on the tube, she pointed at Willow. "I'll do your test first, then the next one for—" she paused to peek at the file "—Luna."

Willow leaned forward and opened her mouth. The other woman swished the swab around a few times inside her cheek, not gently, and withdrew it. Quickly, she tucked it inside the tube and sealed it.

Strange how something that didn't hurt at all could have the ability to destroy her life.

"You see? No big deal." The technician opened the second test.

Easy for her to say when she had nothing hanging on those test results. Willow slid a glance to Asher, who pressed his lips into a firm line. Clearly, they'd found something else they could agree on.

"The results will show how your alleles, the variant forms of each gene the lab will study, compare to that of both infants. The results will look at probabilities, and the conclusions will say you are 'excluded' or 'not excluded' as the biological parent."

"You mean it won't be definitive?" Asher asked.

"Well, probabilities of up to 99.99 percent are pretty definitive."

Willow braced herself as the woman leaned toward her daughter with a swab. Luna usually protested when the pediatrician came anywhere near her with a tongue depressor, so she surprised her mother by barely squirming. On the other hand, Harper let out a shriek and tried to push away the swab when her turn came. Good thing they hadn't placed bets on the girls' reactions.

"You're fine, angel," Asher crooned as he cradled his daughter to his chest and brushed back her hair.

For a moment, Willow picture them in another place

and herself as the lucky recipient of his ministrations. If she was the woman in his life, would he touch her with that same level of care, as if she was precious to him? Would he glide his fingers through her hair and whisper that it was okay to rely on other people sometimes?

"You're free to go whenever you're ready," the tech announced as she sealed the fourth tube. "We should have your results in about a week."

"A week?"

Asher's sharp tone startled Harper and yanked Willow away from the image that had no place in that room nor in any other part of her life.

She couldn't be having romantic thoughts about this man at this time. Or ever. She might have lost control of her good sense for a few seconds, but that had to stop now. In just seven days, they would have the answers to their questions. And if the results came out the way she prayed they would, she could forget she'd ever met the tempting Asher Colton.

Chapter 9

After the tech left with her tubes containing genetic truths and their futures, Asher couldn't get out of that examination room fast enough. It was too small. There wasn't enough ventilation. Something.

He hurried from the room, glad he'd skipped the stroller and just carried Harper. Even she had reacted to his stress, crying out from a mouth swab when she'd barely made a peep after her six-month vaccines.

"It's almost over, sweetie. Everything's going to be just fine."

Why did he keep promising her that? He had no idea how everything would turn out or if he would ever be able to make anything *fine* again. Strange, he'd thought he was handling the situation okay, even though he'd had to keep his personal issue from his family, particularly Marlowe and his mom. A bomb scare had seemed like enough of a Colton crisis for one day.

So, why had Willow's mention of the unusual occurrences at her childcare center been enough to push his fragile equilibrium over the ledge? The lights, sirens and that bomb-squad vehicle from the day before should easily have eclipsed a mildly threatening note and a bogus complaint. Why did it matter so much to him?

"Hey, Asher. Wait up?"

He'd already bypassed the elevator and had descended a few steps down the stairs to the first level, but at the sound of her voice, he stopped and looked over his shoulder. Willow stood at the top of the stairs with Luna's stroller. The diaper bag was in the seat, but she carried the child.

"What is it?" His sharp tone startled him as much as it clearly had her. "Sorry. Uh. What do you need?"

"You okay?"

"Sure. We're good."

She studied him until he took one step down. "Yeah. Me, neither."

"It was strange. It seems like a test that could crush all of us should at least have stung."

She made a strange face.

"Are you sure that Harper's *didn't* hurt?"

He reclaimed the step he'd ceded.

"You don't think—" At her grin, he stopped. "She definitely won't want to have her ears cleaned for a while."

He should have left then. It would have been his wisest choice, but when had he ever gone for those?

"Are you taking the elevator?" Without waiting for her answer, he climbed the last two steps until they stood together on the landing. After passing by her, he headed for the bank of elevators. He reached for the button, but she must have had the same idea as their fingertips brushed when they touched the plastic.

She jerked her hand back.

"Sorry," they chorused.

The lights above the doors indicated that all four cars were on higher floors.

"Was that all you wanted?"

She shot a glance from his hand to his face and back to his hand that he held wide. He immediately lowered it.

"I just wondered if you needed something else. Besides checking on me."

Willow cleared her throat and bent to lower Luna into her stroller. The infant kicked her feet and fussed, so she lifted her again.

"I was just thinking about what you said."

"Which thing?" he asked. "I said a lot of stuff. Too much, if we're being honest."

"The part about 'Anonymous' getting around."

"It was just a joke. Mostly."

"Well, I think you might be right."

"Because someone who sent a nastygram to your business wouldn't want to sign his John Hancock? Or that someone revealing dirty little family secrets or threatening to blow our place sky-high wouldn't want to wear a mask?"

"When you say it that way, it makes perfect sense. No self-respecting lowlife would raise his hand and say, 'Hey, over here. It's me.'"

"That would save both of us a lot of trouble if they did."

She seemed to accept that, which, for some reason, calmed him. He didn't need her questioning when he was suspicious enough for them both.

"Let's talk about something else," he said as the doors of the world's slowest elevator slid open. "Did you ever decide if you can find a spot for Harper at Tender Years?"

She had just parked the stroller in the back of the elevator, while he'd stepped over to select the floor, but at his words she spun around.

"Wait? You *want* Harper to come to the center? I thought you were insisting on in-home childcare."

"I need something right away. There are plans for a day-care center for staff at Colton Oil, and I might be able to get in on that eventually, but for now, yours might be the best choice."

"Why would you want to bring her to *my* center after everything I've just told you?"

"Compared to a shooting and a bomb threat? Anyway, Mustang Valley's not a big place. The town isn't overflowing with options."

"Well, when you put it that way. Flattery and all." She rolled her eyes.

"Seriously, Tender Years has a great reputation. Four and a half stars on Clamor, a *day-care*-review app. Sort of like Yelp for childcare."

"You read those?"

"I'm pretty keyed into local day-care issues, at least lately. Anyway, Harper and I just lost our third nanny in twice as many months."

She pursed her lips. "Hate that missing half a star."

"Perfectionist much?"

"Always. And whatever that complaint said about the center, it wasn't true."

"I know."

She'd been staring at the floor, but at his comment, her gaze lifted, and her eyes appeared to search his for answers he couldn't give. In this period of uncertainty, he was surprised he could be sure of anything, and yet he was. She would never put the center she'd worked so hard to protect during her marriage at risk with shoddy business practices. He wasn't sure why it mattered to her that he believed in her, but he liked that it did.

Seconds ticked by. He knew he should look away from

her, should pierce that bubble that held them as effectively as the three walls and the door of the cramped elevator. He couldn't. Worse, he didn't want to.

The doors broke the spell for him, yawning wide. He stepped out and, without looking back, held the door open for Willow. As he continued toward the exit, she pushed the stroller behind him.

"If you still want the spot, come by the center before we close tomorrow at six thirty to fill out the paperwork."

"You mean you found one, even with that *lengthy* waiting list and all?"

He couldn't resist looking back this time. She scowled at first and then shrugged. He couldn't blame her for lying about the opening. As if the situation wasn't uncomfortable enough between them, depending on the DNA test results next week, it could become unbearable.

"Was that the real reason you came after me? To tell me about the spot?"

"Remember, I can only hold it for you until tomorrow night. You'll need to bring her immunization records and contact information for anyone allowed to pick up your daughter for you."

"Sounds good."

"And you need to know that you'll be expected to follow the rules for picking her up on time, unless there's an emergency."

"Like a cow having a rough delivery?" He grinned.

"Bigger than that."

"Pregnant cows are pretty big."

She frowned again as she passed him. Did she think he'd been serious when he'd joked about his cattle?

"Don't worry. I'll be there tomorrow before you close, and Harper will be picked up on time every night, no matter what I have to do to make that happen."

Finally, she nodded. Whether she was thinking about her dad or her deadbeat ex when she looked at him like that, Asher had a sudden need to prove to her that he wasn't like either of them.

"So, I'll see you tomorrow night."

He swallowed as the impact of her words hit him. She either hadn't noticed that they'd planned a date of sorts or didn't want him to know that she had. She pushed the stroller down the hall without looking back.

Still in her mom's arms instead of the seat, Luna stared at them, cautious but curious.

Asher couldn't look away until they'd disappeared around the corner. Willow hadn't said why she'd changed her mind and agreed to give Harper the spot she'd clearly had all along. Well, let her keep her secret, and he would keep his.

He'd told himself he'd agreed to place his daughter at the center only because he had no choice. He'd even informed Willow that he had to find a childcare provider immediately, which wasn't exactly the truth. Dulcie and Neda adored Harper. Neither would mind helping to care for her a little longer, if necessary.

Why was he so determined for Harper to take her place at Tender Years? He could make all kinds of excuses about her needing stability and the chance to be around someone who had expertise in child development. He could even tell himself he just wanted to keep an eye on Luna after the two odd instances Willow had mentioned. The child could still be his, after all.

But he suspected the truth might be a little more basic than any of those things. He was enrolling his daughter so he could be near Luna's mom. And so that he could see her twice a day, every day.

Chapter 10

Asher tugged the reins to slow his favorite gelding, Dancer, the next afternoon. He hoped to more closely match the slower pace of Tally, the mare Jace rode. Still keyed up from the DNA test and the discussion with Willow the day before, he wished he could take Dancer out and let him fly across the open field, the shadow of the Mustang Valley Mountains calming him as they went.

Even if Asher wouldn't get that opportunity, patrolling the property with Jace would take his mind off his plans to see Willow again later that night. At least he hoped it would. He slowed the horse and looked over his shoulder.

"Doing all right back there?"

Jace closed the distance between them until his horse reached Dancer's right flank.

"Sure. I'm great. Just getting used to Tally. She's so different from all the other horses I've ridden. There's something wrong with this saddle, too."

"Yeah, those things can be awkward."

Since it would be impossible to keep a straight face, Asher didn't look back at him as he answered. Tally had to be the gentlest mare in the whole Triple R stable, and they were barely cantering. Not only that, Jace had mounted the horse from the *right* side. Every experienced rider knew to mount a horse on the "near side," which was another term for the left.

Why couldn't Jace just admit that he was a novice? There was no shame in that. A lot of people weren't comfortable or were inexperienced in the saddle. It also wasn't Jace's fault that he hadn't been raised on the ranch, where he—

Had the word *belonged* almost sneaked into Asher's thoughts? He reflexively yanked on the reins, causing Dancer to jerk his head back. When had he started to believe that Jace really was his brother? Why couldn't he just stay neutral until the test results came in, like his brothers and sisters had been doing?

He leaned forward and patted the horse over its mane. "Sorry, buddy."

Again, Jace rode closer to him.

"You never said anything about my hat."

This time Asher had to hold back a laugh. Still, his mom had always told him that someone fishing for compliments must need a good catch, so he obliged. "It looks great."

"You think?"

"Sure." Well, the cattleman crown was fine, anyway. The turquoise conchos and studs on the tooled-leather hat band might have been over the top for a work hat, but Asher didn't mention that.

"Ainsley said she liked it when I picked it out."

"She took you to Shiny Buckle Western Wear?" Asher didn't know why he'd asked when it was the only place, besides the feed store, where Jace could have bought a hat for miles.

"She offered."

"Nice of her." Not surprising, either. After all they'd been through lately, his sister was probably stress shopping.

"You told me I would need a hat. Guess I'll put it to good use if it turns out I'll be around for a while."

"I did say that."

"It was also great of your family to let me stay in the mansion until the results come in. I was serious that I'd be happy to get a hotel."

Asher shook his head. "It's no problem."

"If I'd had any idea the DNA test would take a week, I would've booked a room right away. I've already overstayed my welcome."

"Just like Ainsley said at dinner, you're our guest. You'll stay in the house until everything is settled."

What his sister hadn't mentioned was that they couldn't have a Colton, even a potential one, staying at the Dales Inn when this whole story came out. Especially after Ace had briefly hidden out at the hotel to avoid press attention.

"Just want you to know that I'm not used to living on someone else's dime. I make my own way. Always have since I got away from Luella."

"Good to know."

Asher would have asked who'd paid for that highfalutin hat, but he didn't bother. If Ainsley had been in a shopping frenzy, she would have insisted on brandishing her credit card. As an attorney, she was used to winning arguments, too.

"I've already told you I'll be volunteering with the rebuilding effort for all the earthquake damage. At least I can give something back to Mustang Valley while I'm in town."

"I'm sure that the families who weren't as lucky as ours will appreciate any help you can give."

He clicked his tongue to encourage Dancer to pick up the pace, but movement along the southeast fencerow caught his attention. A few ranch hands, who were supposed to be doing regular inspections along the property perimeter, were gathered in a single spot instead.

"What's going on up there?" Jace called from behind him.

Asher's phone buzzed in his pocket before he could answer. He clicked on the call as the name of one of his ranch hands appeared on the display.

"What's going on, Rex?"

"Sorry to bug you, boss, but someone cut through the fence on the southeast border of the new pasture. We have a couple hundred head hightailing it to the mountains or even El Paso."

Asher's breath seemed to freeze in his lungs, his heart punching against the wall of his chest. Someone was trying to sabotage the ranch. First, the bomb threat and now *this*? Could it even be connected to that fateful email sent to Colton Oil or to the attack on his dad? What was happening to the Coltons?

"Dammit. We're not far. We'll be there in five."

He sent an apologetic look back to Jace. "I've got to handle this. Catch up when you can."

He lifted his weight slightly from the saddle, leaned forward, nudged Dancer with his heels and loosened his grip on the reins, letting his mount know it was time to gallop. He couldn't get there fast enough. Someone had threatened the ranch and the animals in his care this time. That he couldn't allow.

Near the fencerow, he barely gave the horse the time and distance to stop before dismounting. Some of his men were already riding off to help herd the livestock, but Rex had waited for him. Asher tugged on Dancer's lead, the horse balking before following behind him.

"Is this the only damage you've found?"

"You don't think this is enough?"

Rex pointed with his thumb to the missing eight-foot section of the woven-wire fencing they used for the grazing fields.

"No, it's plenty. I just wanted to know if it was worse."

"I'll ask Marty, Tim and Jarvis to continue riding the fences to check for any additional breaks."

The two men traded worried looks over the amount of destruction the vandals could have caused to the livestock. Then Rex reached for his phone and sent off a quick text.

Asher stepped farther down the fencerow to examine the extent of the damage. Rather than a section with the horizontal wood top post or one with the diagonal wire brace, the vandal had cut through one of the more vulnerable panels on both sides, effectively creating an open gate for the cattle.

"At least the vandals cleaned up the extra fencing for us before they left." Rex reached for the cut section that had been rolled and placed outside the fence.

Though his employee was only trying to cheer him up, Asher gave him a dirty look.

"Yeah, they were downright charitable."

The thuds of approaching hooves announced that Jace had finally caught up with him. Jace pulled hard on Tally's reins, and the horse jerked her head back and whinnied in protest.

"What happened up here?"

Jace lifted his leg from the stirrup and awkwardly climbed down, from the right side again. Good thing the mare wasn't a runner, or she might have taken off since he failed to grab her reins. He glanced at the rein in Asher's hand and reached for his mount.

Rex pointed to the gaping hole in the fence. "Somebody cut it. Several cows escaped."

Jace blinked several times and pulled the brim of his hat lower. "Why would anyone want to do something like that? Wait. Not the new mothers and the calves?"

Asher shook his head, though he appreciated that at least someone was concerned about the animals.

"No, we kept them in the pasture closer to the out-buildings."

"Well, that's a relief, but it's still awful. What are you going to do now?"

That was the big question, and he had no idea how to answer it. His family couldn't seem to do anything to stop this series of attacks. Would they escalate until someone else was hurt? Or worse? He had a job to do, though. He would start there.

"I need to get the truck so I can repair the fence. Rex will guard the opening until I return, while the others chase down our stragglers."

"Why don't you let me?"

Asher had been scanning the pasture for escapees, but the other man's words brought him around.

"You want to track the cattle? Because I hate to tell you, but this…" Asher gestured toward him and the horse.

Jace shook his head, his lips lifting despite the gravity of the situation. "You think I want to ride? We both know I'm a lousy horseman. My only real time in the saddle was the pony rides at the county fair."

"Good. I was worried." At least Jace had come clean about his lack of experience.

"Don't be. I was only offering to guard the fence until you make it back with the truck."

Asher tilted his head and squinted. "What if a cow decides she wants out?"

"You'll give me some suggestions for how to talk her out of it. Hopefully, they'll even work."

"Well, Rex needs to be out herding our strays. You're sure you want to do this?"

"Sure, I am. I'm your…well…*guest*."

Swallowing, Asher glanced at Jace and quickly looked away. He wasn't the only one who'd begun to believe, perhaps even to *hope*, that the DNA test made them brothers.

Rex mounted his horse and pulled his hat lower over his eyes. "So, it's okay with you two if I head out?"

"Yeah, go. We've got this."

As they watched the ranch hand ride off, Asher gave Jace some suggestions for guarding the opening. At the next post over, he demonstrated how to remove Tally's bit from her mouth and tie the reins around the wood and through the interlocking galvanized steel wires.

Jace got it right on the second try.

"You know, I have zero experience with that, either, but I'd love to help you repair the fence. If you're okay with it, I'll even serve as watchman around the ranch and the house whenever I'm not assisting with the earthquake rebuilding efforts. With all the stuff happening lately, it sounds like you could use some extra hands around here."

He hated to admit that Jace might have been right about the last part. They needed to hire more security. "It sounds like you're going to be busy for the whole week."

"It's better than sitting around waiting for the hospital to call with the test results," Jace said.

Now that Asher could relate to far more than Jace could possibly know. He'd been driven to stay occupied, even before this most recent discovery, so he couldn't blame the other man for the same need.

"So, how do we begin?"

Asher blinked, then shook his head.

"Right. I need to get the truck, the extra fencing, tools and the fence stretcher."

"I'll be here, fending off Bessie and Buttercup."

"Good." Asher mounted Dancer and guided the horse in the direction of the stables. But as he stepped away, he spoke over his shoulder. "Thanks, Jace. I appreciate it."

"Hey, Asher."

He'd started away again, but he glanced back.

"If you need someone to talk to about whatever happened with that call the other day, well, I'd be happy to listen. Your brothers and sisters are, you know, busy."

"Thanks."

Asher nodded before turning and giving Dancer's reins more slack. He wasn't normally a sharer regarding his private matters, but this week he'd already poured his guts out to one person, and he was tempted to open to another. He'd almost confided in Jace when he hadn't shared the information with his confirmed brothers and sisters. Maybe he wasn't ready just yet, but he sensed he could trust him.

As he leaned forward and urged Dancer into a faster pace, he tried to compartmentalize those other thoughts that he had no time for right then. This land and these animals were his responsibilities as much as Harper was, and now he couldn't separate them. Whoever had brought fear to the Colton Oil offices had expanded that darkness to the ranch now.

Where his daughter lived.

Asher nudged the animal into a canter, grateful that he'd chosen a mount that loved to run. He would take care of his responsibility there, but then he had to get away from the ranch at least for a little while. And he would spend that time with the one other person who might understand how scared he was.

Chapter 11

Willow ground her molars as the buzzer to her apartment sounded for the third time that night. When would it sink in for the guy that she didn't plan to answer? He'd already tried the doorbell outside the front-door business entrance several times, which also triggered the one upstairs. She'd ignored that, so now Asher had climbed the exterior stairs to her home.

Why had she told him Harper could have the spot at Tender Years in the first place? She should have known better than to believe that he would show up before closing time, as he'd said he would. Men never came through on their promises. Especially ones whose whole lives had been about their "adventures," whether they were dads now or not.

"I told him not to be late."

Luna didn't appear to have an opinion on the matter, her face smeared orange from the squash baby food dinner she'd just devoured. She just kept banging her baby spoon on her high chair and smearing her free hand in what remained of the Os cereal on the tray.

The buzzer hummed for a fourth time.

Luna stopped and listened before resuming with her banging.

"This guy just doesn't get it." Willow bent to peek through the oven window at her lasagna, though she'd checked it two minutes earlier.

"I am not—"

The buzz even interrupted her declaration.

"That's enough."

She marched to the door, unlocked it and yanked it open. "Don't you get it? I'm not answering."

Asher stood on the landing looking back at her. Something, besides the summer-weight checkered shirt he wore, was different about him, but she couldn't place it. Harper, perched on her dad's hip, beamed back at her. Now, bringing the baby with him, that was cheating.

"It looks like you did answer."

"After you rang five times, plus the three downstairs, it was either that or call the cops."

"Does that mean you're inviting us in?"

"You didn't have to bring Harper to register her."

"Think she's old enough to stay at home alone?"

"Is anyone at the Triple R ever *really* alone? How many people live on that property? Eight or so in the mansion, plus staff and ranch hands?"

"Been thinking about this a lot?"

He grinned, but the expression didn't quite reach his eyes. Had something happened? What was she missing?

"Do you make a point of knowing those kinds of details about all your clients?"

"I don't know that much." Her cheeks burning, she

cleared her throat. "Anyway, you aren't even a client yet, and you're already showing up late."

"I'm sorry about that. Technically, though, it wasn't to pick up my kid." Asher gave his daughter a meaningful look, which she rewarded with a pat to his face from her slobbery hand. He barely winced.

"Still. I gave you until six thirty. I even waited fifteen more minutes, something I didn't have to do." She showed him her watch, which read seven fifteen.

"Thanks for waiting, at least a while." He lifted his free hand, palm up. "Please. Let me in and hear me out before your air-conditioning bill doubles. I have a good explanation."

With a sigh, she pulled the door wide enough for him to pass through without squeezing the baby. "It had better be good. It was also unfair for you to bring Harper along."

"Never claimed to be a dumb guy." He paused and slowly scanned her living room. "Hey, this place is great. Did you decorate it yourself?"

Willow considered making another snarky remark, but she always lost when they sparred verbally. Instead, she took in the space as he had, trying to picture it through a wealthy outsider's eyes.

He probably didn't love each piece as much as she did, but maybe he could appreciate the combination. The downsized comfy sectional, rustic industrial wood tables with matching square-jar lamps and the painting of a Texas longhorn steer showed her attempt at New York City chic. The baby swing and the standing infant activity center announced that she was a mom.

"I liked the challenge of it in this tight space."

"Well, you're good at it," he said. "I like the painting."

"How could I have guessed that?"

"What can I say? I'm a cattleman."

She shook her head. "You were going to share that amazing excuse, I mean *explanation*, of yours."

He didn't appear to be listening as he strode right past her, following the baby chatter into the kitchen. The squeal told her just when Luna recognized their guests.

Willow was still shaking her head when she rounded the corner. Asher was bent in front of Luna's seat, so their daughters were on the same level, but he straightened when he noticed Willow in the doorway.

"Squash, I presume?" He indicated Luna's messy face.

"Good guess."

"And what's that incredible smell in here?" He glanced toward the oven.

This time she couldn't help but to smile. She could stay immune to flattery for only so long. "It's my lasagna."

"Homemade?"

She nodded.

"You mean you raced out of work and whipped that up—" he paused to gesture toward the oven "—in the thirty minutes since you left *the office*? Feeling like a slacker here."

Earlier in the week she would have felt compelled to mention that with a full-time cook at the ranch, he never had to "whip up" anything if he didn't want to, but now it didn't seem right. He was trying awfully hard to be funny. Maybe he really did have a good excuse for showing up late.

"You know, it wasn't too hard to slip up here to preheat. And, for the record, since making lasagna is such a pain, and I'm cooking for one, I always prepare a few pans at the same time and freeze them."

"That's smart." He shot one more look at the oven.

"Would you like to stay for dinner?" she heard herself saying.

When had she gone from refusing to let him into her place to inviting him to join her? She hadn't even heard his explanation yet.

"You sure you have enough?"

"There's plenty. You two haven't eaten yet, either?"

He shook his head. "Well, she did. Formula, cereal and strained peas, right, sweetie?"

"Yum!" the adults both said together and laughed.

"And I won't have time to stop anywhere else before I do my other errand tonight," he added.

"Here. Give me a minute." Willow left the three of them in the kitchen and descended the staircase to the center below. She returned minutes later, carrying a second high chair for Harper.

"Great idea."

Asher lowered the infant into it and handed her a teething toy. When Willow passed him a box of cereal, he dropped a handful of pieces on the tray.

She opened the refrigerator door and pulled out a bag of mixed greens and a large tomato. "Here, let me throw together a salad. Meanwhile, you can tell me what made you miss what was probably a fine dinner on the Triple R and show up late here after you promised you'd be on time."

"It was kind of an emergency."

She paused from slicing the tomato to repeat his joke from the other day. "A cow had a difficult delivery?"

"No, someone cut down the fence, and we had about two hundred head of cattle running all over southeastern Arizona."

"*Deliberately* cut?"

"Sliced out like a new gate."

She couldn't help shivering as he filled her in about their discovery that afternoon. The situation had nothing to do with her or Luna, and yet the attack felt personal to her.

"Were you able to get all the cattle back inside their pens?"

After handing Asher plates and cutlery to set the table, which he did well for someone probably performing the task for the first time, she carried the salad bowl to the table. Then she pulled the small pan of lasagna from the oven and set it on a hot pad at the center.

"If you mean pasture, then yes. We think we have them all. But it took us hours."

"Which is why you're late and why you're starving now."

"Yeah, you'll have to forgive me if I make a pig of myself with your lasagna."

"You wouldn't do that, would you?"

"I might."

She grinned as she slid into the seat next to his, and then she blinked as the truth fell into place. "Wait. You didn't bring Harper here because you had to or even as a cute shield for being late. After the damage you found in the field, you just wanted her with you."

He'd started to lift the first slice from the pan, but at her words, his hand stilled.

"Can you blame me? Too many things have happened to my family lately. They must be connected somehow."

Finally, he lowered the spatula without dishing out the lasagna to either of them.

"What do you mean?" she prodded when he didn't start again.

"The email to the board saying that Ace wasn't a real Colton. Someone shooting my dad. The bomb threat. All three things were awful, and they all jeopardized my family members, but tonight? This one was different. It happened on the ranch. We live there. My *baby* lives there."

His voice broke on his last comment, and her heart

squeezed on his behalf. Asher was watching his daughter instead of her, his shoulders drooping as if the weight of his family's problems all rested squarely on his back.

"I forgive you for being late to sign the forms tonight. You can still register Harper at Tender Years."

When Asher turned back to her, he was almost smiling.

"If my excuse worked, then it was all worth it, right?"

"Some people will do anything to make sure they're not stuck on a waiting list."

His lips spread wide, and it was there again, that spark that flashed inside her whenever he was around. Dangerous, yet utterly appealing, two traits she'd learned to avoid in her well-ordered life. Sparks from flint and steel produced fire, which could consume everything in its path. She couldn't afford to take a risk like that again, not when she had a child to protect.

Her thoughts pushing her up from her chair, Willow reached for the dish Asher still hadn't served. She scooped portions out for each of them. With the drumbeat of two six-month-olds' fists on high chair trays as background noise, she used tongs to place salad onto her plate and passed him the bowl. He went through the motions of giving himself some and even ate a little, but he seemed miles away from her kitchen table.

"Guess I should have told you it was store-bought if it's that bad," she said after several minutes.

Asher's head jerked, his eyes widening. "What? Oh, I'm sorry. It's delicious."

He took another bite, pausing to savor it with closed eyes, before setting his fork aside.

"Well, good. I was worried I should give up cooking."

He shook his head. "No, don't do that. It's just that I'm—I don't know…"

"Furious? Worried? Scared?"

"D. All of the above. You don't ever want to know what it's like to want to protect your child from danger and have no idea where the danger is coming from."

She understood that better than he thought, but then didn't seem to be the time to remind him about the threats she'd faced. They seemed trivial when compared with the bogeyman coming after his family.

"Do you really think all those things are connected?" She twirled her fork in the remaining sauce on her plate as she considered it. "Because if they are, could the incidents happening here be somehow connected, as well? Maybe the same person?"

He didn't answer, so she continued.

"No. That didn't make any sense. We hadn't even met when I received that letter. And the complaint had to have been filed before—"

Her breath caught, and her jaw went slack as another thought appeared like a too-close lightning flash. Slowly, she shifted to face Asher, whose eyes were as wide as hers had to be.

"The switch," they announced together.

At the sharp sound of their parents' voices, both infants stopped pounding long enough to look at them with wide eyes. Willow held her breath, waiting for the chorus of tears to begin, but Luna returned to her banging, and Harper played along.

In a lower voice, Willow spoke aloud the question that Asher had to be thinking, as well. "Is it possible that whoever is trying to hurt your family gave the phone tip about the switch? That maybe the girls weren't switched at all? Like the bomb threat, maybe it's just another hoax."

Her words kept coming faster and at a higher pitch until her voice cracked over the last part.

Asher held out his hands above the table in front of him,

fingers splayed, and bounced them, his hands never quite contacting the table in a signal for her to calm herself.

"No, I will not calm down." She settled back in the chair, crossing her arms, her palms clammy against her biceps.

"Just wait," he said. "Let's think about this a minute. If someone called the hospital with a claim of a switch, why would they be so willing to believe them?"

He held up his hand. "Wait. Don't answer that. Obviously, because the other allegation they'd received was later confirmed."

Willow loosened her arms and rested her hands on the edge of the table. "Anne Sewall had no choice but to take the claim seriously until it could be disproven. Guilty until proven innocent."

Asher pushed his nearly empty plate away and planted his elbows on the table, gripping his hands together and resting his chin on top of them. He rolled his lips, as if considering what she'd said.

"How would some outsider know that our daughters were born that day?"

"Ever heard of social media?"

"I'm not on it."

"Doesn't matter. Can you say that no one in your family posted *anything* the day that Harper was born? Selina Barnes Colton, public relations guru, didn't blast a 'welcome to the newest Colton' on Colton Oil's social media accounts?"

"She did," he said with a frown.

She studied him for several seconds. "Don't you *want* the switch to be a lie? Or at least a mistake?"

"Yes, I want them to be wrong. I want the babies we brought home from the hospital to be the ones who should have been in our homes all along. I just don't want *you* to be caught up in any of this. I mean you and Luna."

"Thanks." She cleared her throat, not sure what to say.

"With everything else going on, I haven't even told Mom or any of my brothers and sisters about the potential switch. I figured all the other incidents had involved Colton businesses. Even the cut fence. But this one, it's personal."

"I doubt your dad would say that the shooting wasn't personal. I mean, if he could." She winced. "Sorry."

Willow took a few more bites of her dinner, though she was no longer hungry. Why hadn't she thought it through before making a joke like that? It wasn't as if his dad was at the ranch convalescing from a golf injury. Though the family wasn't talking about it, no one knew if Payne Colton would ever come home from the hospital.

Asher reached for his plate again and finished off the last of his lasagna.

"Yes, he would say it was personal," he said after a few minutes. "He'd also be furious about it, if he'd only wake up."

"He will," she found herself promising. Strange for her to say those words about a man she'd spent so many years and so much energy hating.

Asher's smile was a sad one.

"Thanks. I *am* sorry, you know."

"For what?"

"That you might be caught up in all of this because of my family."

"We still don't know that. And we won't until the DNA results come in. We have no proof there's a connection between the circumstances with your family and the threats here."

"That's why I'm going to hire a couple of guards to watch your place during the daytime. Just for extra peace of mind. Then for nighttime, the two of you should move into our place—"

"I can't accept help from you, and we're definitely not going to stay at the Triple R." She'd already said hogs would have to take flight before she would even *visit* the ranch.

"You wouldn't be with Harper and me, specifically. There's plenty of space."

She was already shaking her head. "Not going to happen."

He settled back in the chair and crossed his arms. "Hear me out. I just need to know that you and Luna are safe."

Something warmed inside her at his words, but she pushed thoughts that he cared about their well-being to the back of her mind. "And I can't move into the same house where my mother was thrown out like garbage."

"This isn't only about you."

They shot glances at the occupants of the two high chairs. Both infants had stopped pounding on their trays and were dozing off, their shoulders swaying and heads nodding.

"Guess our conversation isn't all that riveting," she said.

For several seconds, neither spoke as they watched their sweet, drowsy children.

"We have to figure out something," Asher whispered. "For them."

This time Willow nodded. As much as she hated to admit it, he was right. No matter how they'd ended up where they were that night, this involved the girls and their safety.

She pulled the tray back and unbuckled her child, who immediately whined.

"It's okay, sweetie." She lifted Luna into her arms, rested the infant's filthy face against her and spoke over her shoulder. "Let's clean them up, change them and put them down. I'll grab a portable crib from downstairs."

"I guess it wouldn't hurt for a while." He bent to unstrap Harper.

"We'll do the paperwork for Harper—" she paused, shrugging "—and then we'll figure out the other thing."

She might have been reluctant to accept assistance for herself, but for the child she loved, she would do almost anything, even take help from a Colton.

Chapter 12

Asher peeked at his watch just as he completed the final form. The chore had taken far longer than he'd planned, but then he hadn't expected Willow to invite him to dinner or that he would be reckless enough to accept.

"Have somewhere to be?"

"What?"

"That's the third time you've looked at your watch in the past fifteen minutes."

"It's just that I expected this to go faster."

"I told you there were a lot of forms to fill out."

She'd also shown him around the center, which had taken some valuable time. Every bit of it appeared to have been well-thought-out, from the infant room where Harper would nap and the playroom with tons of developmental toys and games to the craft room and the large activity space for when it was too warm or cold to play outside.

After spending all day in a fun place like that, Harper probably wouldn't want to come home at night.

Willow wasn't paying attention as he scanned the facilities again. She flicked through all the forms he'd completed, arranging them in some specific order and then slipping a paper clip over them.

When she caught him watching her, she gestured toward the stack.

"All the paperwork has to be perfect according to state requirements. I know it's a lot, but it's important for me to have all this information in case something happens with one of my charges and I am unable to reach the parents. I usually have clients print out the forms from my website and fill them out before they come in."

"You mean you gave me a special privilege? A Colton, no less."

That she shifted under his stare made him grin. It also proved he should get on the road. Soon.

"It was special circumstances."

He would give her that. Nothing about the way he'd ended up at Tender Years could be described as *ordinary*.

With another glance at his watch, he pushed back from the tiny kidney-shaped table and unfolded his cramped legs from the even smaller kid's chair.

"I do have to get going."

"Okay."

She followed him as he climbed the interior stairs to her apartment and was only a few steps behind when he reached the closed door to the tiny nursery.

"But I thought we were going to talk about, well, you know, safety," she whispered.

"I know, but I have to get to the hospital before visiting hours are over. I'm trying to take my turn visiting Dad more often." He blew out a breath.

"I'd planned to go over last night, but then ten more cows delivered. Then it was supposed to be this afternoon after I finished checking the fencerow. You know how that turned out."

"Don't worry. We'll wait to talk about it Monday. When you drop off Harper. Or when you pick her up."

His fingers closing around the doorknob, he looked back over his shoulder. "I don't think we should wait. We need to handle this now."

He couldn't blame her for the confusion in her eyes. Yes, he was overwhelmed. What was she supposed to do about it? She probably would ask him why he hadn't dropped by his father's room either time they'd been together at the hospital that week. How could he tell her he'd been too caught up in his personal drama to face the guilt that came with each visit to his dad's bedside?

"But you have a lot of other obligations, too."

"My first commitment is to my child." He whirled to face her but indicated the room behind him with his thumb. "Until we know for sure that Luna definitely *isn't* mine, then I need to protect her and you, too."

She opened her mouth to protest, but he lifted his hand in a request for her to pause.

"I know. You two are just fine. You don't need anyone."

Willow nodded. "At least you remember."

"But your personal safety is only part of it. The business you've worked so hard to build could be jeopardized, as well. Don't you want to protect that?"

When she didn't respond immediately, he suspected he'd gotten through to her.

He opened the nursery door, flipped on the light and stepped inside. The two infants lay sleeping peacefully in side-by-side cribs, one high off the floor, the portable squeezed in next to it. He couldn't help pausing to watch them, these sweet, innocent babies who knew nothing of how they'd either had their lives dramatically changed by someone's mistake or they'd been used as pawns in a cruel game.

"It's a shame to wake her," Willow said from behind him.

"I can't just leave her here."

"Have you thought this through? Were you planning to take her to the hospital? Have you brought her there before?"

"Yes, I've thought about it." Well, not technically. "And, no, I haven't brought her before. I haven't had to."

All the other times he'd visited his dad in the past four months, there'd been someone at the house who could watch Harper. This time was different, since he'd been too worried to leave her on the ranch when he'd left.

"It should be fine, anyway. Kids are allowed to visit direct relatives."

Willow shot a look his way, reminding him that they still weren't sure whether Harper was related to any of the Coltons, but at least she didn't say it out loud.

"You're right about that, but Harper's under a year old," she said.

"What's that mean?"

"A baby under twelve months old doesn't have a fully developed immune system. Some patients there are very sick. Harper could pick up an infection from one of them, or, if she's coming down with a cold, she could infect one of them."

"Why do you have to know so much about babies?"

Willow leaned over the end of Luna's crib since the room was too packed for her to slip in beside it and brushed back her daughter's sweaty hair.

"Same reason you know about livestock and farm machinery. It's my job. My degree is in early childhood development, too."

"Well, what do you want me to do? I can't take advantage of you by asking you to stay here with my daughter this late at night. I haven't even brought her to the center one time, and I'm already breaking the rules."

"You're not asking for anything. And that's not what I'm suggesting, either." She held up her index finger. "Give me a second."

Willow pulled her phone from her back pocket and typed out a text, her thumbs flicking over the keys as fast as any teenager he'd seen. She'd only returned it to her pocket when it buzzed, so she took it out again and glanced at the screen.

"Good. Candace said she can be here in two minutes."

"Who's Candace?"

"My best employee and dearest friend. She lives right down the street and is headed over to help out."

"It takes both of you to watch two *sleeping* babies?"

She chuckled at that. "You need to get to the hospital, and we should discuss our daughters' safety. Sooner rather than later."

He drew his brows together. "What are you saying?"

"That I'm going with you."

Why had she thought this would be a good idea? Willow stood outside the door as Asher pushed it open and stepped inside. Across the room, she caught sight of a woman sitting in a guest chair at the foot of a hospital bed.

Payne Colton's bed.

Hadn't she had enough of this hospital in the past few days without choosing to come again to visit the room of her mother's sworn enemy.

She could tell herself that it was only about discussing

the welfare of those babies sleeping back in Luna's nursery, but she'd hardly said anything after reaching his truck.
She'd barely *breathed* inside that cramped space where the
scents of his cologne, sweat and hard work melded into
something much too appealing for her own good.

Asher hadn't spoken, either, but he'd probably just been
too preoccupied with handling so many problems at once.
Was that why she'd offered to go? Because focusing on
his issues for a while would be easier than thinking about
her own?

"…this is," his voice traveled from inside the room.

Suddenly, Asher was back to her at the doorway. He
looked different as he'd stopped by her restroom before
they'd left and had slicked back his hair with water. Had
he made that adjustment for his dad's benefit, even if his
father wasn't awake to notice it?

"You coming in?" he asked.

"Oh, right."

She stepped farther inside, walking as close to the wall
opposite the bed as was possible without flattening herself against it. A single-patient room, of course, it had rich
wood accents and a recliner that looked suspiciously like
leather instead of the usual plastic-chic decor. Maybe a
celebrity room would have the best equipment that money
could buy, but none of it had purchased Payne's recovery
from the coma.

A thin brunette Willow immediately recognized as
Ainsley Colton waved at her from a straight-back guest
chair that looked out of place against the rest of the ame-
nities.

"This is—"

"Hey, don't I know you?" Ainsley asked, interrupting
her brother's second attempt to introduce them. "Aren't
you Willow Johnson?"

"Uh. Yeah." In addition to it having been a few years since she'd heard that name, she was surprised that Asher's sister knew it. Most royalty weren't familiar with commoners. "It's Merrill now."

"I don't know if you remember me, but I'm Ainsley."

Willow cleared her throat. "Yes, I remember."

Ainsley looked back and forth between them, clearly curious about seeing them together. "Willow and I went to high school together."

Asher shifted and cleared his throat, gripping his hands together. "Ainsley's the corporate attorney and on the board of Colton Oil, and Willow owns the day-care center where Harper will be going, but it sounds like you know each other already."

"We passed each other in the halls a few times, anyway," Ainsley said.

Willow wasn't sure what to do with the discoveries, first, that she hadn't been as invisible as she'd once believed in high school and, second, that Asher was uncomfortable having his sister seeing them together. She tilted her head so that she could see past the privacy curtain to the bumps of the patient's feet.

"Sorry to hear about your dad," she said to them both.

"Thanks," Ainsley said.

For a few seconds, Asher's sister stared at the patient, and then she turned back, her eyes shiny.

"He's a fighter, though. He'll be back to drive us crazy at the office before we know it."

The truth hung in the air among them that Payne had already been lying in that bed for nearly four months, but no one gave it a voice.

"He's looking better every day," Ainsley said.

Despite her reluctance, Willow stepped forward so that she could see the patient. If the way he looked now was an improvement, she couldn't imagine how horrible he'd appeared in the beginning.

She'd never seen Payne Colton in the flesh before, but this man looked nothing like the towering multimillionaire whose photo filled local newspaper pages. Small and frail, he hardly resembled the evil nemesis from her childhood imagination, either. His familiar head of white hair looked clean but stood up in all directions. Though his usual beard and mustache had been shaved off, silver whiskers sneaked out from the edges of his oxygen mask.

Willow swallowed over yet another discovery: a hospital bed could serve as a great equalizer. Outside it, he might have been the powerful Payne Colton, but between its sheets, he was just another patient, a host for an IV tube and the subject of vital-sign monitoring. Ainsley stood and crossed to the door. "The nurses keep getting after us for having too many visitors in the room. We're only allowed two at a time, and we've had as many as five, so if you two will be staying awhile, I'll escape a tongue-lashing this time and head home."

"That's fine. You can go."

As Asher stepped around the side of the bed and rested his hand on his father's arm above where the IV line was taped, his sister glanced back at him.

"I didn't know you were *friends*." She pinned him with a curious glance before turning it on Willow.

"It's not—" Asher cleared his throat. "I mean we're not…"

His gaze went from his father to his sister and back.

"Let's go out in the hall, and I will explain." Though Ainsley had been ahead of him, Asher brushed past her on the way out the door. Willow would have mentioned that Payne probably wasn't listening, but she doubted it would go over well with his children. She was still deciding whether to stay or follow when he leaned back in and gestured with a circular motion for her to hurry. He gave his sister a few of the week's highlights he must not have shared before, from the hospital's call about the possible switch to the DNA test and his decision to place Harper at Tender Years.

"I didn't want to add more stress to the family after the bomb threat and the vandalized fence," he explained.

His sister shot a glance at Willow that made her wish she'd stayed away from the conversation.

"She already knows everything."

"You shouldn't have shared."

He shrugged. "I did. She's caught up in at least part of this mess, anyway."

Willow raised a hand. "You know, I'm right here."

"Sorry." Ainsley lowered her head and rubbed her temples as if she was developing a headache, but then she straightened again. "*Two* baby switches?"

"We didn't believe one was possible," Asher said. "Look what happened there."

"Why didn't you tell me any of this before?"

"I couldn't share it while we were still waiting for the bomb squad to determine if someone had really planned to blow up Colton Oil."

Ainsley crossed her arms in a classic older-sibling move.

"You still should have."

"Maybe. But I hadn't realized there might be a connection. I still don't know if there is."

"Or if Harper's really yours."

The raw look in Asher's eyes caused a lump to form in Willow's throat. She was intimately familiar with the pain of that possibility.

His sister patted his arm in the awkward way of siblings who didn't often touch each other.

"She's mine. I know it," he said and then cleared his throat.

Ainsley nodded. "Where is she now? At home with Genevieve?"

Willow stepped forward and answered for him, not sure if he was ready to speak again. "No, she's at my place with my friend Candace and my baby, Luna."

"So, why are you *both* here?"

Willow rushed on, making up her story as she went. "He's, well, *we're* both concerned about the girls' safety. He mentioned hiring a private service to patrol around my business and my apartment above it, especially at night."

"Makes sense, particularly if, um—" Ainsley paused, as if trying to remember, "—Luna is—well, if the test produces unexpected results."

Willow didn't have to ask who the attorney was in the Colton family.

"What do you think about me getting some security guards?" Asher asked Ainsley. "I thought I'd let you weigh in, but I'm going to do it, anyway."

She gave him a mean look.

"Thanks for at least asking my opinion. I agree with you, by the way. In fact, we need to beef up security at the headquarters and ask the ranch hands to do more patrols on the property. If these incidents are related, and it's becoming more difficult to believe that they're not, then someone wants to hurt us. Who could possibly not like the Coltons?" Ainsley chuckled.

Asher exchanged a secret look with Willow, and though she braced herself for him to share her story, he paced up the hospital hallway instead.

"Have you spoken with Jace today?" Ainsley asked him when he returned.

"He helped me fix the fence." He lifted a shoulder and lowered it. "You know, I think he might be the real deal."

"You mean the 'real Ace' like everyone keeps saying?" she asked. "I know I'm trained to look at the evidence, but I think you might be right."

Ainsley began to pace herself and then spoke over her shoulder. "Jace is just so, I don't know, *different* from the guy I thought was my big brother all these years."

"If he *is* our brother, then it isn't his fault that Luella Smith switched him and Ace. It's not our Ace's fault, either. Just dumb luck."

"With a whole lot of human assistance."

Willow shook her head. "Thanks for reminding me that I was lucky to be an only child."

They chuckled at her joke and then quieted, probably as lost in their thoughts as she was in hers. The Coltons had always seemed to lead such a charmed existence, insulated with the cosmic protective dome of fat trust funds. It was clear now that they had as many problems as anyone else—more than some—and money only amplified them.

Ainsley startled her from her thoughts as she stepped in front of her and held out her hand.

"It was nice officially meeting you, Willow. I don't think we were ever properly introduced in high school."

"I'm pretty sure no one was." She gripped her hand and smiled.

Ainsley's gaze shifted to her brother. "Want me to tell the others about this?" She pointed her index finger and rotated her hand back and forth between them a few times.

"No, I'll let them know."

Asher's sister was talking only about the possible switch of their babies and not anything specific between the two of them, but when his gaze snagged hers, the electricity that sparked inside her had nothing to do with their children.

Ainsley must have missed whatever had passed between them as she wasn't smiling when she spoke to her brother.

"Thanks again for asking my opinion. Usually, we would have gone to Dad over a question about adding security." She paused, sending a wistful look toward the hospital room door. "Or at least Ace. But everything is different now."

"Yeah, as the second oldest, you get your chance to shine."

She shook her head. "The biggest opportunity I never wanted."

Chapter 13

"Have I told you recently how much I adore you?" she said as she applied a wicked red lipstick to the perfect bow of her lips. At least that was how someone had described them the other night.

Her caller chuckled on his end of the line, oblivious.

"As a matter of fact, you haven't."

"Well, let me begin now."

She spent a few minutes puffing him up and getting him worked up as she carefully coiffed her hair for another man. It wasn't wasted time, not when any means to this end would be well worth the investment. No one could take something that belonged to her. Woe to the few who'd tried.

The words came easier, anyway, as she pictured her man for tonight, someone who knew how to treat a lady. Unlike her caller, with his tape-repaired glasses and chronic halitosis. If not for his big, beautiful *brain*, she would have swiped left to make him disappear a long time ago.

"You're going to love how I did this."

While he blathered on about some technical nonsense that no one outside labs or computer companies cared a whit about, she applied quick bursts of hair spray. Was this supposed to excite her or something?

"You're amazing," she said when he finally stopped talking.

"Do you think we can get together tonight? I can tell you exactly what I'll do to—"

"Now, let's not get ahead of ourselves, my love. We have to stay focused, or we'll make mistakes."

"I don't make those."

"That's why I chose you, honey. To be mine." She added the last almost too late.

"When can I see you again?"

"Soon. I promise. Now let's both get some rest. We have so much more work to do." Well, he did anyway.

He finally acquiesced, and she was able to cut the call with a singsong "sweet dreams."

She hung up just in time, it seemed, as her doorbell rang.

Asher climbed into the driver's seat of his pickup in the hospital parking lot and gripped the steering wheel, his shoulders curling forward and his chin dropping to his chest. That night's visit with his father had been tougher than any he'd experienced in weeks, and he wasn't sure why. Could it have been that some part of him hoped Dad would wake right then so he could introduce him to Willow? If she was the reason, he had bigger problems than only a bomb threat and a vandalized fence.

"It's still so hot tonight," she said.

Willow slid off the sweater she'd worn over her sleeveless blouse and skirt in the hospital's air-conditioning, and all he could think about was how soft that exposed skin of her arms would feel. On his fingertips and his lips.

When he didn't respond, she glanced over at him. "You okay?"

Other than realizing he was getting in over his head with this independent beauty *and* that it might have to do with more than her sexy curves and all that dark hair? Or that he'd already learned a lot about her, and he craved more details? If not for all those things, he was just fine. He'd told himself he would never let another woman get close to him, yet, for a reason he couldn't explain, Willow tempted him to break his own promise.

Still, he straightened and glanced her way. Her delicate nose and chin, along with those beautiful curls, were outlined in both light and shadows coming from the parking-lot lamps.

"I'm fine. It's just tough sometimes." Letting her believe that this was only about their time in his dad's hospital room was a coward's way out, but it was easier than admitting the truth.

"It's so hard to see our parents when they're frail like that. I had a tough time with it before Mom died." She jerked her head back suddenly. "I didn't mean... That's not what I was trying to say."

"Don't worry. I understood what you meant." He was quiet for a few seconds, and then he added, "Every time my phone rings, I'm praying that it will be the news that he's finally awake. Then I'm terrified to answer because there could have been some complication, and he'll just be..."

Asher didn't finish his words. He couldn't think about that awful possibility after he'd looked at his father through Willow's eyes that night. Dad wasn't getting better. He was just existing, with oxygen filling his lungs and an IV drip feeding him.

"I know it's hard, but you can't think like that," she said. "You have to be strong for him, just like you are for Harper."

"You, of all people, have to know who my dad is. He's not a perfect guy. He put the company and the ranch ahead of not just me, but all his kids. I can't remember a single time he ever took me outside and threw a baseball with me."

"Do you even *like* baseball?"

He cleared his throat. "No. But that's beside the point."

Asher shifted toward her in the seat, his right leg coming up on the upholstery. "He's the type of hands-off parent I'm determined *not* to be for Harper, and yet—"

"You love him," she finished for him, turning to face him, as well. "He's your dad."

"He's my dad. I guess it's pitiful, but I want him to wake up so he can see that I'm a good father. A better one than he was to me."

"Harper was born a few months before your dad was shot, right?"

"Yes. So?"

"Then he *knows*."

"What do you mean?"

"I've only just met you, and I can see it." As she spoke the words, she covered his hand with her own.

Asher swallowed as he stared down at their fingers. When he finally looked up again, she was watching him. Was she as surprised as he was that she'd reached out to him? Did she just feel sorry for him after seeing his dad in the hospital, or was it something more?

Willow slowly withdrew her hand, but the atmosphere inside the cab had changed. The air was heavier, the space more intimate. Like the first flicker of a flame during a candlelit dinner, something had ignited, and there was no reclaiming that candle's pristine wick before the brush of the match.

"I mean I've seen you with Harper. You're a wonderful dad. She adores you. I think she has good instincts."

"You're a great mom, too."

Not giving himself time to second-guess, Asher leaned forward until they were only inches apart. Her eyes were wide as she stared back at him, but she didn't look away, didn't back away. Her full lips called to him, begging for him to lean just a little farther, to close the tiny chasm, but still he waited. No matter what he wanted, and, oh yeah, he wanted, it had to be her choice.

Her tiny nod was all the permission he needed.

He dipped his head and claimed her lips, sinking into their almost impossible softness. No slow, polite introduction, his big *hello* came with the glide of mouths, a dance of tongues and a brush of teeth. Bells of caution clanged in his mind, but he tuned them out, lost in the sweet taste of her, the texture of her lips, the call of her sighs.

His splayed hands slid through her hair as he continued to delight in and then devour her lips. She returned his kisses with equal determination. A battle of equals where both were favored to win.

When even lips weren't enough, he scooted from behind the steering wheel and slid his hands over her bare shoulders to draw her across his lap. He paused to cheer his genius for insisting on a bench front seat and then brushed his hand along her smooth, lean calf as he took her lips again.

He couldn't get close enough or kiss her deeply enough. He wanted more and, unless his instincts had gone south in his months of celibacy, she was a more-than-willing partner.

Suddenly, she pulled her head back, but she had to take a few breaths before speaking.

"Now let me get this straight. Did you just kiss me because I'm a good mother?"

"No, that's not—"

She grinned then. "If good parenting is an excuse to be kissed, maybe I should prepare myself for random strangers to stop me on the street. You should get ready for it, too."

Willow was only joking, and yet the thought of anyone kissing her didn't sit well with him. That should have served as a warning of high-voltage proportions, as if he needed another one, but he was ignoring them all.

He leaned in and took her lips again, this time in a slow and sensual exploration that had her shifting her bottom on his lap to move closer. When he pulled away again, he smiled.

"I kissed you because I haven't been able to think of anything else since I walked in that office and saw you sitting there in those shorts." Well, that wasn't entirely true since he'd been imagining a whole lot more than just kissing her over the past few days.

"Is that so? You weren't thinking about that beautiful baby sitting in my lap or the little angel you carried in your arms? Just me and my...shorts?"

He shook his head. "That's not it. Sure, I was thinking about the girls, and—"

She stopped him by tilting her head and taking his mouth, kissing him as if it had been the only thing on her mind for days, as well. Her hands slid over his shoulders until they met behind his neck, where she sank her fingertips into his hair.

As his one hand brushed up and down her silky arm, the other took a more adventurous journey to the hem of her long, full skirt. He inched it up slowly, pausing to skim his fingers over each inch of newly exposed skin. She eased his progress by sliding her knees wider.

Then just as his fingertips brushed over the tiny bit of cloth at the juncture of her thighs, and he smiled against her lips as he noted the dampness, Willow jerked her head back and pushed forward off his lap.

"What are we doing?" She shook her head as she slid her feet back into her flip-flops. "We can't do this. Oh my gosh. The hospital security car is right over there."

She pointed through the window to a small white car patrolling the next lot, its yellow light flashing.

"What if that driver made it over here? What would we say we were doing?"

Asher tried not to chuckle, but he couldn't quite remove the mirth from his voice. "I think they would figure it out all on their own."

"It's not funny. I'm a business owner in town. A child-care-center owner. I can't be caught playing show-me-yours-I'll-show-you-mine in the hospital parking lot."

"Was that what was just about to happen here? Darn. We were interrupted too soon."

She folded her arms over the chest that had so recently been pressing against his.

"Go ahead. Keep joking. But I know my business can't handle negative publicity, and probably the last thing your family needs is more of it."

He swallowed. It always came down to that. He was first, last, *always* a Colton. She was right that they couldn't afford any more scandal right now. As with every other decision in his life, the family had to come first. Now he had to figure out how to quiet another potential fire-cracker, the one they'd just ignited together, before it blew up in their hands.

Chapter 14

Willow stared silently out the windshield as Asher drove his truck from the hospital parking lot and continued up the main street. What could she say about the activity she'd not only allowed but had been an enthusiastic participant in, right out in public? How could she have behaved so brazenly and carelessly outside the same building where her DNA and her daughter's genetic material were still under scrutiny?

What could she tell Asher when her pulse had yet to slow completely, and she was still warm in places that had no business heating up for him? She was grateful for the darkness in the truck cab as the skin on her face and neck probably were still pink, having been abraded from the stubble on his chin. It was all she could do not to skim her fingers over her lips that felt swollen and sensitive.

How had she let this happen? She was a divorced mother. A respected local business owner. Unlike a sex-

crazed college student with few obligations, she was up
to her throat in them. And yet she'd been minutes, maybe
seconds, from taking on a sexy cowboy in every sense of
those words in the front seat of his pickup.

That he was a Colton should have been the worst part.
No, that trophy went to the truth that given a less public
setting, she would have enthusiastically continued the activity she'd interrupted before.

"Hey, you were supposed to turn back there," she announced after he missed her street.

"Just give me a second."

He drove three more blocks along the town's deserted
main drag and pulled into a parking space in front of Lu-
cia's Italian Café.

Willow sank down into the seat and crossed her arms.
"If you think we're going to just pick up where we left off,
then you've got another *think* coming."

It didn't matter that she'd just considered the same possibility. Even now her skin still tingled from the delicious,
rough touch of his calloused fingertips, reminders that he
was a man skilled in working with his hands.

Maybe it had been a while, and she'd forgotten the *zing*
of a first embrace, but something about being in Asher's
arms had felt different to her. Was she the only one left
wondering if a kiss could be more than just a kiss?

"You're safe here under the streetlights. I just want to
talk to you." He wrapped his fingers around the steering
wheel. "I'll even keep my hands right here, if that makes
you more comfortable."

It didn't. That was the hell of it.

"Go ahead. Though I don't know what we have left to
talk about."

"I'm sorry about…kissing you. I shouldn't have done
that."

She waited for him to fairly share the blame with her over what had happened in the truck, but he studied his hands instead.

"Okay. You've apologized. Now can you take me home? I'm sure Candace wants to get back to her place, too."

"Give me a minute. I'm trying to say something, okay?"

"All right."

Asher shoved his hand back through his hair. He didn't seem like the type of guy who'd ever be bashful about speaking his mind, but this must have been important to him. If she'd been happy to let him put his tongue in her mouth and his hand up her skirt, she could at least take a moment to hear him out.

He turned to face her, breaking his promise about the steering wheel.

"I think we should get married."

The words rang in her ears, strange and discordant. "Are you serious?" she managed finally.

"Now hear me out." He held up both hands, palms facing her. "We wouldn't do it automatically. Only if we find out for certain that the girls were switched."

"At least it wouldn't be an *automatic* decision."

He crossed his arms.

She lifted a hand in surrender. "Go ahead."

"Getting married would be the best solution. We'd have the chance to be with both girls without disrupting their lives."

"No disruptions at all?" Was he even thinking this through? The girls' lives would be thrown into chaos, particularly Luna's. Not to mention Willow's, if he suggested that they all live together on the Triple R.

"Well, only *a few*. And for us, it wouldn't be so bad. We'd get along. We're already almost friends."

Rather than look at him, Willow tilted her head back,

shaking "no" against the headrest. This was not the *difference* she'd imagined when he'd kissed her.

"You know, Asher, little girls dream of one day receiving a marriage proposal just like that one. What it lacks in romance, it makes up in sheer pragmatism."

"It's not like that. It would be a good thing for the girls."

"Thank you for your lovely offer, but I'll have to decline."

"We don't even have the DNA results yet."

"No, we don't," she said. "But if our girls were switched, and that's still a big *if*, we can work out a legal arrangement. We could even have joint custody of Harper and Luna."

Her idea didn't sound like the best plan, but it was better than her initial worry that he would try to take full custody of both babies. His suggestion would still net him two babies, plus a bonus bride-of-convenience.

He shook his head, closing his eyes. "We'd never be able to keep the story out of the newspapers."

"Is that what your big proposal is about? Don't worry. I won't go to the tabloids. I don't need their money. Or yours."

"I know you don't. And you wouldn't. But can you imagine what a great story a hungry young reporter could find in two switched babies in one family? Particularly if it's the *Colton* family."

He had a point. She hated to tell him, but the press would have a field day with that story, whether they were married or not.

"I don't think you're looking at this as the perfect solution it could be," he continued.

"Probably not."

She had to give him credit for his determination. Xavier had never begged her to marry him; she'd done so of her own volition. Asher might not have needed her to put a roof over his head like her ex had, but he still wanted something from her.

He must have known that he was wearing her down. She'd opened her mouth to tell him that if he'd stop asking, she would at least consider it, when he reached for her hands.

"We could make it work. We've already proven that our marriage could be, you know, *interesting.*"

Willow pulled away from his touch. Earlier images that had been delicious and colorful drained to soot. She knew the moment Asher recognized his mistake because his shoulders jerked.

"That's not what I meant."

"What exactly did you mean? Did you kiss me as a *test*? Were you checking our chemistry? Since you're proposing a loveless marriage, did you want to make sure that we're at least entertaining together in bed?"

He wrapped his fingers around the steering wheel again. "I just meant that we could have fun together."

"Why'd you even worry about that? If you're suggesting a marriage of convenience, you must know that you could outsource the 'fun' part, like my ex did."

Asher leaned his head forward, his hair falling across his cheeks. "I don't know what you expect from me."

"I haven't *asked* you for anything. But I can tell you this. I made a mistake once. I won't marry another man who doesn't love me."

Memories of the hurt and humiliation that Xavier caused flooded her thoughts.

"I also won't marry for security like my mom did, even if it ensures that my child will be with me full-time. I won't marry the wrong guy like she did."

He held his hands wide. "I'm not the wrong guy. I'm

honest and dependable. And, you said it yourself, I'm a good dad."

He looked away then. They both knew what had happened after she'd said that. Finally, he turned back.

"I promise I would be a good father for both girls, no matter which one of them is my biological child. I want to give them two parents who will love and care for them."

"It's not enough."

He crossed his arms and slumped back in the seat. "It has to be enough because it's all I have to give. I'm not looking for a real marriage. I asked for that once, and I got burned."

"I'm sorry you're so jaded. But if you stay closed off, you'll miss the chance for real happiness when it comes along."

He rolled his head to the side to look at her. "Thanks for the relationship advice, but I don't have the luxury of worrying about my heart. I have a daughter to think about."

"That's what I'm doing, too. I am a role model to Luna, and I take that job seriously. I watched my mom pick the wrong man for the wrong reasons and end up with nothing but sadness."

She shook her head to clear those memories of her mother's muffled crying late at night.

"If and when I ever marry again, I will choose the right guy for the right reasons."

"What the hell were you thinking, going rogue on the plan?" he said none too quietly the moment she answered the phone.

"Well, that's a fine way to say hello. I sure hope you're not at the grocery store or in a coffee shop."

He harrumphed.

"I'm smarter than that. I'm outside. No one's around. For once, give me credit for knowing what I'm doing."

"Sweetie, of course you do."

"That's better. Because you know you can't complete our little project without me. Don't forget that."

How could she if he kept reminding her? She'd never relied on a man for anything, and she hated having to do it now. "We're in this together. We're partners."

"Now, tell me why I didn't know the bomb threat was coming."

Bomb threat? Her breath caught, and she winced over her lack of control. Had he heard her gasp? She needed to think. Maybe this was something she could use.

"Ingenious, by the way," he said.

The breath she'd been holding came out in tiny puffs. "I thought so."

She hadn't exactly confessed, a good thing since she didn't have the basic details of the threat yet. How was she supposed to keep the upper hand with her *partner* if he caught her in a lie?

"As long as you didn't make the call to the Colton Oil headquarters on your cell so the police can track you."

"Do you think I'd make a mistake like that?"

"You? No way. You're an expert at the game."

Unfortunately, they didn't appear to be the only ones playing it. Just how many enemies did these people have? She didn't care who the real caller for the bomb threat was, as long as he or she didn't get in her way.

"What about all the other little happenings around town? Did you hire someone else to do it?"

"Can't a girl have a *few* secrets?" she purred.

"Not about—"

"Really, honey." Her matter-of-fact voice was back, but she didn't care. "Don't worry about the other things.

They're just distractions from your real purpose. Remember, you're one of the most critical parts of our whole plan."

"I guess you're right."

She always was. He would do well never to forget that.

Chapter 15

Spencer parked his patrol car that sunny Monday afternoon inside the community of pricey condos in the city's industrial zone. Light brick exteriors, manicured lawns and a view of the mountains to die for, the neighborhood was an odd fit for Mustang Valley. Still, as a haven for young professionals who worked during the day, it was the only spot in town where a parade of officers in marked patrol cars could serve a search warrant in broad daylight.

As if on cue three other vehicles—most of his department's fleet—pulled in behind his car, and the officers approached him.

"You ready for this?" Senior Detective P.J. Doherty said when he approached him.

"I'm more than ready to have a break in this case. Aren't you?"

"Oh, you know we are," Junior Detective Kerry Wilder

answered for the both of them, while tucking a stray strand of long red hair back under her hat.

"Especially you," P.J. said to Kerry, his impish grin in full force. "You have to be sick of investigating reports involving that branch of the Coltons. Have you reconsidered your decision to marry into that family?"

"Rafe isn't like Payne. And no."

Spencer blew out a breath. "Now that we have that settled, can we serve this warrant before Harley Watts comes out of his darkened computer room and tries to escape out his back door?"

"How do you know it's dark?" she asked.

"Just a guess."

A pretty good one, he figured. With as much time as Watts had been spending online to post his ramblings on social media, dotted a few times with references to Colton Oil, he couldn't have been typing in a bright space. Too much glare would cause eye strain.

Officers Lizzie Manfred and James Donovan joined him next to his car. All checked their Kevlar vests and their weapons.

"Now, none of Watts's convictions were for violent crimes, right?" James asked as he adjusted his duty belt.

Spencer shook his head. "Just financial. Identity theft and such with his techie skills, but still felonies."

It was a good thing that he had those convictions, though. Without them and Watts's parolee status, they never would have been able to get a warrant, based on his online comments alone. Free speech and all.

With weapons drawn, three of them carefully approached the front door. Lizzie and James covered the back. Kerry took the lead.

She pounded on the front door. "Mustang Valley Police. Open up."

Nothing. They waited for several seconds, listening closely for movement inside. Still nothing.

"You think he isn't home?" P.J. asked.

"Our research shows he's online at various times throughout the day and night," Kerry said. "Maybe he just isn't answering."

Just then, footsteps came from inside.

"What do you want?" a voice called from the other side of the door.

Kerry spoke in a tone just above a speaking voice. "Mustang Valley Police Department. Mr. Watts, we need you to open up."

"Nah. I don't think so. I know my rights. Not without a warrant."

"Well, you're in luck since that's just what we have."

A pasty-skinned, twentysomething, with brown hair in need of a trim and black, plastic-rimmed glasses, yanked open the door. "What the hell for? This is police harassment."

Instead of addressing his accusation, Kerry held out the folded sheet to him so he could see for himself.

"You're not going to find anything. I'm clean. I'm on parole. Do you think I would do anything to go back to prison?"

"We'll see, sir." She stepped past him into the house.

While James guarded the home's occupant, the others executed the search warrant, hunting for any electronics and printed materials pertaining to Colton Oil.

Kerry stepped into the pitch-dark room where Watts had been working and flipped on the light. She exchanged a look with Spencer, who grinned over his prediction about the darkened computer area. He'd been at this job for a while.

Lizzie was already working her computer magic, invaluable to the department, at the desk. They moved to other rooms to continue the search, but she quickly called them back in.

"Here it is," she said as they crowded around her.

From Watts's "sent" box, she produced an email from "Classified" and with the subject line "Colton Oil CEO Ace Colton is not a real Colton."

"You think it's the real thing?" Kerry asked Spencer.

"I don't know, but it's enough for an arrest and to confiscate the laptop."

They returned to the living room to cuff Watts and read him his Miranda warning. Kerry did the honors.

"You have nothing on me," Watts spat.

"I'm sure the judge will want to see the email from 'Classified,'" Spencer said.

"I was hired to send that email for a friend."

"What friend?" Spencer thought it might be worth a try to ask. "Just tell me what you know, and I'll try to get a deal for you from DA Karly Fitzpatrick."

"No way. I'm no snitch. You know what they do to snitches inside?"

"But you're going to spend years in prison this time."

Watts shrugged despite his handcuffs. "If you really have on me what you think you do, I'm going back either way. Might as well stay loyal, don't you think?"

At the man's smile, Spencer ground his teeth.

Despite that they'd finally made an arrest in the case after four months, no one was ready to celebrate as they put the suspect in one of the cars and headed back to the station. Spencer squeezed the steering wheel tighter than was necessary as he drove. Four months and countless hours of work, and they were back to where they'd started from. With nothing.

* * *

On Harper's second day at Tender Years, Asher rang the bell with a good fifteen minutes to spare before closing. And just like the day before, Candace answered, while Willow appeared to be conspicuously MIA. Sure, he'd seen the center's owner in passing during both morning drop-offs, but she'd been too busy to acknowledge him. Or unwilling.

"Well, hello, Mr. Colton."

"Hi, Candace. Remember, I told you yesterday that I'm just Asher."

A grin split her round, pleasant face. "Oh, right, 'just Asher.' Forgot that. I'll try to remember for tomorrow."

She probably should since she would be the one answering the door again. Guess he couldn't blame Willow for avoiding him after the proposal that never should have been.

"Would you like to come in out of the heat while I get your little darling?"

She pulled the door wide to let him in, quickly closing it behind him. "Stay here, and I'll be right back."

Candace disappeared into the back of the house. She hadn't smirked when she'd spoken to him the day before or then, but he couldn't help wondering how much Willow had shared with her about his lame offer.

Why had he suggested it anyway? That their steamy and far-too-brief session in the hospital parking lot had muddled his brain, along with sending several of his body's systems into overdrive, wasn't a good enough excuse. Had some part of that proposal been about more than only convenience?

Willow had still committed to keep Harper at the center, as agreed, but she would probably try to renegotiate and get as far away from him as she could after they received the results later that week.

Especially if they learned that the switch had been just another hoax and that she and her daughter were only collateral damage in a war that had nothing to do with them. Strange, how the thought of that left him numb. Did he want the babies to have been switched just so Willow Merrill was forced to continue dealing with him? What kind of swine was he?

Candace whisked back into the room so quickly that someone in the next room must have had his daughter ready with her diaper bag for a fast handoff. He had a good idea who was on the other end of that pass.

"Here's your sweetheart."

She tried to switch Harper into his arms, but his daughter had her fingers wound tightly in the woman's black-and-silver ponytail.

"Guess she must like it here."

The older woman laughed as she carefully unraveled her hair from the infant's tight grasp. "Your daughter has a good grip."

"I would think that hair like yours would be a liability in your business."

"Nah. It's not so bad. The babies love it, and sometimes they need something good to hold on to when their parents drop them off in the morning."

She was finally sliding Harper from her arms into his when Willow hurried into that room, carrying a huge cardboard box with a photo of baby wipes on the outside of it.

"Are they gone?" she said before she caught sight of them. "Oh. Hi. Thought *everyone* would have left by now."

He couldn't help smiling as he settled his daughter on his hip. "I gathered that."

She lowered the box to the floor. "So, um, Harper seems to be settling in well here."

"She's used to a lot of different people taking care of her."

Willow licked her lips, seeming unwilling to meet his gaze.

"That's a good thing. She's a flexible young lady."

Alicia, a midtwenties brunette with rust-colored skin and short hair, entered the room from the opposite side of the house, carrying Luna. After glancing at the box on the floor, she handed the baby to Candace and then leaned close to whisper in her ear.

Candace glanced nervously after her as the other woman walked away. "Have a good evening Mr.—I mean Asher."

With a quick wave, she followed the path the other woman had taken.

"What was that about?" Asher pointed to the empty doorway.

Willow shook her head and rolled her eyes. "They're always a little odd when single dads are around."

"You have a lot of those?"

"A couple."

She shot a look over her shoulder in the direction her staff had gone.

"Are you going to stop avoiding me soon?"

"I haven't been—"

She shifted her gaze to his face. He grinned back at her. She answered with a shrug.

"Look, I'll pretend I didn't ask, and you can pretend you didn't shoot me down."

She crossed her arms and shook her head. "It's only a few more days now."

He nodded, swallowing.

"Well, have a good night." He headed toward the door.

"Are you going to visit your dad in the hospital again?" she asked from behind him.

Was she trying to delay his departure instead of rushing him out the door?

"After dinner. Mom said she would watch Harper."

Neither mentioned what had happened when they'd visited Payne together, but that memory hung in the air between them, an uninvited presence in the room.

He'd just turned to the door again, when a sound behind him brought him back around. All of Willow's employees stood in the doorway, odd expressions on their faces. Candace had passed off Luna to Tori and had a tablet and a stylus in her hands instead.

Willow's gaze moved from her employees to the tablet and back. "What's going on?"

Candace rolled her lips inward as she took a step forward. "We thought you'd want to see these."

"A one-star review!"

Willow knew she would upset Luna if she didn't keep her voice down, but she couldn't help herself as she stared down at the Clamor app, open on the tablet. Her heart was beating fast enough to explode in her chest.

"Unfortunately, not just one," Candace said.

The older woman reached over and slid a thumb up the side of the screen, bringing up a series of reviews, each with a clear dearth of stars.

"Oh my gosh. One-star, two-star, one-one-one? How did this happen? How did you even find this?"

Tori slid forward, bouncing and shushing a nervous Luna. "Little Derrick's mom told me we should check it out. It didn't seem right to her."

"That's because it isn't."

Willow blinked at the sound of Asher's deep voice. For

a second, she'd forgotten that he was still there, but relief filled her that he was.

"'Unsanitary conditions'? 'Uncaring staff'? 'Questionable disciplinary practices'?" She glanced up at him over the screen. "It's all garbage. None of it's true."

"I know that." He crossed over to her and used his index finger to gesture from Harper to Alicia, who nodded and lifted the child from his arms.

He extended a hand toward the tablet that Willow held. "Do you mind if I look at it?"

She waited as he scrolled through the damning words. Was she hoping he would know how to fix this when she didn't have a clue?

Asher glanced up again and pointed to the screen with the stylus. "Trolls. Good ones, too. Look. None of these reviews have the same date. A few appear to have been written last summer. Is that possible?"

Willow shook her head. "I don't check it every day, but none of those were there last month. Or even last week."

"Right. You said you had a four-and-a-half-star average."

She leaned in close enough to see that the number had dropped to one and a half. "How can this be happening? Who would do something like this?"

"You said the letter you received warned you they would destroy your business. Well, they're giving it their best shot."

She gripped her head in her hands. "What can I do?"

Candace stepped forward and crossed her arms. "You mean what can *we* do?"

The other two women automatically nodded, and Asher did the same.

"First, I would contact the Clamor app's customer service department and contest these reviews," Asher said.

"You can tell them that despite their varying dates, the posts were all added in the past…week?"

"That's right," Willow said.

Candace took another step forward. "Second, we need to draft a letter to give to all of our current parents, letting them know about the issue and that you're challenging these allegations."

Asher had begun to pace, but he stopped. "Right. That will help ensure that your other current clients stay with you."

The look he shot Willow's way seemed to say that he and Harper would stick around as long as she wanted them there.

"You should also have your webmaster or webmistress add a note on your website," he continued.

Alicia lifted her free hand. "That's me."

Willow shook her head. It all seemed like such a bad idea.

"Not everyone even checks Clamor reviews. We could just report it to the company and not say anything to the clients until after it's repaired."

"You sure you want to do that?" Asher asked. "One of your clients already brought it up to your staff. You think there aren't others or that they won't talk to each other? If I were you, I would try to get ahead of the story."

He returned the tablet to her and held his hands wide as if his suggestion was so simple that one of her daycare kids could have made it. Nothing was simple about this situation.

"Doesn't sound like the Colton approach to handling negative news to me."

"Because it's not. But, just like now, I wasn't the person in charge of making those decisions."

This time she was. He was reminding her of that. She

wasn't the infant inside her mother's belly this time, who'd become homeless because of others' decisions. Nor was she the pregnant wife who'd just found out her cheating husband was leaving her, too.

Tender Years was both her home and how she supported her family. She might not be able to control what someone tried to do to it, but she was responsible for how she responded to it. She planned to fight back. And with this much support, she wouldn't have to do it alone.

Chapter 16

Asher hurried through the living room in the mansion, his boots making entirely too much racket on the shining wood floor for someone so late to dinner. Why couldn't his family be like others that never found time to share a meal together? No, not the Coltons. Even with their busy schedules and the chaos swirling around them, they still managed to eat together several times a week.

Tonight, though, he would have given anything just to eat macaroni and cheese upstairs in his third-floor suite with Harper.

"It's about time you got in here," Rafe called out as Asher rounded the corner into the formal dining room.

Most of his siblings and a few of their future spouses were sitting in chairs spaced along the ornate table, his mother in her usual place at one end. Their dad's empty seat, at the head of the table, served as a constant reminder of his absence. No one dared take that spot.

Asher slid into the empty chair between his mother and five-year-old Evelyn, better known as "Evie," the soon-to-be stepdaughter of his brother Callum. Asher forced a smile and tugged on one of the child's long pigtails, earning a giggle. Still, all he could think about was backing out of the room and returning to his suite.

He wasn't ready to face all of them and the mysteries swirling among them. Particularly now that he was aware of another set of happenings at Tender Years that could be connected to those involving his family.

"Where's my granddaughter?" Genevieve asked before he could unfold his napkin.

He unhooked the baby monitor he'd clipped to his waistband and held it out to display that the power was on. "Already bathed and already down for the night. She had a long day, so she'll be easy for you."

Callum held up his arm to look at his watch. "Well, we're just glad we didn't try to hold dinner for you. Otherwise, we'd all have been eating cold fried chicken."

Grayson pointed to the bones on Callum's plate. "Don't worry, brother. He had more than his share while it was still hot. And Jace didn't starve, either."

Jace glanced up from his plate, littered with bones, and set aside his half-eaten chicken leg. He lifted his hand to lick his fingers but wiped them on his napkin instead.

"Sorry. I couldn't help it. Every time I eat one of Dulcie's delicious dinners, I'm convinced she can't top it. Then she does."

Asher couldn't help chuckling. With praise like that, Jace was probably winning over staff along with the rest of the family.

"You still could have saved some for the rest of us."

"You snooze, you lose," Callum answered for Jace.

Laughter spread around the table. There hadn't been much levity among them lately. Asher liked the sound of it.

Genevieve held up both hands to restore some semblance of the order she preferred at family dinners.

"Can we let Asher get something to eat so he can make it to the hospital before visiting hours are over?"

"That's right," Ainsley said as she lifted the still half-filled tray of Dulcie's award-winning fried chicken. "I'd forgotten it was his turn."

Ainsley handed the platter to Callum's fiancée, Hazel, who then passed it to Callum. With the help of her future stepdad, little Evie was the next to pass the plate.

Finally, it landed in Asher's hands. The sides of mashed potatoes, green beans and country corn bread that followed were all colder than the cook preferred to serve them, but he'd been late, after all.

"So, Asher, what kept you?" Ainsley asked too casually. "Was there a problem at your new day-care center? What's it called? Tender Years?"

Asher swallowed a bite of chicken and his annoyance and then wiped his mouth on a napkin. "Good memory. But, everything's great there. Harper's loving it."

He caught his older sister's attention and frowned at her. Sure, he hadn't gotten around to telling the whole family yet about the possible second baby switch, but he didn't plan to unload all the information on them at dinner. Particularly not Mom.

With as much as she'd had to deal with lately, he owed it to her to deliver the news gently that her first grandchild might not be related to her. Maybe he would even wait until the DNA results arrived so that he could offer the question and the answer at the same time.

He hoped Ainsley would stop trying to push him into sharing before he was ready, but he doubted he would get that lucky. An attorney to the core, she was used to winning every argument.

His stomach sank as she folded her hands on the table in front of her and smiled benignly.

"I had the chance to meet the owner of Tender Years the other night when Asher brought her to the hospital." She grinned at Asher. "Well, meet her again, I guess. I went to high school for a little while with Willow Johnson. Oh. Right. It's Willow *Merrill* now, but she wasn't wearing a ring."

He frowned at his sister again. It was a good reminder that he should never get on her bad side. He either had to tell them the whole story right then or let them wonder about a romance between him and Willow. Coward that he was, he chose silence…and speculation.

Grayson leaned forward and rested his forearms on the table. "I think I remember a Willow from school. She was the class behind me. Dark, curly hair, right? Real pretty?"

"How pretty?"

At her question, Savannah Oliver, Grayson's brand-new fiancée, leaned forward from her seat beside his and lifted a brow.

Asher straightened in his chair, as well. He knew it was an observation from a long time ago, but it still didn't sit well with him that his half brother had been checking out his friend. Was that what he should call the woman he hadn't stopped thinking about since they'd made out in his truck the week before?

He tried to be casual, sliding his fork into his chicken breast and pulling off a chunk, but his brother wasn't paying attention to him, anyway. Ainsley, on the other hand, was watching him with open curiosity.

Grayson reached for Savannah's hand and laced their fingers together. "For me, no one comes close to you."

Rafe pulled an imaginary weapon from a pretend holster and aimed it at his brother. "Hands up. It's the mushy police."

"Oh, you would have said something just as lovey-dovey to Kerry if she weren't working long hours at the police department lately," Marlowe pointed out.

"You would, too, if Bowie wasn't out to dinner with a client," Rafe said.

Marlowe shrugged, not denying it. "Anyway, didn't your fiancée tell you it's not safe to point weapons at people, even if they aren't loaded?"

Again, laughter spread around the table as several of her siblings agreed that they both would have been as syrupy as Grayson if their future spouses were there.

Asher expected his mother to hush them again. Instead, she pinned him with her incisive stare.

"You brought a woman to the hospital?"

She'd been more protective of their father the past few months than even their brothers and sisters. He took a closer look at her, taking in the blue-black half circles of exhaustion that had formed beneath her eyes. The strain was getting to her. She was already dealing with so much that he couldn't bring himself to give her one more thing to worry about.

"Willow, uh, just came along as a favor to me. I needed to finish with the day-care center paperwork, but if I didn't get to the hospital right away, I was going to miss visiting hours."

"That was kind of her."

His mother's gaze narrowed, showing she wasn't buying it. Just like when he was a kid, she could always tell when he was making things up. He scrambled for a better explanation but settled for a subject change instead.

"Have we heard anything more about Jace's DNA test?"

He addressed the matter while trying to ignore the heat of his mother's gaze on him.

Ainsley shrugged. "If you'd been here earlier, you would have already heard this, but I got a call from the lab that there's another delay. They said the test had to be repeated."

"You've got to be kidding. First, the delay and now a repeat?" It gave him an idea about what he and Willow would be facing in a few days, but he didn't mention it.

Jace shook his head. "Yeah, I was so sorry to hear it. And I offered again to move to the Dales Inn, but your mom and brothers and sisters asked me to stay put. Is that still okay with you?"

Asher nodded. "Yeah. It's fine."

Ainsley appeared poised to try a third time to get him to talk about Willow and the possible switch, but a cell phone rang before she had the chance.

"Okay, who has the phone at the table?" Callum called out.

A chorus of not me's rang out.

The "no-phone rule" was one of the few battles that Genevieve Colton won at her dinners. Usually.

"Then whose is it?" she asked.

With an apologetic expression, Marlowe produced a phone from beneath the table. "Sorry, Mom. After the bomb threat…"

Her words fell away as she glanced at the display. Without looking up again, she clicked the screen to answer the call.

"What's up, Daniel?" She nodded with the phone at her ear as she struggled to her feet, as if the person she spoke to could see her. "Which mystery are you talking about, and what did you find out about it?"

"Okowski?" Ainsley mouthed. At her sister's nod, she added, "Put him on speaker."

Marlowe shot a glance at her mother for approval and then lowered into her chair again, set her phone on the table and clicked the speaker button. With so many unusual happenings at Colton Oil, they all wanted to hear what the company's information technology director had learned.

"Go ahead, Daniel. You're on speaker with most of the family. You caught us all at dinner."

"Hello, Coltons."

They called out greetings at once.

"We have a lead on a dark web connection to the anonymous email about Ace. Should I wait to inform the board in private, or should I tell you all now?"

Everyone waited for Marlowe's lead since, as Colton Oil CEO, it was her call. She glanced around the table at her siblings and their partners, and then her gaze paused on Jace.

"I'll step out," Jace said. "I need to make a call anyway."

She nodded at him apologetically.

Genevieve lifted a hand to him as he walked toward the living room. "You'll be back for dessert, won't you? We have Dulcie's double-chocolate cake."

"Wouldn't miss it. I'm already salivating." He continued from the room.

As soon as a click announced the front door was closed, Marlowe addressed the phone on the table.

"Okay, you can speak freely. It's just family now. I'll update Selina afterward."

Asher leaned forward. "So, tell us. Who was it?"

"The police found a link to a guy named Harley Watts."

Rafe shook his head. "Daniel, this is Rafe. I don't recognize the name."

"Yeah, me neither," Daniel said. "But the police were

able to connect him to a few references about Colton Oil on a dark web board where illegal activities are bought and sold like want ads."

Asher planted his hands on the edge of the table. This meandering story was getting them nowhere.

"It's Asher. Cut to the chase, man. Did he write the email or not?"

Daniel's chuckle came through the speaker. "Yes, the police found the email to Colton Oil that said, from 'Classified,' right in his sent box. They arrested him."

"Guess he wasn't much of a computer expert, after all, if the police were able to catch him," Marlowe said.

"Right about that, boss," Daniel said. "Watts refuses to give the identity of the person who hired him. He is being charged under interference with commerce laws for his implied threats of exposure of the secrets affecting the structure of Colton Oil."

Marlowe puffed up her cheeks and blew out a breath. Her skin was ruddy again, like it had been after the bomb threat. Their mother wasn't the only one dealing with a lot lately.

"That's great, Daniel. Do you think the district attorney will be able to convince him to cooperate in the investigation?"

"It's not looking likely."

Ainsley rolled her eyes. "Why wouldn't he cooperate? He could face up to twenty years in federal prison if convicted."

"That's true, but he probably realizes that the information investigators already have on his computer will connect him with other convicted felons on the clandestine board. The DA will petition for his parole to be revoked." Daniel sighed audibly. "I guess he figured it wouldn't serve him well to talk."

"Just our luck," Rafe called out.

Grumbles of agreement all around the table announced their common frustration as Marlowe ended the call. Too many questions, never enough answers. It was the story of their lives lately, and the rest of them didn't even know the full tale.

Marlowe glanced over at Rafe. "Did you know anything about the arrest?"

"Me? Kerry doesn't tell me anything about her job. She says it wouldn't be professional, but I think she just doesn't want me to worry."

For several minutes, no one spoke as they ate a few more bites and sipped their wine.

Asher even considered making the announcement about his personal mystery right then. It wasn't as if their spirits could get any lower.

Then the five-year-old, who'd been sitting so quietly beside him, shifted and came up on her knees so she sat as tall as some of the adults.

"Did someone say 'dessert'?"

Jace strode through the door then, tucking his phone back in his pocket. "Yeah. What she said."

"You sure timed that one," Grayson said.

Again, the room filled with laughter. The moment had passed, and Asher hated admitting his relief that it had. He would tell them all about the possible baby switch. Soon. Individually instead of en masse. Anyway, he would share his story with at least one family member that night.

Maybe Payne Colton had dropped the ball dozens of times during Asher's childhood, but right now he could do one thing from that hospital bed that he'd never done before. Something Asher needed more than he could ever know. He could be a good listener.

Chapter 17

"You're looking better today."

Asher shook his head as he patted his father's pale hand on top of the blanket. He didn't know why he said that every time he visited. It wasn't true. Dad looked the same. Broken. Fragile. Words he never would have used to describe the mountain that was Payne Colton.

"On second thought, you look like crap. I want you to wake up right now and get back to work. We need you."

He scooted the chair closer to the bed and waited. Payne's chest rose and fell in the same monotonous and assisted rhythm as before, his regular heartbeat drawing a squiggly but relatively even line on the heart monitor. Asher lifted his father's hand and squeezed, but when he released his hold, it dropped with a soft thud back to the sheets.

Asher gripped the plastic bedrail instead, squeezing so hard that his knuckles flashed white. What had he expected? That his father would pull a Lazarus and wake up right then? Sure, Dad would have liked to make a statement like that, but wherever he was, he must have felt safe there, as he didn't seem ready to return yet.

"Okay, then. Stay there if you need to. But just for a while, okay? Remember your grandbaby, Harper? She's getting so big now. You're missing out on the chance to see her grow."

He pushed aside his own resentment that elbowed in every time he thought of his dad. Besides, they now shared something in common that no father should ever face.

"I finally understand how you were feeling when you found out that Ace possibly wasn't yours. The hospital's said the same thing about Harper and me."

Even recognizing that this was a one-sided conversation didn't stop him from pausing and waiting for his father's response.

"Deep in my soul, I know she's my child, but then you thought the same thing about Ace. *Felt* the same thing. Yet you were wrong."

He couldn't bring himself to put to words the question swirling in his mind that he could have been mistaken, as well.

"I'm a lousy son, but part of the reason I wanted you to wake up was so you could see that I'm a good dad. Maybe better than you." He shook his head, a sad smile pulling at his lips. "I know. It's terrible."

His voice broke on the last. He lifted his chin and tilted his head back and blinked several times. He had to stay in control, at least for his daughter's sake.

"I met Willow because of this mess. She was here the other night, but you were too rude to wake up and give her a proper hello."

He paused again, hoping, and then finally he continued.

"You'd like her, I think. She's a take-no-prisoners person. Kind of like you."

He grinned at the comparison. Until he'd spoken the words, he'd never realized how true they were. She was strong-willed and single-minded in her determination to keep her business and the security she'd worked so hard to build for her family.

Just like Payne had.

Asher blinked again in the muted lights that illuminated his father's bed. No matter what he could say about him, he never should have doubted that Payne had made so many of his decisions to protect not only the business, but also the family. Maybe that had been his way of showing the children he loved them. Had Asher been looking for more, to the exclusion of seeing what was already there?

"I asked her to marry me. Can you believe it?" He shook his head, still finding it hard to believe himself.

"Yeah, she turned me down flat. I'm zero-for-two in the proposal business. First, with Nora, though that was more of a suggestion than an actual proposal, and now Willow. She said she didn't want to marry someone who didn't love her."

He propped his elbows on top of the bedrail, clasped his hands together and pressed his thumbs to his forehead just between his eyebrows.

"Can't blame her, I guess."

He also couldn't admit that her rejection had stung, nor that his feelings about Willow weren't as indifferent as he would have liked to believe. Was it because they were trapped together inside a puzzle where the pieces might produce a picture that neither of them wanted to accept?

"She'll get over it." But would he?

He continued to update his father on the rest of the

recent developments involving the family, from the possible baby switch to the bomb threat to the damaged fencing. The list included the unusual events at Tender Years, though he admitted he still hadn't worked out whether there was a connection between those and the attacks on their family. Sure, he glossed over a few details, but a gentleman never kissed and told.

A strange peace filled him when he'd finished. Whether it was a message from his father that everything would be all right or just his own mind's reprieve from the worry, he wasn't sure, but he was relieved anyway.

A pile of cards on the bedside bureau caught his eye. They had been stacking up since so many friends and business associates wanted to offer their well-wishes, and only so many flowers could be crammed in one room.

Asher crossed to the pile of cards and rifled through them. Marlowe had been handling them until then, having Payne's admin, Dee Walton, send thank-you notes for the cards and flowers. Obviously, they'd gotten behind.

He carried the stack over to the bed, opening and reading the sentiments, both printed and handwritten, inside each one.

"You definitely have a lot of friends, Dad," he said after reading a flowery comment. "Or a lot of people who owe you a favor."

He grinned at that. His dad would have gotten a chuckle out of it, too. His chest squeezed that he might never hear that full-throated laugh again, but he shook his head, pushing the thought away. It wouldn't help anyone.

To distract himself, he opened the next get-well card, its message on the front as benign and well-meaning as all the others. But at the note written in block uppercase letters inside, his breath caught.

Oh, too bad you won't get well because I'll be back to finish you when your family least expects it.

Could this be from the same saboteur who'd called in the bomb threat and cut the fence? Or was this from the real shooter? Was he finding connections where they didn't exist, or missing real associations at everyone's peril? Even Willow's?

With fumbling fingers, he reached for his phone and found the personal cell number for MVPD Sergeant Spencer Colton.

Spencer answered on the second ring.

"What's going on, Asher?"

His distant cousin didn't bother with niceties. They'd rarely spoken to each other before the past few months, and now they were in regular contact.

"Can you come to Dad's room at Mustang Valley General as soon as possible?"

"What's going on?" he repeated.

"Can you just *get here*?" Asher hated that his voice rose at the end of the question, but he couldn't help himself.

"I'm already on my way, so just slow down and tell me—"

"I'm not going to slow down. Just get here." He blew out an exasperated sigh. "Someone's planning to kill my father."

Asher knocked but didn't wait for an answer before hurrying into Spencer's office at the Mustang Valley Police Department building late the next morning. He dropped into a visitor's chair adjacent to the desk piled high with file folders and loose papers.

"Did you learn anything more about the card I found last night?"

The former soldier in his dark blue uniform stared at him from across the desk, his blue eyes narrowing. Spencer closed the dark file folder he'd been studying and rested it on top of the pile.

"Well, hello again, cousin. Since we filed the report only twelve hours ago, I don't have much to tell you yet. We sent it to the lab, but chances are slim that we'll be able to pull a print. You and the hospital staff touched that card, too."

"Well, what are we supposed to do while we wait?"

"We already have an officer outside his hospital room door, one we can't really spare, I might add. So why don't you head back to the ranch and let us do our jobs?" Spencer stood as if attempting to dismiss him. "Anything else I can do for you today."

"You can tell me what you know about Harley Watts."

"Why do you want to know about Mr. Watts? And why didn't you ask last night at the hospital?"

"We were both a little busy dealing with the newest threat to my dad's life, don't you think? Sorry about calling your direct line, by the way."

"Yeah, we have this thing called 911 that residents can use to access the emergency dispatchers. You might have heard of it. Usually, it works pretty well for us." He settled in his chair again. "But I guess I can forgive you."

"That's generous of you."

"It's the kind of guy I am. Besides, your branch of the Colton family tree might be straining my department's overtime budget for officers investigating these cases, but at least the work is interesting. Better than writing up dog-licensing infractions."

When Asher frowned at him, Spencer shrugged, unrepentant.

"As I told Daniel Okowski, Watts has been charged with—"

Asher waved his hand to stop him. "I've already heard that part from Daniel at dinner last night. I want to know how a lowlife like Watts can afford a beautiful condo in the industrial area. Daniel copied me on the research he's been doing about Watts. I drove over and got a look at the place."

"Already, this morning?" The sergeant pointed his pen at him. "Are you trying to take over my job? You don't see me out on the Triple R, birthing calves or slaughtering cattle."

"Just trying to hurry things along. I had to do *something*. Marlowe and Ace both own units in that community, and I can tell you they're nice, too nice for someone without a job to afford."

Spencer grinned. "Have you been looking at Watts's social media too?"

Asher lifted a shoulder and lowered it. "I know how to use a computer. Obviously, so does he if his charges involve the dark web. Maybe that's where he earns his money, sending messages for other people who don't want their identities known."

"We're looking at all of that."

"Well, are you checking out the recent incidents at Tender Years? Maybe he could have been involved in those, too."

Spencer shook his head. "Now I don't know what you're talking about."

"Willow Merrill, the owner, probably didn't file a police report. Maybe she should have."

"What kind of incidents?"

"A threatening letter was delivered to her place of business."

The law-enforcement officer lifted a brow. "I'm not

sure you understand how this dark web thing works, but that seems a little low-tech to me."

"What about an anonymous electronic complaint with the Department of Health Services when it's supposed to be impossible to do without the filer's name? And what about a Clamor smear campaign, where tons of reviews show up the same day, all showing different dates and appearing to come from a variety of sources?"

"Now, those would require some expertise," Spencer said. "They also hint that she really pissed somebody off."

"That's what I told her."

"Since when are you and Ms. Merrill friends?"

Asher crossed his arms. "She's my daughter's day-care provider, and we found out our babies may or may not have been switched at birth."

"No way. Again?"

"Some families are just lucky, I guess." He filled the sergeant in on the details from the hospital. "It's possible that the call about the switch and the other strange events at the center might somehow be related to the threats involving my family."

Spencer gestured to his stack of files. "As much as I don't want to add to our backlog of cases, you should tell Willow to file a report. Whether or not any of the things are connected, whoever's trying to get her attention might not stop."

The sergeant stood again, indicating the meeting was over. "I guess we have even more to look into, so we'd better get started. Unless there's anything else…?"

"There's one more thing. I think you should look into the Affirmation Alliance Group."

"You mean Micheline Anderson's self-help organization? Why that group?"

"Harley Watts just happens to be a member. He talked

about it all the time on social media. Daniel's research mentioned it, as well."

"Sure, we saw that, too. But that's no big deal. Many community members are involved with AAG. Anyway, the group has done a lot of good in helping people since the earthquake, even putting victims up at that huge guest ranch on its property. Have you ever seen that place? Fancy log-cabin exterior. Huge open lobby with a triangular roof." Spencer held his hands wide. "And what about Micheline offering a location for the evacuees after the bomb threat at Colton Oil?"

"I'm not saying AAG doesn't do good. It's just that if Harley Watts is involved, then maybe there's, I don't know, *something*."

"Fine. I think you're barking up the wrong tree, but we'll check into the AAG as soon as you Coltons stop calling us every day." He shook his cousin's hand. "You know, you could have been a fine police detective. In fact, I'm glad you had an interest in ranching because you'd probably have had *my* job."

"I don't want to be a detective, but I'm motivated to find the answers on one case." Asher tilted his head back and forth, considering that.

"Well, make that a few cases. It's my dad in that hospital bed and my siblings who were targeted in that bomb threat. Willow and the girls might be caught up in all of this because of me. Even the cattle are my responsibility."

Spencer patted his shoulder and then guided him out through the squad room.

"I know you feel responsible, but you need to let us take it from here, okay?"

Asher nodded, and then he pushed back his shoulders.

"I will, but you need to know that if whoever this is trying to get to the people I care about, they'll have to go through me first."

* * *

Asher stepped to his spot in front of the massive television in the mansion's family room. His requested audience, consisting of his mother, siblings, a few of their future spouses and one possible brother, lined the two brown leather sofas and the pattern side chairs. He cleared his throat and began.

"I've called you all here because—"

"It had better be important. Dulcie made chicken and noodles, and she said fifteen minutes until dinnertime," Grayson announced. "I'm not eating cold noodles."

"Just give me a minute, will you? And it is important."

Grayson's grin slipped away as he sank back into the buttery leather.

Ainsley leaned forward and gestured for Asher to continue. "Well, go ahead and tell them. Finally."

He nodded, surprised that she hadn't done it herself several days before.

"I wanted to give you an update on a mystery I've been facing this week."

"Just you?" Rafe piped. "Don't you think the rest of the family has been dealing with this, too?"

"Not *this* mystery."

The group appeared to lean forward as one to hear him better. He took a deep breath, reminding himself that speaking the words aloud wouldn't make it true.

"It's about a possible baby switch." He raised a hand before any of them could interrupt him again and say that Ace's switch was a fact, not a possibility. "Involving Harper."

"Harper?"

This time it was his mother calling out. He held his hand up again to slow the onslaught of questions.

"A week ago, an administrator at Mustang Valley Gen-

eral called to inform me that Harper might have been
switched with another baby born November 2."

Marlowe splayed her hands over her belly. "You've got
to be joking? Again?"

Her husband-to-be, Bowie, slid his arm around her and
squeezed.

Asher smiled despite his nervousness. "I said about the
same thing when I heard it. Willow was pretty shocked,
too, but we went the next day for the DNA test—"

"Wait. That's how you know Willow?" Grayson asked.

Callum propped his hands on his knees. "And you
waited a whole week to tell any of us this?"

Asher's younger brother might have said "any," but it
was clear from the hurt look in his eyes that he meant him.
Asher was already worked up enough himself tonight without having to worry about wounded feelings.

Instead of asking Asher another question, Rafe directed
one to his future wife, Kerry, who sat next to him.

"Did you know anything about this?"

She shifted in her chair, her eyes narrowing. "I keep
telling you I can't share anything about any cases I'm
working on."

"But this is about my *family*."

She shook her head and let it fall forward. "Almost all
the cases we're investigating lately involve the Coltons.
And I won't be telling you about any of them, either."

"She told you, brother," Grayson said, earning a laugh.

When attention turned back to Asher, questions came
at him from all sides, each trampling the one before. One
comment, though, edged its way around the others.

"I'm really sorry you're dealing with this, Asher."

His siblings stopped and looked at the man who'd spoken the words. Jace. He was the only one who seemed to

get that this wasn't about them. It was about Harper, Willow, Luna and him.

"Yeah, he's right," Marlowe spoke for the group. I'm so sorry you're facing this. We know Harper's yours. We're certain of it."

The others murmured their agreement.

"When do you get the results?" Bowie wanted to know.

"If the hospital doesn't have to repeat your test, too," Jace said.

Again, chuckles spread around the room. No one could argue that the hospital had more misses than hits with their family lately.

"Are you handling this okay, Asher?"

Genevieve watched him with a mother's concern, though she already had enough to worry about.

Finally, his family gave him the chance to fill in the details about the possible switch and the impending results. He finished just as Dulcie announced that dinner was served.

Asher walked with the others into the dining room, though he was certain he wouldn't be able to eat anything. Strange how telling the rest of his family hadn't given him as much relief as he'd hoped it would, even if they had his back, like always.

The appointment for receiving the test results still hung over him like a rain cloud following him alone. Yet he wasn't by himself in this. As he'd recognized the week before, there was only one person who could understand his fear that night, could feel it all the way to her bones. He couldn't worry that it might be a bad idea. He had to go to her.

Chapter 18

A flat sound yanked Willow from a troubled sleep. Her buzzer? Her alarm clock? She blinked into a darkness that suddenly had become sinister, its shadows stretching from walls to floors, its sounds shrill and disturbing.

Had those who'd threatened her business and her home decided that the negative-review campaign wasn't doing its damage quickly enough? She'd sensed that someone had been watching her the past few nights. Had it been more than just her already spooked imagination?

The digital clock on her bedside table read only ten thirty. She'd been asleep no more than a half hour. Would someone try to get to her while her neighbors with later bedtimes might still be awake to hear her screams? She slid from beneath the sheets and stepped over to her bedroom window. The dark sedan that had been parked outside her house for the past few days was still there, her two posted security guards likely drinking coffee and watching from inside it.

She crossed to the bedroom next door to hers, carefully turned the knob and tiptoed over to the crib. Luna slept sweetly on her back, her fisted hands above her head, her legs forming a diamond-shape opening from her diaper to the touching bottoms of her feet. Her child safe, Willow could finally breathe normally again.

She was almost convinced that she'd dreamed up the sound that had awakened her, but just as she climbed back into bed, someone knocked at the door. Were the security guards even inside that car across the street? Had she been too quick to assume that she and Luna were safe?

After pulling on her lightweight robe, she scanned the shadows in her room for anything she could use as a weapon. A plastic hanger? An empty laundry basket? She didn't even have a soiled diaper handy to toss in an attacker's face. She settled on the golf umbrella in the corner. She could use it to shove someone over the railing at the top of her outside stairs if she hit hard and fast.

But at the door, she paused, flipped on the porch light and leaned toward the peephole. Asher stood there, glancing back over his shoulder. After unlatching the bolt, she threw open the door.

"What's going on? Did something happen with Harper?"

He shook his head. "She's fine. Marlowe offered to stay with her so I could get out of the house."

"That was nice of her."

"I know it's late." He cleared his throat. "Did I wake you?"

As she shrugged to answer, she followed the line of his gaze to her robe that had fallen loose despite her best effort to cinch it. The V-neckline of her simple silk shift peeked out along with the shadow between her breasts. The garment's hem skimmed her thighs.

She wrapped one side of the collar over the other and knotted the belt.

He cleared his throat. "What's with the umbrella?"

"Uh, thought it might rain."

"You mean since the region averages about a quarter inch in the whole month of May? Sure you didn't plan to whack me with it?"

"Guess you'll never know."

He glanced over his shoulder into the night, his arms tight against his sides. "Were you worried someone else was out there? I talked to the guards when I came. Have you received more threats?"

"Nothing like that. Though I was a little concerned when my door buzzer went off so late."

"Sorry about that. I didn't mean to frighten you. I shouldn't have come."

He kept shifting his weight from side to side in a way that made her as uncomfortable as he appeared.

"Why are you here?"

He didn't speak for so long that she was convinced he wouldn't.

"Tomorrow."

At his single-word explanation, Willow swallowed. Like her, Asher had been thinking about the test results they were scheduled to receive the next day. How she'd managed to rest when the shadows beneath his eyes suggested that he hadn't slept in days, she wasn't sure.

"Would you like to come in?" She stepped back and made room for him to pass.

"Thanks."

He closed the door and gestured to his boots, asking if he should remove them, but she shook her head.

He clearly needed to talk to someone, and since she was the only other person who could relate to what he was going through, he'd come to her.

"It'll be okay, you know."

"Will it?"

"I don't know. I just said it because you looked like you needed to hear it."

"I did."

She headed into her kitchen but slowed and spoke again. "Did it help?"

He stopped in the doorway between the living room and the kitchen, bracing his hands on the door frame. "Want honesty or kindness?"

"Kindness."

"I feel completely better."

"At least you're being honest."

The heavy air between them seeming lighter for a moment, Willow crossed to the counter, stuck a filter in her coffee maker and added several scoops of dark roast.

"Neither of us will be sleeping tonight if we drink all that," he observed.

"You don't look as if you've slept much lately, anyway, and I probably won't now."

"Sorry."

"You keep saying that." She set two mugs on the counter, along with teaspoons, napkins and a bottle of fancy creamer from the refrigerator.

He eyed the bottle. "You remembered."

"What?" Her gaze shifted to the items on the counter. "Oh. You like the sweet stuff."

How could it have been only a week since they'd been introduced in a body slam of circumstances and had commiserated over coffee at Java Jane's? Now she couldn't picture a time when she didn't know Asher and Harper, when their lives weren't connected with hers and Luna's by either the truth or a lie.

"I don't have any whipped cream, but hopefully this will satisfy you." She coughed into her elbow. "Your sweet tooth, I mean."

Their gazes connected, but she quickly looked away, ignoring the spike in her pulse. That sizzle between them never knew when to stop shooting off sparks. Now would have been a good time for a dousing to put out that fire.

Asher filled both cups and added an ample pour of creamer in his. When he held it up to offer her some, she shook her head. She kept the stuff for her staff in the kitchen downstairs, but she could offer no explanation for the bottle in her apartment. Had she been expecting him? Hoping?

After he put the bottle away, he carried both mugs to the table and sat.

"I finally told the rest of my family about Luna and Harper just a few hours ago."

"What was your hurry?" She rolled her eyes as she took her first sip. "It took me a while to catch on the other night at the hospital that you hadn't told anyone before Ainsley."

Immediately, she regretted that she'd brought up that night, when it served as a reminder that the evening had ended with steamed-up windows on his truck.

She coughed into her shoulder. "How did they take it?"

"They said I should have told them sooner."

"If you stalled until tomorrow, you could have avoided telling them altogether. Well…depending."

"Yeah, *depending*."

Could this conversation get more awkward? It was as if each lane change they made led only to another pothole. The air in the room seemed heavier than before, as well.

"But after last night, I knew I had to tell them everything."

"What happened last night? There's something else?"

"I found a card with a death threat in Dad's hospital room. Someone, maybe the original shooter, promised to finish the job."

"I'm so sorry." She leaned in, tempted to touch the hand that he'd wrapped around his mug. Would he pull away from her compassion if she did?

"Thanks. The police were guarding his hospital room at first, but now we've hired round-the-clock guards. I also talked to Sergeant Spencer Colton about the threats to your business. I thought police should look at the possible connection to the incidents facing my family. He wants you to file a police report."

"Thanks. I will. I appreciate the security service, too. I have to keep our girls safe, them and all the children at the center."

"Are you scared?"

Willow couldn't look up from her mug, her fuzzy image staring back at her from the shiny black liquid. His words matched the subject they'd been discussing before, but he had to be asking about only one mystery now.

"About tomorrow? Sure. Aren't you?"

"Terrified."

She lifted her gaze and met his again. Just like his one-word answer minutes before, this one was brutally honest. She couldn't decide whether to feel privileged that he'd confided in her or scared she wasn't strong enough for him to rely on.

Willow smiled, hoping to reveal neither of those impulses. "I was probably more afraid when I first received the news."

"How is that possible?"

She tilted her head to the side. "I was still picturing some high-powered couple who might fight for custody of *both* babies if we found proof that they were switched."

"Why would anyone try to do that?"

"The reason powerful people do all the inexplicable things they do." She shrugged. "Because they can. I'm a single mom, still sometimes struggling to make ends meet. I'm an easy target."

"That's what you were thinking when you found out I was a Colton. Then you had even more reasons to be upset."

She shook her head. "Don't remind me."

"Why didn't you think I would go after custody of both girls? Because I was a single parent and not a part of a couple?"

"I *did* think that you would at first."

"What changed your mind?"

"I got to know you and found out you weren't the monster I'd always pictured in my mind."

"Thanks, I think."

"And any guy who'd propose marriage as a solution, well, it's hard to stay worried about his motives."

"Yeah, about that, I'm sorry for asking."

"Forget about it." Even if she couldn't. Even if it still stung every time that she thought about it.

"It's just that the thought of not being with Harper every day… Well, you get it."

"I do."

"But it's more than that. While I was sitting with Dad last night, all I could think about was when we found out that Ace wasn't his child. My siblings and I were focused on the scandal and the chaos, but Dad lost his *son* that day. After he'd already lost the child's mother."

"That must have hit so close to home for you. First Nora—"

He shook his head before she could get the rest out.

"It's not like that. Yes, my ex will always be important to me. She was the mother of my child, after all, but we were never—" He stopped himself that time and shrugged.

"Yeah, I get it."

From the beginning, their situations had been alike but different, their wounds from betrayal like a T in the road, two points meeting through the turn and continuing on their own rocky paths.

He was quiet then, sipping coffee that must have grown cold and staring at a place where only he could see.

"You know, I wasn't happy when I got Nora pregnant. I wasn't ready to be a parent."

"Then you stepped up and became a great dad."

Asher shook his head as if he couldn't allow her to smooth out the jagged edges of his pain.

"I just keep thinking that my sweet Harper, the child I love more than I thought I was capable of caring about anyone or anything, might not even be...*mine.*"

As his voice broke, his misery clear in his damp eyes, Willow couldn't stop herself from reaching out to him this time. She placed both of her hands around the tangle his fists had formed together. For several seconds, he stared at that connection before looking up again.

"You'll still be a father to Harper," she blurted before she could stop herself.

"Just like I'll always be a mother to...Luna." Her voice cracked as she spoke her child's name, perhaps for the last time while still believing they were biologically linked. Her chest squeezed so tightly she was convinced that the pain would crush it. "We will. Somehow. No matter what."

He stared back at her, searching for a guarantee, the thing she had no ability to give.

"I want to believe that."

His raw whisper touched her in the deepest part of her soul.

"Then believe it," she said.

For several seconds or minutes, Willow stared into his eyes, a guarded man's wounds openly displayed for her, with hope lingering just out of reach. Then she did the only thing she could think of to soothe his pain.

Leaning in close, she touched her lips to his. Only when she tasted salt did she realize that she was crying. Or, maybe, they both were.

He didn't pull away, but he didn't commit, either, only staring back at her with shock and something she couldn't define. She kissed him again, her mouth slightly open and connecting with the dampness just inside his parted lips.

When Asher slid his hands out from between hers and uncurled his fingers, a lump formed in her throat. Had he refused the comfort she'd offered and needed as much as he seemed to? He surprised her, though, as he leaned closer. Those work-roughened hands that she'd been unable to forget since that first time he'd touched her glided up her arms on the outside of her robe until they came to rest on her shoulders.

His fingertips pressed into her flesh as he drew her to him. Then he closed his eyes and dipped his head to take control of the kiss, brushing his lips over hers several times before tracing the line between her lips with the tip of his tongue. She opened for him on a sigh.

He claimed her mouth with desperation, but she was no docile passenger on the journey, her need strong-arming her judgment, her patience stretched taut and then fraying.

Asher painted a line of nips along her jaw, up the side of her neck and to that sensitive place behind her ear.

"You're so amazing," he breathed against her damp skin.

She wasn't sure when she'd gone from kissing him while seated to standing and facing him. When had her robe wrestled its way open again, her bare feet becoming sandwiched between his boots? When had she begun to find those boots sexy, anyway? She didn't care as she stretched up to meet him when he dipped his head to take her mouth again.

Her arms scaled his and wrapped around his neck as she fit herself intimately to him, each feminine curve finding its home in the unyielding planes and the impatient fullness of him. While one of his hands remained at the small of her back, anchoring her to him and making her certain of his desire, the other hand slid inside her robe.

His fingers skimmed the side of her nightie over the lower curve of her breast, her waist and her hip, awakening skin that strained for his touch. Then he slid his hand around her, splaying his fingers over the fullness of her bottom.

It wasn't enough. Willow wanted more. She wanted everything that Asher Colton was willing to give.

When he broke off another heady kiss, she let out a frustrated moan. Asher smiled against her cheek.

"You're killing me, Willow. I haven't wanted anyone like this—well, in a long time." He cleared his throat, straightening slightly. "Tell me to go home if you don't want to do this. Just say the word and I'll leave."

"I don't...want that."

Immediately, Asher's arms went up as if he was facing a police officer's weapon, and then he lowered them to his sides and stepped back.

Willow blinked several times. What had just happened? She'd struggled to get the words out, but she'd said them, right? She'd said she didn't want him to leave. Had he changed his mind? Then her own words repeated in her head. *I don't...want that.* She swallowed. He'd misunderstood, she'd misspoken, or some crazy combination of the two.

"Sorry." He didn't meet her gaze as he backed up farther. "Um, I'll see you tomorrow."

"Asher, wait."

He paused. "Look, this is embarrassing enough. Can we just—"

"Please, listen. That didn't come out the way I meant it."

This time he faced her and waited. "Well, what did you mean?"

"I was trying to say that I didn't want you to go."

He drew his brows together as if he couldn't trust what he'd heard.

"What are you saying?"

She cleared her throat and lifted her chin. "I want you to stay."

Chapter 19

Asher didn't bother with words as he reached her in three long strides, his mouth taking hers before his arms had even closed around her waist. She responded to his kiss with a desperation that inspired him and terrified him at the same time.

Was this the two of them just trying to escape their fears over answers that tomorrow would bring and situations that would never be as easy to navigate as she'd promised they would be? No, he wouldn't think about those things then, not with lovely Willow wrapping herself around him, inviting him in. There was no way in hell he wouldn't accept her invitation.

"How about we relocate?"

"Sounds…good."

He grinned at her breathless response as her fingertips pressed into his back.

Without asking where to go, he scooped her up in his

arms and headed for the closed door of the only room he hadn't visited in her apartment. Her bedroom.

"Always the gentleman cowboy, aren't you?" she asked as he turned the knob.

He pushed open the door, twisted and carefully tucked a shoulder so she wouldn't hit her head.

"Not always. A few minutes ago, I was considering pulling you down on top of me on the floor."

"But you really would have stopped and headed right out that door if I hadn't..."

He studied her for several seconds, her question surprising him. Then he nodded. "Yes, ma'am."

From her smile, he would have thought he'd made the most profound statement in the world. In the shadowy room, he lowered her to the bed, where she sat and flipped on the table lamp next to it.

As he sat next to her and reached for his boot, he paused. "Still sure?"

That her only answer was a nod didn't make him feel confident, but after he slid off his boots, she reached for the hem of his T-shirt and shimmied it up his chest and over his head.

"Guess you are," he said.

She cleared her throat. "Maybe a little less talk and a lot more action?"

"Wouldn't want to disappoint a lady."

He dipped his head and took her mouth again, and he was lost. Each taste, each touch only made him crave another. And then one more.

He pushed the robe off her shoulders and down her arms, letting it pool around her hips, before tracing his fingers along the spaghetti straps of her nightgown. Her eyes fluttered closed as he followed the line of the garment's neckline to its modest vee at the center.

He dipped his fingertips beneath the cloth, the silk no match for the smoothness of her lovely tawny skin. Nor, he was surprised to discover, could memories of gymnastic sex from his past compare to the moment when he slid his palm beneath the weight of her breast, floating his thumb across its peak. He swallowed Willow's sigh.

Asher closed his eyes, trying to dissect those feelings over the haze of his own relentless need for her. Was this time different for him? Did she matter more to him than the others had? But he lifted his lids in time to catch sight of her pulling the flimsy nightgown over her head.

Whatever he'd been thinking about before fluttered away as he stared at the most beautiful woman he'd ever seen bare, let alone touched. And he planned to take his time in saying a fine, leisurely greeting to all those spots of skin as she introduced them.

Slow must not have been on her agenda, however, as with the next intoxicating kiss, she pressed him back on the bed and draped herself over him. He was about to explode, still half-dressed.

He rolled with her to his side to correct that problem, but her hands slipped in to cover his belt buckle first. His front teeth sank into his lower lip, and he gripped the comforter, but he managed to avoid taking over as she worked the buckle and the button of his jeans. A slow hiss escaped him as her fingertips "accidentally" grazed him as she worked.

He wasted no time in standing to shuck his jeans and boxers, while she wiggled out of her panties next to him. He reached for his jeans again and the wallet inside but stopped just as he opened it.

"Damn. I don't have—I stopped carrying—"

Instead of answering, she leaned over to the bedside table and opened the drawer. From it, she produced a box of condoms. He glanced from the box to her face that had deepened in color and then back to the box.

"I'm a single mom. It's important for me to be responsible if, you know, anything ever happens."

"Well, good thing one of us was thinking ahead."

"You might need to blow the dust off that package."

He chuckled before taking a good look at it. She hadn't purchased them with him in mind, but he was strangely relieved that the box hadn't been opened. He turned away to cover himself and then stretched out next to her.

"We don't have to be in a hurry." He didn't care if his body clearly disagreed.

Again, Willow seemed to have a different idea, kissing and curling herself around him with a need like the one he was trying to contain in himself.

"Please. It's been so long," she breathed against his neck.

"I'm here to please."

Yet her words troubled him as he brought them together, and they began to move in tandem toward an ecstasy they could seek and find in each other. Willow couldn't know how right she was. It had taken him so long, in fact a lifetime, to get there, but he suspected that in her, he had found home.

He hadn't believed anything could frighten him more than the next day's test results could, but his temptation to want more from Willow than any agreement or handshake type of marriage told him just how wrong he was.

For the second time that night, a sound pulled Willow from her sleep, this one from somewhere nearby. As she blinked against the harsh light of the lamp, she reached for the other pillow and the man who'd held her close as she'd drifted off to sleep. Her hand landed in the depression where Asher's head had once rested.

She sat straight up in the bed, her upper body uncovered, bedsheet puddling around her hips. Asher stood across the room, fully dressed and balancing on one foot while stuffing his other in a boot.

Immediately, she reached for the sheet and tucked it under her armpits, though she wasn't sure why she bothered when he'd already seen and sampled everything she could hide. Had he been trying to sneak out while she was sleeping like some guy after a one-night stand? Even if, technically, at least so far, this *was* a one-nighter?

"Heading out soon?"

Asher startled and then turned back to her. He appeared to note the sheet under her arms, and then his gaze darted to the side.

"Sorry." He cleared his throat. "I didn't want to wake you. It's getting late, and I need to get home."

Her gaze flicked to the clock, which read just after one in the morning. He was right. It was late, and, like her, he had a child waiting for him at home.

"Marlowe's probably waiting up for you with Harper."

"More like asleep on the couch in my suite, but, yeah, she's waiting."

After having little success getting his boot on while standing, Asher sat on the edge of the mattress, slipped on both and then stood again. He took several steps away from the bed and gestured back to it. "That, well, was… amazing."

"Yeah." She chewed the side of her lower lip. "It was."

Her skin still tingled with the memory of his calloused fingers and soft lips discovering, adoring and memorizing her form. She still could recall with absolute clarity the perfection of his body, the scent and taste of him, his sheer masculinity. Her hand lifted, as of its own accord, to lips still sensitive and swollen from his kisses.

"Sorry about the five o'clock shadow. I should have shaved…before, but I wasn't expecting to, well, you know."

"No problem."

Though he'd appeared nervous before, confident Asher returned then as he stepped toward the bed again. "I guess you'll have to marry me now and make an honest man out of me."

Willow's pulse pounded in her chest. "I guess the only way you'll know the answer to that would be for you to ask me again."

It would be different this time, she told herself, as she tried to inconspicuously wipe her sweaty palms on the sheet. His lovemaking had been so tender. He'd touched her as if she was precious to him. She'd finally recognized the truth in her heart that she was falling in love with him, Colton or no. Had he realized that he felt the same way about her?

"Will you marry me, Willow Merrill? Will you take on this crazy, unpredictable world with me and our two girls? It doesn't matter whether Harper is mine and Luna is yours, or the other way around. I just think we could make a great family together."

Her gaze connected with his and held for seconds or minutes as she took in his sweet message. Then she held her breath, waiting for the words that mattered most. The *three* words that would make the difference between a business transaction and a lifetime commitment.

His gaze flitted to the window. "I mean, we've just proven how amazingly compatible we are, haven't we?"

An anvil seemed to lower on her chest.

"Are you saying that because we're good together *in*

bed that we should just call in the minister and cut the wedding cake?"

He crossed his arms over his chest. "I've definitely heard *worse* reasons to get married. We already have two amazing daughters to raise. We love them both. Now we know that our private time will be comforting, as well."

Willow pulled the sheet tighter over her chest and drew her knees closer to her body. She'd been unclothed for a few hours, but she suddenly felt naked.

"You're still offering me the same marriage of convenience that's no more romantic than mating one of your cows to a bull?"

"The cattle probably think it's romantic."

"That isn't funny," she spat.

His smile disappeared. "Come on, Willow. Don't you get what I'm offering you? Security like you've never known. For you and Luna."

How dare he use her biggest fear against her.

"Oh, I get it, all right. Just another opportunity for the Coltons to buy whatever they want."

"That's not fair. When have I ever tried to buy you or Luna?"

You're doing it now. She wanted to shout the words, but it already hurt so much just to think them. Why he'd even mentioned her, she didn't know, when all he really wanted was her daughter. He had to guarantee that the child would be in his control in case the test confirmed she was a Colton heir. If not, at least he could secure quality, *permanent* childcare for his own child. Even after their lovemaking that had meant so much to her, for Asher, nothing had changed.

"Please give this a chance, Willow. I will promise to love your daughter, whichever one she turns out to be, as my own. I'll commit to support you, emotionally and physically."

But you won't promise to love *me.* The unspoken words gripped her heart, tearing strips of flesh slowly, agonizingly, instead of ripping all at once.

"I even promise to be faithful to you," Asher continued, oblivious to the pain he'd inflicted. "That's more than you can say about a lot of people."

She shook her head. First, security and then Xavier's infidelity. Had he listened to her stories only to use them as ammunition later? Despite the humiliation that made her wish she could curl into herself and disappear, she met his gaze, daring him to look away.

"Look, I know that this is a good offer for someone like me. A single mom with no father herself and no family support system at all. A *Colton* wants to marry me. Wants to provide a wonderful life for my child."

She shook her head as twin tears slid from the outside corners of her eyes. "But I can't do it."

Anguish covered her as an image of her young, pregnant mother stole into her thoughts. Willow tried to push the picture away, but her mom only continued to twirl in that fantasy dress, those lovely baubles bouncing, as she dreamed of a life she would never have. Now Willow had the chance to live a life filled with every luxury and comfort her mother had longed for, as long as she was willing to give up the only thing that really mattered.

It wasn't enough. Not close to it.

"I'm sorry, but I'm going to turn down your proposal again." She wiped her tears with the corner of the sheet. "I will never marry again without love."

His crossed arms appeared to squeeze tighter.

"You're asking too much of me. You're asking for more than I can give."

"I know I am. But I also know that I deserve more than you're offering. Every woman, every *person*, does."

He opened his mouth as if he was about to say more but clicked his jaw shut instead. Then he gripped the doorknob.

Over his shoulder, he spoke once more. "I'll see you at the hospital tomorrow. We'll get the results and go from there."

With that, he strode from the room. After a few seconds, the loud click of her apartment door filtered through the apartment. He was gone.

As she pulled the sheet high, she gave in to her earlier temptation, rounding her shoulders and drawing her knees up tightly against her. The tears came, hot and fast, but instead of trying to wipe them away, she let them fall.

In a few hours, she would go to that hospital with her head held high, but now, just for a few minutes, she allowed herself to grieve. So like her mother and yet so different, she would mourn the life she'd dreamed of and would never have.

Chapter 20

By the time that the upstairs side entrance finally opened again at Tender Years, her eyes were bleary over staring at the door for so long. Beyond that, her ears must have been bleeding from listening to him talk for the past few hours. Didn't the guy ever shut up?

"Oh. Look. He's coming out. Think he's got an extra spring in his step after all that time?"

His horselaugh over his own joke could have made any *Revenge of the Nerds* character proud. Where had she found this guy? Oh, right. When you scoured the dating apps for computer whizzes who might be convinced to try their hacking skills, you couldn't get too choosy.

"Would you hush? Do you want to alert the neighbors? Or the rent-a-cops up the street?"

"Sure, I can be quiet, but can you?"

He reached over and planted his hand at the top of her thigh on her shorts, a smooth move he'd been going with all night. This time she grabbed his hand and squeezed hard. She'd been pawed enough, thank you very much.

"Ouch!" He yanked it back. "You could have just said you weren't in the mood."

Could she say that every time he touched her? Not if she wanted to keep her employee content and striving for that next big promotion.

"Sorry. I was just distracted." She put his hand back on the spot herself.

"Because Asher Colton's wasting all that beautiful money on the town babysitter?"

If he said, "and not on you," he would be singing soprano for a month. She would never get that lucky, to be able to snuggle up with one of the Colton boys in a duvet filled with cash. She was smart enough to know some prizes were out of reach. The guy sitting next to her would find that out soon enough, too.

For now, though, she still needed him. She wouldn't even have known for sure the identity of the gentleman caller if not for his special skills in accessing the Arizona Department of Transportation's database.

"How'd he get past those security guards anyway?"

For a few seconds, she stared at his ugly profile, wondering how he could be that stupid.

"You saw him talking to them, didn't you? They either knew him or were working for him."

He chuckled at that. "Oops. Guess I missed that. I must have been watching someone else when he walked by the car. You pointed him out when he climbed the steps to her place."

"Right. I forgot."

She couldn't blame him for that anyway. At least he recognized a good thing when he had it, unlike some other people she knew.

"Is there anything you can do to revive the app campaign?"

He shook his head. "You saw it. Most of the new reviews have already been taken down. And there's too much focus on the one account for me to try to put them up again right now."

"That's disappointing."

She applied her best mom's tone, and, like she'd predicted, her discouraged assistant perked right up next to her.

"The campaign wasn't working anyway," she said. "There hasn't been any drop-off in the number of cars lined up here in the mornings and afternoons."

"I told you that competition is low here. Besides, the reviews weren't up long enough to have a good impact."

"Then what about the complaint filed with the state?"

He shrugged, his hand pulling away from her thigh. "I've been looking, but I haven't seen any more about it. Like it's been squashed or something."

"So, what you're telling me is we're at a big fat nowhere now."

"Not nowhere, exactly. The place is under more scrutiny. And parents who were paying attention are questioning their decisions to send their kids to Tender Years."

She smacked her palm on the steering wheel and faced him, hating his wide eyes behind those glasses. "You say it like it's some great feat. Kind of sounds like a failure to me."

"I'll think of something. You know I have mad skills. You told me so yourself. Just give me a couple of days."

She grinned into the darkness. If only all men were as easy to guide as this one. "You're right. I do know that I can count on you. But in the meanwhile, I have another idea. I'm going to need a little help from you to pull it off."

She filled him in on the new plan, one that would require even more care and discretion. Was he up for it? She
doubted it, but she had few choices, and none as pliable as
this one. Besides, her time appeared to be running out if
Willow Merrill was hooking up with one of the Coltons.

"Do you think the security guards will be a problem?"

"We've been sitting here monitoring them for hours,
and they haven't noticed. What do you think?"

"Guess it should be a cakewalk."

Something like that. Either way, it was time for them to
turn up the heat or forfeit the plan. And she wasn't about
to back off from anything until that woman felt some of
the burn she deserved. If her friend there couldn't handle
it, she would take care of it herself.

Just as she had a little more than a week before, Willow sat in Anne Sewall's office at Mustang Valley General, waiting for somone to show up and for her life to
possibly be changed forever. At least this time she hadn't
been forced to drag her daughter along for the bumpy ride.

She and Asher had made what she still believed was
a good idea to have Harper and Luna sit this one out and
allow the adults to handle it. Since Asher had dropped off
his child right on schedule at the center, Willow didn't have
to question whether he'd keep his end of that bargain. So,
what kind of mother was she to wish that Luna was in her
arms just then as a distraction? Not one worthy of a flower
greeting card on her first Mother's Day in a few days.

Willow braced herself as the sound of Asher's familiar heavy footfalls in the hall outside announced his arrival. Anne appeared in the doorway first, nervous hands
pushing her glasses up on her nose. Asher followed her
in. Still not ready to see him again after the night before,
Willow focused on the floor. Unfortunately, that gave her

a perfect view of his boots. The last thing she needed was a reminder of those boots in her apartment, first holding her bare feet between them and then, later, tucked under her bed.

"It's good to see you again, Asher," Anne said. "Please have a seat next to Willow. Once everyone is here, we'll get started."

Everyone? Willow glanced sidelong at him as he lowered into the seat, but he was focusing on the hospital administrator, who still stood behind her chair. Asher sat straight, his hands gripped in his lap. Could even Anne recognize the chilly atmosphere in the room where the temperature seemed to threaten frostbite?

Another set of footsteps, these with a quick clip of high heels, filtered in from the hallway. Soon, Ainsley stood in the open doorway.

"Come on in, Miss Colton, and have a seat."

For the first time, Willow noticed that a third guest chair had been added to the room.

"Willow, I'd like you to meet—"

"Thanks, Anne, we've met," Ainsley said, interrupting her. She leaned past her brother and waved. "And thanks, everyone, for waiting."

Willow lifted a hand to wave back, but she had the sudden sense that she was surrounded. Had Asher invited Ainsley to attend as his sister, attorney or both?

Ainsley wore a dark jack and skirt and a prim blouse, and, yes, heels. Even Asher was dressed up for him in a white dress shirt and a pair of tan trousers. In fact, on closer inspection, his boots weren't even the ones he'd worn the night before, but a dressier, shinier pair.

Somehow, that made Willow more nervous. She'd taken special care with her own clothes that morning, telling herself the summer dress, sweater and flat sandals were only for receiving the results and not as armor for facing Asher again. Either way, she still felt underdressed, ill-prepared, outmatched.

"I have your results right here." Anne indicated two sealed clasp envelopes placed side by side on her desk. "I will read off the results and then provide each party with copies of all the documents. Then if you need further explanations, I'll call down to the lab. They promised they would make someone available for us."

"Awfully accommodating for a team that can't seem to finish a different set of results," Ainsley grumbled. "Or at least get them right."

"Miss Colton, I am so sorry about—"

Ainsley lifted a hand to interrupt Anne again.

"As you were saying about my brother's case…?"

Was her use of the word *case* intentional? Had Asher changed his mind after Willow had rejected his second proposal? Was he considering going for custody of both girls, after all?

Anne cleared her throat as she lifted the first envelope and broke the seal. As the woman withdrew the stack of papers from inside, Willow held her breath.

Strange how she still longed to reach out to Asher, though he still hadn't looked at her and hadn't made any gesture of support to her. They'd gone from enemies to friends to lovers and back, and part of her still needed for them to at least be allies.

The administrator pushed up her glasses again and studied the first sheet for several seconds. When her expression gave away nothing, Willow was tempted to rip it out of her hands.

"In the case of the child, Harper Grace Colton, the alleged father, Asher Colton, is not excluded as the biological father with a probability of paternity of 99.9998 percent."

"*Not* excluded?" Asher asked.

Ainsley patted his arm. "It means that you're her dad."

"That's what the Combined Paternity Index ratio shows," Anne agreed.

Asher's breath whooshed out, and he leaned forward, planting his elbows on his knees and catching his forehead in his splayed hands. "I *knew* she was mine."

Anne looked back to the paper and began reading again. "The alleged mother, Willow Merrill, is excluded as a biological parent."

The results were what Willow had known in her heart all along, so she couldn't explain her nervousness as the administrator opened the second envelope. Did she expect confetti to fall out along with the announcement that though Harper wasn't hers, Luna wasn't, either?

"In the case of Luna Mariana Merrill, the alleged mother, Willow Merrill, is not excluded as the biological mother."

"Thank God," she called out, the voice sounding as if it had come from someone else.

Anne said more about overwhelming statistical probability backing up the claim when comparing specific alleles from Luna's DNA against Willow's and then other unrelated women. But for Willow, the words *not excluded* repeated on a loop.

"So, the results say I'm Luna's mother?"

"Yes, they show the statistical likelihood that you are." Anne's expression was carefully blank as if she understood the tightrope she walked.

"And they're definitive?" Willow asked again.

"Yes. She's your child."

This time, the older woman smiled. Willow could only

nod. The memory of Luna's sweet face as she'd left her that morning filtered through her thoughts, her heart squeezing. But then the toothless grin of a second infant trickled in, clamping her chest even tighter.

Had she become attached to Harper, as well? She'd known all along that confirming she was the mother of one baby would mean losing the other. She just hadn't expected it to hurt so much. She brushed her hand over her face, her fingers coming away wet.

Ainsley startled her by reaching out and planting her hands on the edge of Anne's desk.

"How can you explain this nightmare the hospital has just put two families through?"

"On behalf of the Mustang Valley General board and staff, I want to apologize for the inconvenience that this situation has caused both of your families," Anne said. "You can rest assured that our security and local authorities are searching for whoever called in the anonymous report and will prosecute if the suspect is located."

"That's the least we would expect from you," Ainsley said.

As the conversation about them continued as if neither was in the room, Willow peeked Asher's way. She caught him staring, but he didn't look away. A lump formed in her throat as she took in his ashen face and watery eyes. How had she reverted to thinking of him as the competition?

Last night, she'd recognized him as the only other person who truly understood her dread while awaiting the test results. Now, only he could relate to the flood of conflicting emotions threatening to pull her under the surface.

His hand shifted as if he wanted to reach for her, too, but then gripped his thigh muscle instead. Had he remembered he was supposed to be angry with her? He'd offered to marry her, no matter what the results showed today. And she'd been right to say no. So, why did emptiness expand inside her over a marriage she hadn't wanted and a proposal she'd rejected twice?

"I can't believe the whole thing was another hoax."

Since Asher had barely spoken until then, all three women startled and looked his way.

"A hoax. Just like—"

"Asher," Ainsley warned.

He shook his head, appearing surprised that he'd nearly revealed family secrets again.

"Sorry."

"Just like what?" Anne separated the papers into two piles, slid them back into envelopes and handed one to Willow and the other to Asher.

Ainsley waved away the question.

"It's not important. My brother here is a little overwhelmed. But we'll want to follow up on this matter. Clearly, someone targeted our family, and we want to know who it is. We'll also need to determine whether to pursue a civil lawsuit against the hospital."

With that, the attorney stood, effectively ending the meeting.

Willow gripped her copy and hurried down the hall. Asher reached her near the exit and brushed her arm to get her attention. Even knowing he was there couldn't prevent her from jumping when he touched her.

"Where's your sister?"

"She had to get back to the office."

"Nice to have an attorney in the family."

The side of his mouth lifted. "We've kept her busy lately."

She smiled back, her heart cramping just a little. "Well, I need to get back to work."

"Me, too. But I wanted to tell you that I'm sorry that you got caught up in this mess."

"You think the hoax was related to the other unusual happenings involving your family?"

"Don't you?"

She nodded. "But what about the incidents at my building?"

"There's a chance that they're unrelated. You might want to think about whether you have any enemies. They probably aren't as obvious or as *plentiful* as ours."

"Thanks. I'll go through my records and see if there's anyone I'm forgetting."

"I'll keep the security guards there for a while, and hopefully, you'll figure it out soon."

"You don't have to do that."

"I want to." His hand jutted out, like it had in Anne's office. She braced herself for the pain and relief of his touch, but he stopped as he had before. This time he slid his fingers in his pocket and gripped his belt loop. "My daughter is still under your care for now, and I want to make sure she stays safe."

"Right. Well, I appreciate it. For her."

Now that their infants' parentage had been resolved, there was nothing left for them to say to each other that didn't involve the day-care center.

With a wave, Asher turned in the opposite direction, as if he'd come in the hospital from a different entrance. Willow forced herself to keep moving forward to her own car, her own life. She wouldn't look over her shoulder and wish she could have accepted less from him than his love.

A part of her heart still went with him.

Chapter 21

"Willow? Over here."

Fighting an overwhelming sense of déjà vu on that afternoon four days later, Willow moved toward the feminine voice inside Java Jane's. Not only was this the second time she'd visited the shop that month, but it also would be her second meeting with a Colton there.

That morning, though, she'd been summoned.

She waved back at the elegantly dressed middle-aged woman with wavy long blond hair, cream-colored skin and a slightly turned-up nose. Even if Willow had never met Asher until recently, she would still have recognized Genevieve Colton anywhere from the local newspaper's society pages. Or because she looked a lot like her oldest son, but Willow wouldn't think about that.

As she stepped up to the table, the other woman stood. She glanced at Willow's extended right hand and leaned in to hug her instead.

"Hi, I'm Genevieve," she said when she pulled back. "I'm so pleased you agreed to meet with me."

Willow nodded. Once she'd hoped for an audience with any Colton to address her mother's mistreatment. She'd never expected something like Genevieve's call. Even if Asher's mother had given her the chance to say no, the curiosity still would have gotten to her. Genevieve Colton had wanted to meet with *her*?

Appearing not to notice the coffee drinkers from nearby tables, who stared openly at them, Genevieve lowered into her seat again and gestured for Willow to take the chair opposite hers.

"I hope you don't mind that I already ordered drinks for us."

Genevieve gestured to the table where two oversize, porcelain coffee cups had already been placed, steaming black liquid filling them almost to the brim. A small bowl containing individual creamers and sweetener packets had been set next to the cup, and two teaspoons were on a pile of napkins just behind them. Clearly, she intended the two of them to be there for a while.

"I should have checked to see if you even drink coffee."

She chuckled and then nervously spun the massive wedding ring set on her finger. Willow hadn't expected Genevieve Colton to fidget.

"I do. Thanks." She pulled the cup to her.

"My son told me about the situation at the hospital. I'm sorry you got caught up in that. I'm glad everything turned out all right."

"Thanks for saying so," Willow said. "And I'm sorry to hear about your husband. I hope he's improving."

"I appreciate that. I just came from visiting him. He did look better today."

Willow waited for her next cue from Asher's mother

because they weren't there to discuss Payne Colton. Genevieve had a faraway look in her eyes for a few seconds, and then she shook her head.

"Where's your daughter? I thought you would bring her with you. Luna, is it?"

She nodded. "She was still down for her nap at the center, so I decided to leave her with my staff. She's not a fan of transitions."

"Don't I know what that's like. Asher was just like that when he was a baby. He was my first, too, though I was a veteran stepmom by then."

"You're not talking about Asher, are you? Laid-back, easy-to-get-along-with Asher?"

Genevieve watched her over the top of her coffee cup.

"Things can change, Willow. *People* can change."

"I guess I believe that."

Whether Asher's mother had been speaking of something specific or just life in general, she wasn't sure.

"It was good that you received your DNA results before your first Mother's Day. Did you get to enjoy it yesterday with your daughter?"

Willow smiled at the memory of splashing with Luna in the baby pool. "I didn't get breakfast in bed, and our brunch consisted of strained peas and peaches, but it was the best day of my life so far. How was your holiday?"

"Lovely, like yours. Except the food at our brunch was better. A mother's time with her children is always precious."

She nodded, though her own mom's face appeared in her thoughts then, causing a lump to form in her throat.

"Your mother was such a lovely woman," Genevieve said. "Kind. Hardworking. I'm sorry that I didn't do more to help her."

Willow startled, shaking the table and causing coffee to swill over the rim of her cup.

"You know who I am?"

"When Asher brought you up at dinner the other night, I remembered your name. You're Kelly Johnson's daughter. There aren't a whole lot of Willows around."

"Asher spoke about me at your family meal?"

Genevieve flashed a knowing smile.

"Well, technically, my stepdaughter, Ainsley, mentioned you to get him to share about the switch nonsense, but my son was trying awfully hard *not* to talk about you, which is almost the same thing."

Willow wasn't sure how those things were alike, but she nodded anyway. "About my mom—it was a long time ago. It doesn't matter anymore." She was trying not to let it, anyway, without much success.

"Of course, it still does. I should have fought harder for her that night. It was a misunderstanding. A harmless game of dress-up. Kelly never would have taken any of it. I knew that."

"Then why *didn't* you do more?"

Willow sat back in her seat and crossed her arms. Since Asher's mom appeared to be determined to share her side of the story, the least she could do was listen.

"I was still finding my place on the Triple R and playing stepmom to four children. And I was a coward. I didn't know yet that Payne listens to the loudest voice in the room, not necessarily the most reasonable one." She shrugged. "I wish I'd known that then."

"No, that lets you off too easily." Willow shook her head hard. "You did nothing, even after that."

"Well, technically, no. Not for a lack of effort, though. I tried to help her right after she left, and when I found out about you, I tried harder. But she wanted nothing from me."

"Can you blame her?"

"No." Genevieve swiped her hand through the air, grinning. "I didn't give up, though. For years, I sent her checks from my personal account every few months. I hoped she would cash them if she ever really needed the money. Do you know what she did? She voided them and mailed them back to me."

None of this made sense. It didn't fit with the story her mother had shared so many times. The one where her connection with the Coltons had ended the day she was booted off their ranch.

"She was much too proud to accept charity from you. From anyone."

"You don't know this about me, but I'm as stubborn as she was proud. So, I kept sending them. I liked to think she mailed back the checks to let me know that you were both all right."

"Why is that?"

Genevieve stirred more sweetener into her coffee, though it was probably cold by then. "Think about it. She could have just torn up the checks without cashing them. Instead, she took the time to mail back each one."

Willow pushed her own cup aside. "Why do you think Mom never told me any of this?"

"I think she was trying to raise a strong, independent woman, and maybe that part of the story wouldn't have helped her narrative. And she never accepted any help, so it wasn't a lie." She gestured toward Willow. "Anyway, it looks as though she succeeded."

"She also kept me hating all the Coltons."

At that, Genevieve laughed. "I hope that isn't the case anymore. We're all just people. My family. Your mother. You. Most of us aren't as good as some think we are and not as bad as others believe."

"So, why are you telling me all this now?"

"You think it's to relieve my guilt? Maybe a little. Mostly, though, it's because you and your daughter are important to my son. I don't want Asher to miss out on something he wants because of something I did, or failed to do, more than thirty years ago."

Her sharp eyes studied Willow until she squirmed in her seat. "From what I can see, you care about my son and his daughter, too."

It would have been useless to argue, so she didn't try.

"How do you know that Luna and I are 'important' to him? What did he say?" Revealing that Asher had twice proposed to her would only make Genevieve's point, so she kept that to herself.

"Remember, we're talking about my son. He's not going to tell his mother how he feels about a woman. At least not without a lot of prodding. On this, though, I knew without him saying a word."

"How's that?"

"Simple. He took you to meet his father."

Asher dropped into the desk chair in his office later that night and shoved recently scrubbed hands through his sweaty hair. He desperately needed a shower after what had felt like a second full day of work, and it wasn't even time for lights-out for those back at the house. Well, except for Harper.

Ten calves had come into the world since he'd shared dinner with the family a few hours earlier, one even requiring the head gate to hold the mother in position and calving chains to pull out her offspring.

Worse, though, than cows refusing to space out their deliveries was that throughout the whole time he'd been assisting with deliveries, a young mom of the human species had refused to get out of his mind. That shouldn't have surprised him. Since their first meeting nearly two weeks before, he hadn't been able to think about anything else but Willow.

"Why didn't you just tell her the truth?" he asked the four walls.

A crunching sound outside his partially open door startled him. He'd finally told Rex, Jarvis and the other ranch hands they could head back to their cabins. Had someone else sneaked into the white metal structure of Barn Three through the small side door? He clearly remembered closing and locking that main barn door, but he was fuzzy on the other one.

Something gripped his insides, and the odd sense of being watched crept up his neck. Was this the time that whoever had been targeting his family would do far more damage than just cutting a fence or calling in a bomb threat?

He unlocked his desk drawer, pulled out a box of bullet cartridges and slid his bolt-action Winchester rifle off the shelf. He seldom needed it, except when he had to protect his cattle or put down an injured one, but he was glad to have it then.

"You've made a mistake coming in here, my friend." He spoke in a loud voice as he opened the gun's bolt action and inserted the .22-caliber rounds one by one into the internal magazine, his hand hovering near the safety. "I'm armed."

"Don't shoot," came a feminine voice from outside the door.

"Willow?" His heart thudded as he unloaded the weapon, his breath coming in rapid bursts. A few seconds more, one poor decision about unlocking the safety, and he could have— No. He didn't want to imagine what could have happened.

"Okay to come in?" she asked through the closed door.

"Yeah. But what are you doing here?"

The door opened, and the most harmless intruder he could have imagined stood there in jean shorts, a T-shirt and sneakers, her hair tied back in a thick ponytail. Instead of looking at him, she stared wide-eyed at the rifle, as if she expected him to turn it on her. He lowered the butt of the gun to the ground.

"Uh. Hi."

Her voice sounded strange, her smile a nervous one. She crossed her arms over her body as if she was freezing in a building that was always sweltering.

Because he was tempted to reach out to her, Asher took his time hanging the rifle back in its rack and locking the box of cartridges in the drawer. He couldn't go to her. Not after she'd made a habit of rejecting him. But that didn't make him want to any less.

So much for getting Willow out of his system by making love with her once. Hell, he couldn't think of the pleasure they'd found together in her bed as anything short of the real deal. If that wasn't a good enough warning for him to back away, he wouldn't be able to pick one out on a billboard.

When he had his thoughts together, he finally turned back to her.

"You shouldn't sneak up on someone like that. Especially lately. We're all on edge. You could have gotten hurt." His gaze flitted to the gun on the wall.

"Sorry. I didn't expect…"

"We have to be on guard. We don't know what we're up against. You or my family."

"I know."

She shook her head as if frustrated with herself.

"Why didn't you knock?"

"On the door outside? I did, but you didn't answer, and it was unlocked. I would have tried your office door, but it sounded like you were talking to someone in here."

"To myself. A habit of the solitary cowboy. You never said what you're doing here. Where's Luna?"

"Candace is with her. And when I stopped by your place, one of the housekeepers—I think her name was Neda—said you were out in one of the barns helping a cow give birth."

That second part was a nonanswer, but she must have had a reason to be there, and she would tell him in her own time.

"Ten, actually."

She tilted her head and squinted her eyes. "Oh. You mean the cows. Busy rancher, handling all those deliveries."

"There were several of us. Anyway, the girls would probably argue that they were working harder than I or any of the ranch hands were. But I still wouldn't stand downwind of me right now."

"I'll keep that in mind. Nice office."

"If you say so." It was about as basic as a work area could be, with a desktop computer, printer, filing cabinets and a bulletin board. The only thing great about the place was that the others usually left him alone when he was working in it.

Willow paced the narrow space, scanning some of the posted safety and cow gestational documents on the wall. Finally, when Asher couldn't wait any longer for answers, he tried asking another way.

"I mean, what are you doing on the Triple R? I thought you wouldn't be caught dead here."

Finally, she faced him, gripping her hands together. "It's not so bad. Anyway, I thought we could talk."

"If you mean about the other night, there's not much left to say. You rejected my proposal."

"That's just it. I've been thinking about what I said. Maybe I was wrong."

Asher rubbed at his forearms that were suddenly tingling. *Wrong?* She shouldn't have said no?

"What do you mean? You said what I was offering wasn't enough."

"Can't a woman change her mind?"

Though "a woman" could, he doubted Willow often did. He didn't have an extra seat in his office, so he gestured for her to sit in his. She shook her head and continued to pace. He leaned against the desk.

"What are you saying?"

She grinned at him, though it was different from her other smiles that he only then realized he'd been cataloging over the past two weeks. There was no laughter in her eyes.

"I'm saying that I've thought more about your proposal, and maybe I'd like to amend my answer."

He shook his head. A response to an offer of marriage should have sounded musical or something. Not flat. Not like accepting a bid for a bathroom remodel.

"You were right," she continued. "We can form a family together. I've grown attached to Harper, and I know you feel the same about Luna. This way we can be with both girls, and they can each grow up with two parents *and* a sister."

Why did it sound so bleak when Willow said it? And a bigger question: Why had it seemed like a good idea to him in the first place? Because they had great chemistry in bed, a couple of kids to raise and could hold a civil conversation?

Sure, it was more than a lot of marriages had. Only it wasn't enough. Especially not for *her*.

Earlier, Willow had said she could never marry without love. Was he ready to use that word to describe the unfamiliar and disconcerting feelings he was developing for her? Probably not. But could he sentence her to life without it if it was something *she* needed?

"Maybe we should think about this," he blurted.

"I have, and your idea is so practical. It's easier this way. No feelings involved. We both know what we're getting into. We're walking in with our eyes wide-open."

That was the problem. His eyes were clear, and the picture before him suddenly looked bleak. She would never be truly happy in a marriage of convenience, and he couldn't bear the idea of giving her that life.

Willow folded her hands together at her waist. "So, all this is to say, yes, I'll marry you."

She glanced up at him with a look so hopeful that he hated to dash it. But he would. For her sake.

"Well, that's the thing. I need to rescind my offer."

"You what!" She jerked her hands wide. "You can't *rescind* a marriage proposal."

"Why can't I? You rejected *two* of my proposals and then come in here saying you changed your mind? Well, maybe I did, too." He stopped, tucked his thumbs through his belt loops and tried again. "Look. I'm sorry. I just realized that it's not right for, well, us."

"You just decided this? I don't even get a vote?" She stalked away from him and then looked back. "And I can't believe you let me go on and on when you were planning to withdraw the offer."

"I'm doing this for you."

The words rushed out before he could stop them. Her glare told him that he'd said the wrong thing.

"Don't tell yourself that this was for me. It has been about you all along. You were hurt once, and now you're wrapping yourself in a suit of armor to avoid being injured again. I hope at some point you figure out what you want."

"I'm a parent. I don't have the luxury of making all my decisions based on my wants or needs."

"And I do?"

"I never said that." He gripped the edge of his desk behind him. "I don't understand. Are we having this argument over a marriage of convenience? Over my taking back an offer I never should have made about something you said you never wanted?"

At that, she blew out an exasperated breath.

"If you think that's all this is about, then you don't know a damn thing about women."

She stalked from his office. Soon the thud of the outside door reverberated through the barn.

He lowered himself into his desk chair again, more spent even than he'd been when she'd arrived. He'd found her anger over his withdrawing the proposal perplexing, but his own feelings then confused him more. Nora's abandonment after Harper's birth had been painful, but this was different. Until that moment, as Willow walked out of the building and out of his life, he'd never felt so completely alone.

Chapter 22

"There. You look more like yourself now."

At Genevieve's words, Asher glanced up from his folded hands and leaned against the bedrail to examine her handiwork. With a pair of professional shears, she continued trimming his father's silvery sideburns with tiny careful snips. It had been two days since Willow had accepted his proposal, and he'd withdrawn it. Since Asher had been unable to get it out of his mind, his mother's request that he would go to the hospital to help with his dad's grooming had come as a welcome distraction. But as Genevieve completed her gentle ministrations, brushing her fingers along Payne's hairline, a lump formed in Asher's throat.

This was what true love looked like.

Did he already know what it *felt* like?

He licked his lips and tried to blink away memories that benefited no one. Even if he did love Willow, what did it matter now? He couldn't exactly renege on the *withdrawal* of a marriage proposal.

"Thanks for meeting me here this time," Genevieve said. "I know it's hard for you to get away during calving season, with all the mamas and the new babies. Especially during the day."

"Don't worry. The guys are holding down the ranch."

In fact, he'd been surprised when she'd asked him to join her. Usually, she insisted that they take turns sitting at Payne's bedside, so there would be a smaller chance that he would awaken alone.

"I still can't believe you've been trimming his hair."

Genevieve brushed her fingers through her most recent work. Though probably uneven, it was better than the shaggy look he would have had after lying in bed for four months.

"What was I supposed to do?" she said. "We can't bring his barber in here and provide material for gossip. We would need a nondisclosure agreement."

She waved away the idea with a brush of her hand. "He'll wake up soon, and then they can joke at the barbershop what a bad job I've done."

"Or hire you."

They both chuckled, a good thing since they hadn't had much to laugh about lately.

"So, I heard that Willow Merrill stopped by the ranch the other night."

Asher had been focused on his mother's progress with the scissors, but he lifted his gaze to catch her carefully blank expression.

"Mother, what did you do?"

"Willow's such a lovely young woman. Smart, too. We had a nice chat. You must have come up at some point."

He was torn between waiting his mother out and begging her to know what was said. But she couldn't be rushed.

"I was sorry to hear you're removing Harper from her day-care center. Your baby probably already loves her."

He didn't have to ask himself how she knew about his plans. People who complained about having no secrets in a small town should try being a Colton.

"Please stay out of it." Could she have been the reason that Willow had changed her mind about his proposal? Had his mother's meddling caused Willow humiliation?

"I wish I could. Unfortunately, I was already involved."

Asher blinked as the truth settled. "You know about Willow and her mom."

Genevieve set the scissors on the bedside table. Then she gathered up the towel she'd been using to collect hair and crossed to the trash can to shake off the clippings.

Finally, she looked back at him.

"It wasn't hard to put it together. Willow's not a common name."

She returned to her chair next to the bed.

"How did you even know what her name was, after—" He shook his head. The last thing he needed was to listen to his mother trying to explain the inexcusable. "Why'd you talk to Willow now, after all this time?"

"Even if it was late, she deserved an apology. I should have helped her mother more than I did the night she was fired."

She scooted closer to the bed and brushed her fingers over her husband's freshly shaven cheek. "He would probably agree now that he overreacted. He's softened a little after all these years."

Asher half expected his dad to wake up and argue that point.

"If he has softened at all, he owes that to you."

Genevieve squeezed her husband's pale hand.

"We all make mistakes, Asher. What we do to repair the fences we tear is a sign of our true character."

"Only you would speak in rancher analogies."

"What can I say? I'm Payne Colton's wife."

Asher's gaze moved from his father to the woman who loved him despite his flaws. He slumped in his chair.

"I think I've made the biggest mistake of my life."

He waited. If nothing else, he'd always been able to count on his mother to take his side. "So, what did I always tell you to do when you mess up?"

"Fix it."

"It's good to know that at least one of my children was listening. I worried that I was whispering into the wind with all of you."

"You? Whispering?" He shook his head. "Never."

This time she laughed, sounding more relaxed than she had in a while. She stopped as her gaze fell again on her sleeping husband. Her smile was for him alone as she brushed her fingers back and forth over his hand.

Then she looked up at her son.

"We can't help who we love, Asher. Or change whatever mistakes brought us to that point. We can only recognize that person for the gift that he or she is, because love and family are the only things that matter."

He patted his father's hand and rounded the bed to drop a kiss on his mother's head. Then he hurried from the room before she had the chance to see how wet his eyes were. Anyway, if his dad awoke right then, he would probably fire him as foreman for the sheer lack of toughness.

Only his mother's words followed him as he passed the guard posted outside his father's hospital room door and continued down the hall. *We can't help who we love.* And he knew. He loved Willow Merrill. It didn't matter how they'd met. Or his track record with relationships. Or even hers. But was he ready to take a risk on love the way his mother had described it? His heart still ached at the memory of Genevieve looking with hope at his comatose father, still believing, no matter how much time had passed, how bad the odds were. If he did take a risk with Willow, could he bear it if he ever lost her?

Asher pulled into his regular spot on the ranch in the line of pickups just as Jarvis Colton emerged from Barn Two. Jarvis, a distant cousin and one of triplet siblings along with Bella and cop Spencer, approached the truck.

"How's it going, boss? Any change with Payne?"

"How'd you know…?"

"Oh. Rex told me you were taking a little time to see your dad. I'm sure you mom appreciated having you there."

Asher shrugged. What would he and the other cowboys think if they knew that, even with everything else going on, his mother had reached out to him instead of the other way around? Anyway, it surprised him that his cousin was asking about nonwork matters. Jarvis had previously refused to discuss his own past.

"Is the news that bad?"

"No. There's just no change, no matter how great everyone keeps saying that Dad looks."

"Sorry, Asher."

"Any new deliveries this afternoon?"

Jarvis shook his head. "No, but Jace has been watching out for one laboring mother in Barn One. He's been super helpful lately and has us on speed dial in case the cow needs some backup."

Asher immediately started toward the barn where Jace was working.

"He's doing fine, boss. Don't worry."

Asher paused. "You're right. I'm sure he is."

"I needed to talk to you about something anyway."

"More problems with the fences?"

"Nothing like that. It's just, well, I have an idea about how to flush out Payne's shooter."

"Your brother's got it under control. At least that's what he said when I went to see him. I was trying to tell him how to do his job, too."

Jarvis shook his head. "Oh. I bet Spencer hated that. He hates when anyone questions his authority, especially Bella or me. But maybe that's just a triplet thing."

"Then why are you trying?"

"Because whoever shot your dad needs to pay for it. And because Mustang Valley will be a much safer place once the shooter is off the streets."

"Okay, I'll bite. What's your plan?"

"It's simple. You just have to let the information leak that Payne is awake. Since your dad probably knows the shooter, or at least *saw* him, the guy will be forced to come and finish the job."

Somehow Asher managed not to shiver over the last part, but he still shook his head.

"That doesn't sound like a good idea."

"Really, it's perfect. Spencer could have some of his officers staking out the place in addition to your security guys. Heck, your story won't even be that far off from the truth, since you all said your dad is improving every day."

"There are a few problems with your premise. First, we can't use my father as bait. What if the shooter's successful? Even with the police and the personal-security service we hired, Dad could still be killed."

Asher's breath caught as he remembered to whom he was speaking. Jarvis wouldn't take that risk lightly. The

Colton triplets had lost both of their parents when they were just ten years old.

"Sorry. I wasn't thinking."

"Forget about it. Anyway, you're right. I wasn't thinking about what would happen if the guy succeeded."

"That's not even the only hole in your plan. MVPD isn't big like Tucson's police department. Chief Al Barco doesn't have officers to spare for surveillance. And the part about it being closer to the truth, well, those reports about Dad's improvement might have been exaggerated."

"So, it's not a perfect plan, but do you have a better one?" When Asher shook his head, Jarvis lifted his hands in victory. "Then, hell, it's worth a try."

"Maybe you have a point. If we used a decoy for Dad, it could possibly work. I would need to run it by my brothers and sisters first, but if—"

"Absolutely it could work. Don't you think so, Jace?"

Asher found Jace standing behind him. How long their houseguest had been there, he wasn't sure.

"Depends on what you're talking about."

"What about the cow in Barn One?"

"Rex took over for me two minutes ago. Guess he didn't trust me to handle it if she really got into trouble."

"That's fair." Asher grinned, both because he had an answer to his question and that Rex was probably right.

If Jace was going to be around the ranch for a while, then he had a lot to learn. Still, every time he came out to the barns or field, he appeared to fit in a little better. Today he'd even traded the fancy Western hat that Ainsley had bought him for a more reasonable work hat. He'd paid for it himself that time.

"It was good of you to help out here while I was at the hospital. Especially with all the work you're doing with the earthquake recovery efforts."

"Just glad I could help. And glad you had that old truck around so that I had something to drive." He stretched his neck from side to side and rolled his shoulders.

"I am a little tired, though. If not for the work gloves, I wouldn't be able to bear the blisters by now." He pulled out the pair he'd tucked in his back pocket and waved them.

"You just need to develop some calluses. Badge of honor around here."

"I'll keep that in mind." Jace shrugged. "I have to keep busy, or I'll go crazy. This waiting is killing me. I can't believe you and Mrs. Merrill already have your results, and we're still waiting for the results on our repeat test."

"They should be coming at any time now, right?"

Jace blew out a breath. "God, let's hope so."

Jarvis might have become bored with the topic, as he took a step between them.

"Back to our discussion. Asher said he wants to clear my idea with his siblings, but how about we try it out on you first?"

Jace's gaze flicked to Asher. "If you're okay with that."

He considered for a few seconds and then nodded. He didn't bother lying to himself and saying he hadn't fully gone from proper skepticism to believing there was a possibility that Jace might be his brother, and then to hoping it was the case.

Asher still didn't want to be disloyal to Ace, but he couldn't argue that Jace would be a different type of Colton from any of the others. The guy was at least *interested* in the ranch part of the Colton world, instead of only the oil business like half of Asher's siblings, or emergency response and personal protection, like the other two.

Jace might need a major ranch education, but Asher also knew of someone who would be a willing instructor.

By the time that Asher had tuned back into the conversation, Jarvis had wrapped up his pitch, even including Asher's suggestion of a decoy.

"Well, what do you think?" Jarvis asked.

Jace appeared to consider for a few seconds.

"If it were me, I would want to guarantee that Payne was safe by having him moved from the hospital to another facility," Jace said. "But, other than that, I think it's a great idea.

"Whoever hurt…Payne needs to be stopped before he comes back and finishes, you know, what he started."

Asher nodded. At first, he'd been cautious about the idea, but Jace was right. They had to stop the shooter instead of just having security guards to protect his father, or he would never be safe. None of the family would be.

"Just give me a minute. Let me talk it over with my siblings."

He stepped away and scrolled through his contacts. Strange how he was still tempted to call Ace first as the oldest, but he resisted the impulse. Ace had enough to deal with lately. Instead, Asher started with Ainsley, and worked his way down the list by age until he reached the twins, Callum and Marlowe.

When he was finished, he returned to Jarvis, who stood near his truck.

"Where did Jace go?"

"Said he had to get back to work."

Asher could have said the same thing about the two of them, but he didn't mention that.

"Well, what did they say?"

"They all agreed with Jace. As long as we move Dad, then they're in."

"What about your mom?"

"She'll go along with us."

Jarvis's skeptical look had Asher scuffing the dirt with

the toe of his boot. The other man was right to question. Genevieve would be the most difficult to convince, since she had the most to lose. But she also was Payne's next of kin and could determine whether they would be allowed to move his father.

"I'll talk to her tonight. I'll make sure she's on board."

"So, do you want me to wait to call Spencer until you have her approval?"

Asher shook his head, fully aware that there would be hell to pay later that night. "No, go ahead."

Immediately, Jarvis pulled out his phone, clicked on a contact and tapped the speaker icon.

"What is it, brother?" Spencer said the moment he answered. "I told you not to call me at work."

Jarvis rolled his eyes. "Well, *Sergeant* Colton, this is official business, and I am calling as a Mustang Valley citizen."

"Oh. What is it?"

Asher leaned toward the phone to announce his presence before a sibling battle ensued. "Hey, Spencer. Asher Colton here. Jarvis is calling on my behalf."

"Our meeting wasn't enough? Look, I know it's taking a while, but the members of our department are doing everything we can—"

"This isn't just Asher," Jarvis said, interrupting him. "I came to him with an idea."

Spencer didn't respond for so long that Asher wondered if the call had been dropped, a common problem in an area with too many mountains and not enough cellphone towers. But, finally, Spencer's voice came through the line again.

"What are you two up to?"

"I just have an idea about how to flush out whoever shot Payne Colton."

"Is that what you do while riding the fences on the ranch? Look for ways to do *my* job? I already know that Asher should have been a cop. If you're vying for my position, too, who will be left at the Triple R?"

Finally, he let Jarvis share his idea. When he finished, Jarvis exchanged a look with Asher as they waited.

"It could work," Spencer said finally. "It's a good idea, Jarvis, but then I'm not surprised that you would come up with it since you—"

Spencer stopped himself, making Asher curious.

"Since he what?"

"Oh, it was nothing," Jarvis answered for him. "With all these investigations happening at the same time, his brain has to be muddled."

"You've got that right. It's nothing," Spencer said. "Right about the muddled part, too. This new plan is the only thing that matters right now. We need to stop this suspect. So, talk to your mother, Asher. Believe me, I wouldn't want to be you when you tackle that subject with her."

Asher lifted a brow over the abrupt change in topic, but Jarvis wasn't looking his way. Did it have something to do with the guy's past? Asher had always figured the guy had a right to his privacy, but now he wondered if he'd failed to ask enough questions of his employees.

"Sure you'll have enough staff to constantly cover the decoy?"

"We'll make it work."

The conversation suddenly awkward, they ended the call. Jarvis made the legitimate excuse that he needed to get back to the barns and strode that way.

What had just happened? His distant cousin appeared to be running from questions Asher hadn't even asked, scuffing up dirt as he went. What didn't make sense was that Jarvis had come to *him*, offering to help. Should he trust that assistance?

Would the man have a reason to want to see Payne dead or to have created any of the mysteries directed at his family or him individually? His gut told him no. Absolutely not. If only that could have made him less suspicious, could have eliminated his sudden distrust of Jarvis and, by extension, Spencer, who happened to be the local police sergeant.

Just what did Jarvis have to hide?

Chapter 23

Willow startled as the doorbell to Tender Years triggered the buzzer in her apartment. Even knowing Asher would be dropping to settle his account that night didn't prepare her for the sharp reality of his arrival. She'd managed to avoid him the past few days, sending Candace or Tori out during drop-off and pickup times, but this she would have to handle herself.

How was she supposed to face him, just over a week since he'd taken back his proposal? Had he figured out the message behind her acceptance of his offer in the first place? She'd said she would never marry without love, and she'd been true to her word. Maybe she'd found her courage after Genevieve had said her son might have feelings for her, but she'd said yes for one reason alone: she was in love with *him*. Completely. Hopelessly.

She'd taken a leap, blindfolded, into an empty pool. Had she ever considered what she would do if she'd gambled wrong? Had she believed her love would be enough for them both?

She opened the door that separated her work from her home life and descended the stairs. She didn't miss that he'd gone to the Tender Years entrance instead of climbing the exterior stairs to her apartment. Images of what had happened the night he'd visited her there were still alive in her memory. They were sharp in both the imprints they'd left on all her senses and their ability to slice her heart.

Was she ready for this? Her life would be easier if she didn't have to see him every day, if only from her office window as he carried Harper up the walk, but did she want to lose even that lingering contact?

She entered the center through the kitchen and closed the door behind her. Flipping on light switches as she went, she continued up the hall to the front of the house. The facility looked as if she was working evening hours by the time that she opened the front door.

"Hello, Willow."

She cleared her throat. "Hi."

Her chest squeezed at the sight of him under the glow of the porch light, dressed in his uniform of jeans and a dark T-shirt, yet somehow looking different. It was more than that he'd used gel to control his hair. She refused to think about that other night when he'd stood on the landing outside her apartment. She'd let him into her home, bed and heart, not close to being in that order.

"You were expecting me, right?"

She nodded.

His lips lifted slightly. "Then may I come in?"

For a few seconds, she hesitated. Would she force him to complete their final business transactions on the porch? Couldn't she be an adult about this?

"Sure. Come in."

She pulled the door wide for him to enter and closed it behind him, but she immediately entered her office. "I have the paperwork on my desk."

Lingering longer than was necessary so that she could take a few deep breaths, she collected the forms and returned to where he stood in the entry.

"I feel like I just filled those out." He pointed to the sheets in her hands.

"Because you did." It didn't seem possible that only three weeks had passed since she'd received that call from the hospital. So much had changed. *She* had changed.

"You don't have to withdraw Harper yet from the center if you don't want to."

The surprise in his eyes had to have been mirrored in hers as the words seemed to have come all on their own. She shifted from one foot to the other. "I mean, she's so happy here."

"It seemed like what you wanted."

She shrugged and licked her lips. "It's just that you've already said what a difficult time you had finding good childcare."

"I'll just have to search harder and offer a higher salary."

"Than the amount you were already paying? You can't just create qualified candidates out of thin air. Do you know how hard I had to search for mine?"

He shrugged. "I'll figure something out."

"And she and Luna are both scooting. They'll be crawling soon. Can you imagine how much fun the two of them would have together?"

Why was she giving him excuses not to leave? Did she *want* to see him every day? Was she trying to make this harder on herself? Or him?

"Yeah, that would have been fun," he said.

"Luna will miss her. So will I." She cleared her throat.

"I know it will be…awkward, but this is about Harper. Not us. She deserves quality care, and you know she can have it here, where there are people who already love her."

He coughed several times into his T-shirt sleeve. "You don't happen to have anything to drink do you? Water? Coffee? Anything?"

"I have some lemonade."

She led the way to the kitchen, pulled a glass from the cabinet and grabbed the pitcher from the refrigerator. Did the fact that he was delaying his departure mean something? It wasn't as if he could leave when she hadn't given him the forms to sign or accepted his final payment.

She handed him the glass, careful not to let their fingers touch.

"This is great. Thanks."

If he decided to keep Harper at the center, she would always have to take care around the child's father. She couldn't extend a polite handshake whenever he visited the center. Or stare at him too long during drop-off. And never could she allow herself to remember the scent of his skin, the taste of his lips or sensation of his touch on her skin.

She knew how tightly her hands were clasped hinted just how tough those rules would be to follow. When she forced herself to release her grip and looked up, she found Asher watching her. She braced herself for the words she should have wanted to hear but suddenly dreaded. *It's for the best.*

"It doesn't have to be this way."

Her breath caught, and her pulse pounded in her temples.

"What do you mean?" she couldn't help but ask when he didn't immediately explain himself. "About the girls?"

He shook his head and chewed his lip, appearing nervous. It didn't fit. This was Asher Colton, who usually exuded confidence through his pores.

"No," he said finally. "Us."

There was an "us"? Had something changed from the other day when he'd humiliated her more than she'd believed possible? If he made that same, sad proposal a *third* time, would she be able to bear the mortification?

"The two of us together, it didn't mean anything, right?" Was she asking for more pain? Like an idiot in a bar, daring all the drunks to punch her in the gut as hard as they could?

"I tried to tell myself that."

She swallowed. "What are you saying? Because if this is just another—"

"I want you," he blurted and then shook his head.

The right and left slide of her chin had to mirror his. Though her body still craved him like a pitcher as part of a fountain, filling but never full, it still wasn't enough. Anything less than all of him never would be.

"No, that's not what I meant. I don't want your body. Don't get me wrong. Your body's great. Fantastic. It's just that..."

His struggle tore at her heart and pulled her lips up at the same time.

He cleared his throat and stared so deeply into her eyes that he must have been able to see straight to her soul.

"I...want—"

Then he stopped, his head jerking to stare at the closed door that hid the stairway to her apartment. *You.* The word ricocheted in her head, booming in its absence. *Please say it,* she wanted to beg. Just that one syllable and then three words more and everything would change for them. The impossible would become possible. A lie could be a foundation for truth.

"Do you smell smoke?"

Her gaze swept to that door. She shook her head, and then she stopped. Because she did smell it.

"Oh my God! Luna's up there! My baby!"

She barreled for the door, but he gripped her shoulder from behind.

"I'll go."

"No! I have to get to her!"

"What you *need* to do is call 911 and let me do this." He pressed his cell into her hand.

She shook her head and moved forward again.

"Please!"

The desperation in his voice cut through her panic, and she hesitated long enough to look back at him.

He shook his head. "I can't risk losing you both. Now you've got to get out."

Without waiting for her to answer, he hurried across the kitchen, collecting items as he went. He rested a pair of silicone oven mitts on the counter and tossed a white tablecloth into the sink and turned on the faucet. After wringing it slightly, he wrapped it around his head to cover his nose and mouth, shoved on the mitts and rushed for the door.

"Please bring back my Luna."

"I will."

He didn't look back as he opened the door and barreled up the stairs. At the top, he pushed open the second door. Willow gasped as smoke poured out, but Asher didn't hesitate as he crouched low and slipped inside.

"I love you," she called after him.

Her heart squeezed with the knowledge that he couldn't hear her. Maybe would never hear the truth that she'd known all along. Her vision smeared with welling tears, she jogged down the same hall she'd followed so recently to meet him. Once outside, she hurried all the way past the decorative blond brick barrier that bordered the street and marked the edge of her property. Then she dialed for emergency assistance.

A sob escaped her just as a loud click came on the line.

"911 operator, what is your emergency?" the woman said.

"Fire" was all she could manage.

The emergency worker spoke calming words as she extracted information and then assured Willow that assistance was on the way. Willow clicked off the call and stared down at the phone in her hands. His phone. She glanced up at the house again. Smoke was already billowing from the upstairs window. Were those *flames* climbing the pretty curtains next to her dinette? Asher had promised he would bring her baby to her. What if he couldn't keep his promise? What if he couldn't get out?

Sirens already blared in the distance. In minutes, the fire trucks would arrive, but would they be soon enough? She couldn't just stand there and wring her hands while two of the people she loved most in the world were inside that building. Maybe hurting. Maybe—no, she couldn't let that happen.

She rushed up the walk again. She had to get to them. Had to save them. Or she would die with them.

"Willow, stop!"

She felt more than heard his words as they slowed her at the bottom step. Had she imagined the sound that seemed to have come from the west side of the house, the section with no access to the second floor? The shrill whirr of the approaching emergency vehicles crowded her brain, forcing out the sound she longed for. With it, her hope.

Her world swam in and out of focus as she was suddenly enveloped in a mob of firefighters in heavy yellow jackets. One of them guided her outside the low brick wall.

"Miss, you have to stay back."

"But my…baby. My—"

"Your *what*?"

Where Asher had come from, she wasn't sure, but he was there, sweat and soot painting his face, a filthy table-cloth-covered bundle in his oven mitt–covered arms. She could only stare at the lump, her hands covering her mouth to hold in a scream. Her knees buckled, her legs no longer having the strength to hold her upright. Someone behind her, probably an EMT, caught her.

Asher rushed forward. Only then could she see the burns on his upper arms where his shirt used to be.

"It's all right, Willow. It's going to be okay."

A female EMT lifted the package from him, and they all unwrapped it. And there *she* was, her jammies dirty, her face and hair sweaty and filthy. Then Willow's wonderful, high-strung, perfect Luna started to cry.

Chapter 24

"We have to stop meeting like this."

Asher grinned at Willow as she stood outside the cracked curtain in Mustang Valley General's ER department, her face still looking as if she'd seen a ghost. Earlier, when he'd emerged from her burning house, she probably thought she had.

"Are you coming in?" he asked when she didn't.

Finally, she slid past the curtain and stepped inside, hugging herself as if she couldn't get warm enough. If only he could take her in his arms and hold her until all those storms disappeared from her eyes. But with these bandages near his elbows, he probably shouldn't be holding anything, even Harper, for a few days.

"Where's Luna?" he asked.

When he gestured toward the guest chair, she stepped over and sat.

"She's sleeping. Candace is with her. The doctors want to keep her overnight—"

Immediately, he straightened in the bed and then gritted his teeth because of the searing down his arms. "She's okay, right?"

Her eyes still damp, she nodded. "It's just a precaution. They want to make sure her lungs are okay. They're getting her bed ready in the pediatric ward. I would have waited with her, but Candace thought I might need some coffee."

"She threw you out, didn't she?"

He hoped that would make her smile, but she only shrugged, hugging herself even tighter. Her gaze moved from the neckline of his hospital gown to the bandages on his arms.

"What did the doctor tell you?"

"These?" He gestured to the gauze. "They're nothing. Barely more than a good sunburn. In fact, the doc's springing me from here as soon as she gets back to sign the release forms."

Willow lifted a brow and then stared down at his hands that were in far better shape than the upper part of his forearms.

"Oh, sorry to say your good oven mitts are toast. Or barbecue. Whichever you choose."

"Please stop joking about it. You two could have been—"

"But we weren't." He shook his head to emphasize his point.

Tears welled in Willow's already puffy eyes, and a lump formed in Asher's throat.

"I'm sorry about your building. Do you know yet about the extent of the damage?"

She shrugged. "Candace was talking to the fire inspector before she came here. He suspects arson. He said there's little structural damage, except the roof. The contents of the apartment? Well, at least they're insured. We might be able to save most of the equipment in the center."

"If someone wanted to hurt your business, then why set fire to your apartment instead of the facility?"

"I don't know, but we were lucky."

He rushed on to prevent them both from considering just how much worse it could have been.

"I couldn't believe that even the outdoor stairs were still standing when the paramedics made me get in the ambulance. I was worried they would fall, so I took the interior stairs and came around the opposite side of the house."

She nodded, yet drew her brows together, as if his explanation offered more questions than answers. Or gave her another reason to believe he'd failed her and her daughter. The lump in his throat grew larger.

"And I'm sorry… I didn't get to her sooner," he managed.

Her eyes were wide as she looked back at him.

"You kidding? That was amazing what you did for her. For *us*. Thank you so much. You didn't have to do that."

"Yes, I did. It was Luna."

Clearly, she still didn't get it. It couldn't have mattered less to him that Luna wasn't his child biologically. She had still become his. Asher loved her almost as much as he loved her mother.

He was tempted to tell Willow right then, his fears be damned, but something outside the cubicle must have caught her attention as she looked toward the curtain's opening. Heavy footsteps followed.

"Knock. Knock."

Asher sat higher in the bed. "Spencer, is that you?"

He didn't know why he bothered asking when he recognized his cousin's voice. They'd spent a lot of time to-gether lately.

The sergeant pulled back the curtain and stepped inside. "Hello, Mrs. Merrill. How's it going, Asher?"

Spencer glanced at his arms as if to answer the ques-tion for himself and then pointed to the bandages. "Been playing with matches again?"

"Do all Coltons have to make a joke out of everything?" Willow asked.

"Sorry, ma'am." Spencer straightened. "I'm here on business, anyway."

"If you've come to ask us if we saw anything suspicious before the fire, I'm not going to be able to help you," Asher said. "I came in through the front of the house instead of the exterior stairs to the apartment."

"I didn't see anything, either, before meeting Asher in the center," Willow told him.

Spencer jotted a few notes in his tiny notebook. "I checked with the guards you had watching the house. They didn't see anything either."

"Hiring them was money well spent."

His cousin shrugged. "Apparently, the arsonist came through the back."

"So, what are you going to do now? Someone is obvi-ously out to get Willow." He shivered at just how close the arsonist had come to succeeding.

"Have you been able to find the connection between the events at Tender Years and the attacks on my family? There has to be something."

"There isn't," Spencer said.

Asher had just been getting on a roll with his suspicions, but at the sergeant's words, he stopped.

"How can you be sure?"

"What do you know?"

Willow's words trampled his.

Spencer held his hands wide. "Because we have a suspect in custody. Arrested right outside the house in the crowd of onlookers. He confessed."

Willow came up from her seat. "Who is it? How do I know him? Why would he want to hurt my business? Or *us*?"

Spencer held out his hands, palms down, and lowered them, signaling for them to calm down. "The suspect's name is Alan Hunter. Ring a bell?"

She shook her head, squinting. "Should I know him?"

"I don't think so. As far as we can tell, Alan didn't so much want to hurt you as he wanted to please *her*."

"Her? I don't understand. Why would a woman want to hurt me?" She stopped and tilted her head to the side. "Wait. Was she an angry former client? Did she leave the reviews?"

"That's what Detective Kerry Wilder is trying to find out right now. We have Ms. Williams in custody."

"Ms. Williams?"

Willow repeated the name is if testing it against her memory bank and making no connection.

"Her name is Audrey Williams. Does that ring a bell?"

The color drained from Willow's face, and she dropped down in the chair again, her eyes closed, her hands forming a steeple beneath her nose.

Asher wished he could climb out of that ridiculous bed and take her in his arms. He didn't care if the local police sergeant was there to witness it.

"You know her, don't you?"

She nodded with her lids still shut.

"Was she a parent of one of your charges?"

This time she shook her head and opened her eyes. The look of misery in them gave him a good guess.

"She was one of the women your ex cheated with, wasn't she?"

Willow shrugged. "I insisted that he break up with her or get out. At least that time, he agreed."

"And she blamed you."

Willow gripped her head in her hands. "This was all my fault. I should have told him to go be with her then, but I'd just found out I was pregnant, and I thought I needed him."

Asher jerked his hands wide, his arms stinging again beneath the bandages.

"No, you're wrong. None of this was your fault." He lowered his hands, but he couldn't keep from fisting them on top of the blanket. "And you never needed *him*. For anything."

Until Spencer cleared his throat, Asher had forgotten he was even in the room.

"Mr. Hunter told the whole story, and it lines up with yours. Ms. Williams blamed Willow for Xavier ending the relationship. It didn't seem to matter to her that they later divorced. She didn't seem to be aware that he is deceased. She appeared shocked."

"She did all those things to us because he broke it off with her?" Willow asked.

"I never said it made sense. She recruited Hunter for her plan of revenge. A technical genius who could do things like hack into the Department of Health Services website to file a bogus complaint and override the Clamor app's security system to destroy a business."

Asher shook his head. "After everything, can you believe that none of the suspicious incidents at your business were related to the equally strange ones affecting my family? Well, except for the switch."

"Yeah. Except for that."

Willow smiled, and then the expression seemed to drain from her face. She glanced at Spencer.

"Then what about the fire?"

"Hunter must have realized he was being used, and her pressuring him into it must have been the last straw for him. As poorly as the arson was executed, he must have wanted to be caught, so he could turn her in, too."

Willow leaped to her feet, hugging herself as tightly as she had earlier. "He did it to get back at *her*? Didn't he realize he could have killed my baby and my—"

She stopped herself and shot a glance first at Spencer and then at Asher.

He battled to keep a straight face and lost. "Your...?"

A pair of white running shoes appeared beneath the curtain, and soon a young nurse peeked around it. "Excuse me, Mrs. Merrill? Mrs. Hill told me I would find you here. We're ready to move Luna into her room."

Asher's doctor appeared behind the nurse, her white coat hanging open, a chart in her hands. "This room is getting full. Too full."

"I agree," Spencer said as he stepped toward the opening in the curtain. "I was just on my way out, Doctor."

The nurse gestured for Willow to follow her.

The doctor addressed Asher. "Now, that's better. Let's get you—"

Asher lifted a finger to ask her to wait.

"Willow? Hold up."

She glanced back. "I have to get to Luna."

"I know you do."

But as she swiveled to go again, he spoke to her back. "But it sounds like we need to talk."

She looked over once more, her tongue slipping out to dab her lips. "We will. Soon."

Chapter 25

Asher tromped through the house's main entryway on his way to his wing, not caring that Neda would yell at him for not taking off his work boots before crossing the tiles she'd just waxed. He needed to get to Harper, not only because he couldn't stand to be away from her since the fire but also since he needed to relieve whichever staff or family member was taking a turn babysitting her.

Though Luna was already out of the hospital and staying with her mom at Candace's house, Tender Years would be closed for a few more weeks for repairs. After five days, he couldn't help wondering how he and his daughter had survived before he'd enrolled her there. The same could be said for his time away from Willow, but he needed to give her a few days to process how her ex still had been able to hurt her, even from the grave.

It still didn't make sense to him why the woman had blamed Xavier's rejection on Willow, even after their divorce. Jilted lovers didn't have to make sense, he guessed. Would it have made a difference if Audrey had known earlier that Xavier was dead? Somehow, he doubted it.

Asher had been giving Willow time to puzzle through the situation, but his waiting time was nearly up. At least he hadn't been forced to pass any of his other siblings or Jace in the hall. He couldn't take more questions. His ranch hands had gotten so bad that he'd volunteered to ride the fences earlier to be alone.

Asher paused outside the entrance to his suite. He wanted time to paste on a smile, so he could spend some quality time with his little girl. He didn't want to admit that he needed to see one of her amazing smiles as much as she required a father who could protect her. Even now he wasn't certain he could do that for her. If someone had gotten to Luna in her own home, how long would it be before someone reached his child in hers?

He pushed the door open.

"Is that you, Asher?" Dulcie called out as she emerged from the nursery carrying the baby. "Someone's been waiting for her daddy."

Harper squealed as she stretched her arms out to him.

Asher started toward her, but at the scream coming from downstairs, he froze.

"What was that?" Dulcie rushed toward the hall.

"No!" He lowered his voice. "Take Harper and hide. I'll go see what happened."

Turning, he stopped again, reached in his pocket and tossed his phone to the cook. "Call 911."

As he ran down the grand stairway from the third floor to the second, he tried not to think about how recently he'd asked another woman to make that same call. Was someone else he loved in danger? Would he be too late to help this time?

When he glanced in both directions on the second-floor landing, he started down again. "Who screamed? Where are you?'

"It's me, Asher."

"Mom?"

"In here."

She seemed to be calling from her suite, so he raced inside. From her scream, he would have expected blood or at least bruises. But from the look of the carefully decorated and always immaculate master bedroom, his mother was the only thing there that hadn't been touched. Dresser drawers lay upside down, their contents scattered across the floor. Her mattress had been flipped off the bed. Even her antique hand mirror had been shattered on the bathroom tile.

"We've been robbed."

He didn't bother telling her how obvious that was. "How did they get inside?"

Asher took in the pile of handled boutique bags on the bed. "Were you out shopping?"

"Just for a few hours."

"That's all it took. How did they get past Jace?"

"Do you think the thugs overpowered him?"

He shook his head. "I didn't see any sign of a struggle, at least at the front door. He probably just stepped away."

Come to think of it, he hadn't seen Jace all afternoon. That he'd been relieved not to have to deal with his possible brother's questions earlier only made him feel guilty now. Where was he?

"Well, what about the alarm system? Was it on?"

She shook her head. "I don't remember if I set it."

But he already knew that answer. They often left it off during the day when staff and family members were regularly coming and going.

"Do you think they're still in the house?"

Asher shook his head. "No. Whoever broke in is long gone by now."

"Who do you think could have done this?"

"I don't know." Was it the person who'd shot his father or involved Willow and him in a bogus baby-switch mystery? Maybe it was the suspect who called in a bomb threat or who let Triple R cattle escape. Could one individual have accomplished so many crimes without dying from exhaustion?

He scanned the top of his mother's dresser, but the bric-a-brac that was usually there had been swiped to the floor.

"What did they get?"

His mother rushed into her side of the his-and-hers closets and dressing room and pushed aside the sliding wall that covered the safe. By the time he reached her, she was already putting in the combination. She pulled open the door, moved jewelry boxes around and then sighed.

"The burglar didn't make it in here. My good jewelry is fine. But I had some expensive pieces on the dresser. They're all gone along with some cash I had lying on top."

"Cash, Mom? Really?"

"I trust our staff. Implicitly. At least I did." She returned to the main room. "We should call the police."

"I already had Dulcie call from upstairs, but we'd better let them know it's not a murder or an active-shooter incident they're coming into." He reached out his hand. "Give me your phone."

She grabbed her purse off the bed and handed her cell to him.

"At least you remembered to take this with you , or it would already be gone and wiped back to factory settings by now."

He dialed the emergency dispatcher to let police know

that though an officer was still needed, the situation at the Triple R wasn't critical. Then he dialed his own phone to let Dulcie know she could bring Harper out.

Just as the cook handed his daughter into his arms in the entryway, Marlowe came through the front door, followed by Grayson.

"What's going on this time?" Grayson asked immediately.

Marlowe planted her hands on her hips. "Yeah, what now?"

"Better check your suites," Asher told them. "We've been robbed."

Grayson climbed the stairs to the second floor. After handing Harper to his mother, Asher took the elevator with Marlowe to the third. Like in their parents' suite, Marlowe's drawers had been emptied on the floor. She rushed over to her bedside dresser that was still intact.

She shook her head as soon as she opened it. "My jewelry is gone."

They both automatically glanced down at her left hand. Her diamond solitaire engagement ring from Bowie blinked back at them.

"Oh, thank goodness." Marlowe blew out a breath. "I've not been wearing it as often lately since my hands are swelling from the pregnancy."

"Good thing you wore it today."

She pointed back to the drawer. "They got the cash I keep in there, too."

"Does everyone in this family leave cash lying around?"

Since they were on the third floor, anyway, they also checked Callum's room, which looked much like the first two. Then they checked Asher's before taking the elevator back down.

"Looks like we've all been hit," Grayson said as they reached the landing.

Marlowe pointed to Asher. "Except for him."

"I told you that Dulcie was in there with Harper. I don't have anything of value in there, anyway. And I rarely use cash."

Marlowe pulled out her phone. "I'll call the others."

Genevieve pointed toward the guest suite. "What about Jace's room?"

"Right. Jace." Asher hurried that way. "A burglar wouldn't know which wings to hit."

The others followed him down the hall but stood back as he pushed open the door.

"It's empty!" Genevieve called out, speaking for everyone.

Asher stepped inside to look around, and the others followed. The dresser drawers had been pulled out like they had been in the other suites, but this time, there were no clothes on the floor. None of the paintings remained on the wall, either.

"What the hell?" Asher called out.

"This place has been wiped clean," Grayson said behind him.

Marlowe marched over to the closet and opened the door. It was empty, too.

Grayson shook his head. "The leather jacket I bought him."

"That hat from Ainsley. The boots from Callum. The clothes from Mom." Marlowe shook her head. "They're all gone."

Genevieve frowned. "I won't even ask about the cash I gave him to tide him over."

Could Jace have been the one who'd robbed them?

Asher shook his head, the sensation that he'd just been kicked in the stomach making him want to double over.

As they returned to the entry, the doorbell rang. Asher pulled open the door. Kerry Wilder stood on the stoop in her police department uniform, her hair tucked under her hat.

"Oh, hey, Kerry. Rafe isn't here, but you don't have to knock. You're nearly family."

She shifted from one foot to the other. "I'm here on business."

"Right," Asher said. "You don't usually respond to calls, do you?"

Kerry shook her head. "I volunteered. Everyone else is getting sick of coming out to the Triple R."

"Can't say as I blame them."

Just as he stepped aside to let her in, Ainsley hurried up the walk. As usual, she was on her cell phone. She clicked off as she stepped inside.

"I forgot something when I left for the office this morning." She stopped and scanned the crowded entry. "What's going on?"

"I hope whatever you left wasn't valuable," Marlowe said.

The others took turns filling Ainsley in on the most recent incident. Her shoulders slumped forward with each detail, but when Grayson announced that Jace was missing, she put her hand to her forehead and squeezed her temples between her thumb and middle finger.

She lowered her hand to her side. "The hospital just called. The results for the repeat test are in."

"Finally." Asher and Grayson said it in unison.

As their take-charge sister, Ainsley stepped forward.

"Okay, let's check to see what's missing from our suites, and then I'll go pick up the results. We can open them together." She started up the stairs and then stopped and turned back to them. "Hopefully, by then Jace will have reappeared from wherever he took off to, and it'll be a misunderstanding we can all laugh about."

Though they called out their agreement with her, the sounds fell flat. Asher wanted to believe it, too, but the circumstantial evidence was piling on top of their hope, threatening to smother it. The answers they'd waited for were about to be theirs. Unfortunately, they would have to deal with the possibility that even if Jace was their brother, he also might be a thief.

"Okay, let's get this over with."

Ainsley rested the clasp envelope on the dining room table and sat a few seats down from her stepmother.

Asher nodded her way and slid into the chair between Genevieve and Rafe. The room was too quiet without the addition of his siblings' husbands- and wives-to-be. Even Harper wasn't around, as Dulcie had taken her off for a bath.

Just seven family members crowded around one end of a cloth-covered table. The absences of both Payne and Ace had never seemed starker or more obvious. They hadn't even asked Dulcie to provide a last-minute meal for them as none of them would have been able to eat, anyway.

When everyone was seated, Ainsley opened the envelope.

"Has Jace reached out to any of you since the discovery of the burglary? If so, we'll wait for him before we read this."

"I tried calling his cell, but it went right to voice mail," Marlowe said.

One by one, they said they hadn't heard from him.

"Okay, then." She pulled the stack of documents from the envelope and read down the first page.

Asher's gut clenched as images of another set of tests results filtered through his thoughts. Conclusions that had both thrilled and unsettled him as he'd confirmed he was Harper's dad but not Luna's. He doubted now that any results on those sheets would give anyone sitting around that table joy.

Callum leaned forward on his elbows. "Well, are you going to tell us what it says?"

Asher lifted a hand to stall him. "Give her a minute. There's a lot of information to digest."

Callum nodded and sat back.

Finally, Ainsley cleared her throat and read aloud, "In the case of the child, Jace Smith, the alleged father, Payne Colton, is excluded as the biological parent."

Marlowe struggled to her feet. "You mean Jace is *not* our brother?"

Ainsley nodded. "That's what it means. On the Combined Paternity Index, it says 'zero.'"

"That jerk!" Grayson called out.

Asher had to unclench his molars to be able to speak. "That's what I thought. At least after what we found this afternoon."

"Me, too." Ainsley tucked the papers back inside the envelope. "He must have had something to do with the delay in getting the DNA results back from the hospital, as well."

Marlowe gripped her hands on the edge of the table as she sat again. "But that would have required help from inside the hospital."

Ainsley nodded. "How else can you explain that our test had to be repeated, and we received our results after Asher and Willow did?"

Something about that bothered Asher, too, but they had to deal with the truth on the documents first.

"We just have to admit that we've been duped by a grifter. Me most of all."

Rafe shook his head. "You don't get to own that. We all believed him."

Marlowe slumped in her chair. "We were all so naive to think the 'real Ace' would just appear out of nowhere. We never considered that there might be people out there ready to take advantage of this mess affecting all of us."

Asher crossed his arms and shook his head, refusing to be let off the hook. Sure, the others had bought him gifts. They were rich. They could buy things for every resident of Mustang Valley if they wanted to. But he'd gone a step further.

"I was worse than any of you. I wanted him to be my brother." He was furious with himself, but more than that, he was ashamed.

Grayson chuckled. "You weren't alone, Asher. We all did."

Rafe held out both hands in a sign for them to hold up. "Well, maybe not all of us."

They all laughed at that, but the sounds rang hollow. Jace had betrayed them all, and Asher felt like an idiot for letting him do it.

Slowly, Genevieve came to her feet, drawing the attention of her children and stepchildren to her.

"I don't want you all to feel sorry for or angry with yourselves over this."

She seemed to be looking right at Asher as she said the second part.

"As awful as it was to be robbed, nothing we lost was irreplaceable."

Ainsley started to speak up, but Genevieve held up a hand to delay her.

"We opened our home and our hearts to someone we believed could be family. You can console yourselves with that. Things can be replaced. Family can't. That grifter wasn't family."

The meeting broke up soon after as they all quietly returned with their thoughts to their suites and homes.

Only Asher's sitting room seemed to shrink on him once he reached it. Back in the dining room, he couldn't bring himself to mention it and add to an already difficult discovery, but now he could think of nothing else. One switched-at-birth report had been fabricated, and the other was real but with an impostor playing the role of the missing baby. Were those things connected?

"I was a chump."

He shook his head as memories of showing off the new spring calves to Jace crept through his thoughts. Had he hoped he would finally have a brother who cared as much about the land and the animals of the Triple R as he did?

Unable to stay on the sofa any longer, he crossed to the nursery and carefully opened the door, allowing light to stream across the room. His beautiful Harper slept flat on her back, her arms raised above her head, the light blanket he'd placed over her already bunched in a corner of the crib. He took a step toward her, but she startled in her sleep, so he remained in the doorway.

Jace had not only taken advantage of his parents and siblings, he'd also likely targeted Asher's precious child, the woman he loved and another child he cared for as if she was his own. Was he positive that Jace was the one who orchestrated the fake baby switch? No. Audrey Williams had a motive to do it in her plans to hurt Willow, but if it was Jace, Asher wouldn't let him get away with it.

Without covering his daughter again since her sleeper was plenty warm, he closed the door and returned to the sitting room with his phone. He needed to get in touch with Rex and Jarvis and let them know they would be in charge the next day. He had to find some answers.

After he made those calls, he pulled up Willow's name in the contact list and stared down at her photo that he'd added to it. As his finger lingered over the call icon, he reconsidered. He'd told himself he would give her space, and even if he suspected he'd finally found the real connection between the mysteries involving his family and hers, he still needed proof.

Once he had it, he would share the whole story with her and apologize for how she'd been dragged into a drama that had nothing to do with her. Then, if she was still talking to him, he would tell her one more thing: he was in love with her.

Chapter 26

Willow carefully climbed the exterior stairs to her apartment and inserted her key in the dead bolt. She didn't know why the fire inspector had locked it, since there was almost nothing salvageable inside. She shifted onto her hip the box of contractor trash bags, a pair of work gloves tucked at the top. They would fill many bags that morning.

"Are you sure these steps are safe?" Candace asked from behind her.

"The inspector said we're clear to come back inside," Willow said over her shoulder. "The building is structurally sound. But I have to tell you, if it wasn't, hugging that handrail wouldn't have made a difference."

Though Candace made a mean face, she didn't release the rail until she stood behind her boss at the top.

"Glad Tori could babysit Luna today."

Willow nodded, but she didn't look back at her. "She said she was glad to have a little extra income. I'm sorry

I'm unable to cover payroll until we're up and running again."

"That's what unemployment insurance is for. Besides, you know I don't need this job. I'm just here for the distraction, and because I adore you and Luna."

"Thanks. We love you, too." She stared at the same peephole where she'd looked out at Asher that night not so long ago. Was everything in her apartment going to remind her of him? "Get ready to be really distracted today."

As she pushed open the door, her breath caught. She'd thought she was prepared to see it. The fire department officials had warned her. That didn't stop the images and the stench from hitting her like a two-by-four to the face. This was the home she'd made for her tiny family, the business she'd built, piece by piece, and that plan that was supposed to provide her with the type of security her mother had never known.

At least this part of it was gone.

Anything that hadn't been burned lay bloated and destroyed from the high-powered fire hoses. Even days later, her tennis shoes squished on the soggy carpeting as she took her first few steps inside.

She swallowed a sob, reminding herself that only things had been inside that building. No one she loved had been badly injured. Luna was unharmed. Even Asher's injuries were minor. None of her employees or charges were hurt. So why did she still have the urge to sit on the floor and cry?

"Wow. I was expecting it to be a lot worse."

"You're joking, right." She whirled to face Candace, who grinned back at her.

"Yeah, it's bad. We'll fill up that dumpster you rented in no time." The older woman scanned the room. "But it could have been a lot worse. And if I'd lost you and Luna…"

Candace closed her eyes and sank her front teeth in her bottom lip.

"Right. We're fine." Willow straightened her shoulders. They could do this.

She tied a bandanna over her nose and mouth, put on the gloves, yanked out the first huge trash bag and handed the box to Candace.

"It was a good idea doing this part first." Candace donned her own scarf, slid on her gloves and spoke in a muffled voice. "It'll make the downstairs look a lot better."

Willow shoved garbage inside her bag, trying not to attach memories to each item as it disappeared inside the plastic. If she did that, they would never be finished. Still, she had to blink back tears as she grabbed what was left of Luna's crib and lugged what she could of it down the steps to the dumpster on the driveway. Her sweet child had been in that bed when Asher had pulled her from the fire.

"Have you heard from Mr. Rancher?" Candace said, her voice indistinct behind the cloth.

She shook her head and pulled off her bandanna, using the inside to wipe the sweat off her neck. As much as she loved Candace, she wished her friend hadn't brought him up this time. She'd already stared at the table where they'd shared coffee, the bed where they'd made love. He was as much a ghost in this space as she and Luna were.

"Maybe it was just too much to expect that anything would work out between us in a high-stress situation like the way we met. I'm the former maid's daughter, and he's a prince from the local royal family. We wouldn't even have met if not for a ridiculous claim about switched babies."

Candace pulled off her scarf. "Yep, and you would have gone on hating the Coltons for something most of them had nothing to do with."

"Some things just weren't meant—"

"And neither of you would have found your one true love."

Willow stopped just as she was about to tie on the bandanna again. "You don't believe in all that, do you?"

"Haven't you ever wondered why I never dated in the ten years that Hank has been gone?"

"I thought you weren't ready."

Candace lowered her bag to the ground, pulled off her gloves and flashed the wedding band she always wore. "It's because I'm still married to *my* love."

For several seconds, Willow could only stare at her. "I'm sorry. I didn't realize."

Candace smiled. "Asher Colton might be 'a prince,' as you call him, but I've seen the way he looks at you when he thinks no one is watching. That young man's in love with you. He put guards on your house. He rescued your baby."

Each of her friend's words caused more tears to fill Willow's eyes until they finally spilled over. Candace was crying, too, twin tears forming lines through the soot on her cheeks.

"And if you say you're not in love with him, I'll call you a liar."

Willow wiped her face on the sleeve of her T-shirt. "I am."

"Then the question is, what will you do about it? Are you going to wait for him to come to you?"

Willow tied her scarf back on, grabbed a trash bag and tossed some of her destroyed clothes inside. Was that what she'd been doing? Waiting for him? She'd stared at Candace's front door that whole first night after Luna had been released from the hospital, expecting him to come, at least to check on the baby. But he hadn't, that night or the next.

Was she brave enough to go to him after he'd had time to conclude that being with her and Luna was too much?

She'd waited for him to make the first move, but hadn't he already done that? He'd been trying to tell her how he felt when the fire broke out. He didn't get the chance, but hadn't his sacrifice to save Luna been the best love letter he could have written?

Slowly, Willow lowered the bag to the floor. "Would you mind…?"

Candace grinned. "If we came back to this project tomorrow? I think it can wait a little longer."

"Then I need to do something I never expected to do once, let alone twice. I'm going to the Triple R." Willow grabbed an overstuffed bag and pulled open the door. "Coming?"

Her friend took another bag and followed her.

"Just a suggestion, but you may want to stop by my place first. For a shower."

Asher stared up at the weathered sign posted above the door of Wilson's Buy, Sell & Pawn. The shop closely resembled the six other establishments he'd already visited that morning throughout nearby counties. Even the hitching post on the edge of the parking lot was the same, though, unlike the others, this one had no horses tied to it.

He didn't want to think about how many miles he'd put on his truck to check out his hunch. It had panned out, as he'd already located a few of his mother's necklaces and a pair of his dad's enormous gold cuff links with the initials "P.C." engraved on them.

It wasn't close to enough. He wanted to find Jace.

Catching sight of a park bench in a shaded area opposite from the pawnshop, Asher crossed the street to take a quick break. He twisted open one of the two water bottles he'd purchased from the local pharmacy as he watched the spattering of shoppers move along the strip of mom-and-pop businesses and even an old-fashioned general store. He drained the bottle and wiped his mouth on his sleeve.

Was he ready to admit defeat? He'd been two steps behind Jace all day, and it appeared he would never catch up with him. With all the cash Jace had stolen from Asher's careless family members, he didn't even have to unload all his stolen goods at once. By now, he could have made it to Tombstone or Bisbee or even crossed a border into New Mexico or Mexico.

But as he continued to study the shoppers, something about a young couple carrying several handled shopping bags caught his attention. He couldn't place the blond guy and his redheaded girlfriend, who laughed and appeared to be wrestling over a Western hat, but something about them struck him as familiar. The woman rested her bag on the ground and put the hat back on her partner's head.

Asher knew that hat, with its fancy turquoise conchos and studs. And blond hair or not, the man wearing it was the same one who thought he could take advantage of the Colton family and get away with it. Jace Smith. Asher didn't need to see his grandmother's antique tea set peeking from one of the shopping bags to confirm it.

The temptation to race across the street and wipe that laugh off Jace's face was so strong that Asher crunched the water bottle in his hand. But he'd already been warned to be smart. He couldn't take down two suspects with the bandages on his arms, anyway. Instead, he tipped his own hat down so he wouldn't be recognized, grabbed his phone and tapped on the number he'd dialed several times that morning.

"What city are you in this time?" Spencer asked immediately. "Did you find more of the missing items?"

At least his cousin had given up trying to convince him

to back off and let the authorities take care of the investigation. He wouldn't have listened anyway.

"I'm in Bilmar. I found him."

"Don't go near him."

"I haven't. He and a woman are inside the pawnshop now."

"Did you call Bilmar Police?"

"That's my next move."

"Let me handle it," Spencer said. "Give me your location, and I will call it in."

After Asher passed along the details, the police sergeant gave him one more warning.

"Now stay put and just watch to make sure they don't leave the pawnshop."

"What should I do if they try to leave?"

"Nothing. Just keep me up-to-date. I'm on my way."

Jace and his girlfriend were laughing again as they exited Wilson's, but they froze as they were surrounded by police, weapons drawn. Asher took a little satisfaction in that, even if he hadn't been able to wipe the smiles from their faces himself.

"Stop. Put your hands up. Police," one of the officers called out.

Instead of lifting her arms as Jace had done immediately, the woman shifted and darted out in an escape attempt. Spencer stepped into her path, unarmed.

"I don't think so, Sasha Quick." He grinned at her surprise. "You and Jason Walters, operating under the alias 'Jace Smith,' are both under arrest."

"You don't have anything on me," she said, struggling as a female officer handcuffed her.

"Are you kidding?" Already cuffed and being led to

the patrol car, Jace called over his shoulder. "This was all her idea."

The officer behind him grinned as he recited the Miranda warning to Jace. "Jason Walters, you have a right to remain silent…"

Unable to hold back any longer, Asher rushed over to them.

"Stay back," Spencer warned.

Asher lifted his hands to show he wasn't a threat. "Please, just give me a minute."

Spencer nodded, and the other officers shifted Jace and his girlfriend to face Asher.

"What are *you* doing here?" Jace asked him.

"Just tracking down my long-lost *brother*. The results are in, you know. We're not related."

"Big surprise." Jace lifted his shoulders and lowered them. "Hey, it was a good con. You've got to give me credit for thinking of it after I learned about the forty-year-old baby-switch thing involving that Luella Smith lady. Sure, it was someone else's game, but why should she be the only one to reap the rewards?"

Jace shook his head, chuckling. "And you Coltons were so desperate to find your 'real Ace' that you swallowed my whole story. My idea to use the name 'Jace' was ingenious, if I don't say so myself. Like the new-and-improved Ace."

He glanced down at Asher's fisted hands and grinned.

"You didn't think I really liked your jerk dad or your filthy cattle, did you?"

Asher's stomach tightened as if the guy had just punched him. In many ways, he had, but at least he wouldn't get away with what he'd done to his family.

"Now you take credit for the plan?" Sasha spat at her coconspirator.

"Fine. It was all *her idea* to have me pose as the baby

switched with Ace." He paused to grin at the woman next to him. "She also came up with the plan to call in the phony tip about the current Colton baby, so you'd all be too focused on that to pay any attention to me while I sucked your family dry until the DNA results came back."

"What about the delay at the lab and the repeated test?" Asher asked.

"She had a friend in the lab, too. Isn't that great? But we won't be sharing all our secrets."

"Oh, don't worry. We'd already figured that one out," Spencer said. "We're expecting an arrest by the end of the day."

Asher wasn't sure he wanted to hear the answer, but he had to know one more thing.

"Why did you do it?"

"You probably think it's all about the money," Jace said. "Well, it wasn't. You all deserved everything that happened to you after what one of your former foremen did to my dad, Bill Walters, when he was a cowboy on the Triple R. They drove him to a heart attack."

"I don't remember the name."

"It was before your time, but that doesn't make any of you Coltons less responsible."

Asher swallowed, again feeling bad for actions of those on the Triple R before he was born or had any impact on the ranch decisions. "He survived, didn't he?"

"Yes, but he was never the same after that. They took my father from me. He was just a shell of a man."

"I'm sorry your father was treated badly, but the atmosphere on the ranch is different now. I'm the foreman, and you know I care about the ranch hands as much as I do the animals and the land," Asher said. "No matter what happened, it didn't give you the right to target my family."

His heart squeezed as he remembered how Willow had

as much reason to hate the Coltons as Jace had, but she'd never struck out at them the way he had.

"Oh, hell," Sasha called out. "Could I have found a worse accomplice for this con?"

Jace glanced over at her. "You needed me. I'm the one who got inside. I'm the one who gained everyone's trust enough to have them letting me provide security, like a fox guarding a henhouse."

"And you wouldn't even have known about the game in the first place if I hadn't been forced to do home care for that gabby retired nurse from Mustang Valley." She spoke to Asher. "Does the name Nancy Hersh sound familiar to you?"

He swallowed because it did. Nancy, also known as Nan Gelman, was the nurse Callum had tracked down two months before, hoping she could lead them to Luella Smith. They still hadn't located Luella.

Sasha shifted to the officer holding her by the arm. "So, you see, your guy here has confessed. You might want to uncuff—"

Spencer raised a hand. "Not so fast, Ms. Quick. Besides the charge for receiving stolen goods, you have a rap sheet a mile long with a few outstanding warrants."

He slid a glance to Asher. "I did a little research on Jace Smith and his associates after the first time you called while trying to track down your belongings."

"How did you find so much information so fast?"

"Apparently, these two don't know a lot about facial-recognition software. Successful criminals need to avoid social media." Spencer stepped over to Asher and tapped him with his elbow. "And, for the record, not only freelancers like you happen to be good at this job."

Asher grinned. "I'll remember that."

The Bilmar officer directed Jace toward the patrol

car, but he twisted his head for a parting comment. "You Coltons deserve everything that has happened to you. The bomb threat, though it should have been the real thing. The lost cattle. A fake baby switch. And you'll deserve it, too, if Payne never wakes up."

The fragile control Asher had over his anger snapped, and he barreled forward, his hand fisted and poised for contact. Spencer caught his arm before he reached him.

"I know it would feel great, but he's not worth it." He indicated the other officers. "Also, you might want to think twice about rushing people who are carrying weapons."

"Sorry, guys." Asher waved to the officers and then got in his own parting comment to the suspects before the doors closed. "Enjoy prison."

As the cars pulled away, he turned back to his cousin. "Thanks for meeting me here."

"Just doing my job."

"Going beyond the call, in my opinion. But it's time for me to get back to Mustang Valley. A little girl there is waiting for me. There's also someone else I need to see."

"I'm guessing that 'someone' also has a baby girl at home?"

Asher only smiled and then waved before they headed toward their own vehicles. Now that he'd located Jace, he could think of nothing else except getting back to Willow. He'd given her enough time, enough space. He had to tell her and Luna that something good could come from Jace Smith's arrival in all their lives.

Chapter 27

"Mom, she's gone!"

Asher chased his voice into Genevieve's suite, where she looked up from her book and smiled.

"What are you grinning about? Didn't you hear me? Harper's missing. I've checked everywhere. My room. The kitchen. The family room. Neda doesn't know anything."

He shot a look out the window as if he would find answers there. "Do you think Harper's been abducted?"

Genevieve didn't even rush as she tucked a bookmark inside her book and set it on the table beside her. "Relax. She's with Marlowe right now."

"Marlowe? What's she doing home? And where are they?"

"She took a few hours off from work. She volunteered to watch Harper for a while."

"Well, she just gave me a heart attack, so tell me where she took my daughter."

Her smile was starting to annoy him.

"If I understood her correctly, they're in a tent they built under the deck."

"Marlowe built a tent?"

"With Dulcie's help, I think."

He backed out of his parents' suite and hurried toward the back of the house. Genevieve followed him from the room.

"Wait. You didn't give the rest of the details about Jace's arrest."

Asher paused, shaking his head. He'd given her no more than the basic information from the road, but now wasn't the time to fill in the blanks. He needed to get to his daughter and then to the woman he loved.

"I will later, okay?"

"That's fine."

Still, she followed him as he reached one of the sets of French doors at the back of the house.

"Oh, Asher. Hope you don't mind, but Marlowe brought along a friend or two."

He drew his brows together and then stepped outside. In the shady end beneath the second-story deck, a play tent had been made of old quilts thrown over a nylon rope, anchored between two six-by-six posts. That the structure wasn't collapsing over its inhabitants signaled that his sister must have received help in building it. Dulcie apparently had skills with play tent construction, as well.

"Marlowe, are you in there?"

A loose flap of material moved. His sister emerged, stooped over, before she straightened.

"What is all this?" he couldn't help asking.

"Just getting a little practice for my own upcoming event." She grinned and settled her hands on her rounded stomach. "And having a little playdate."

As if responding to her comment, the side of the make-shift structure rippled with movement from inside. The squeal that joined it sounded strange to him. Not like Harper at all.

"Was this your idea?"

"Not really." She pulled the flap farther open for him. "Come inside."

As he bent to enter the tent, several things suddenly made sense. His mother's knowing smile and hovering. His sister's uncharacteristic choice of activity. Even the happy-baby *cheep* that hadn't sounded like his child.

Not one but two infants scooted around on the blankets covering the cement slab, and just beyond them, sitting cross-legged, was the woman he'd been dying to see.

"Hello."

Her voice squeaked when she spoke. He could relate to her nervousness. His hands were so sweaty that he had to wipe them off on his jeans.

"What are you doing here?"

This time she smiled. "Didn't you hear? We're in our tent, having a playdate."

"I mean why are you *here*? On the Triple R?"

"We came to see you two."

"And how long have you been here?"

"Two hours or so."

As their gazes connected, his heart thudded in his chest. She'd not only come to see him, but she'd *waited* for him. Another delighted squeal, this one from his own child, split the silence. Like always, Harper reached out her arms to him.

"Your baby wants you to join us." Willow's tongue darted out to dampen her lips. "I do, too."

Asher glanced back at his grinning sister as he slid off his boots. "You coming in?"

Marlowe shook her head, holding back a smile. "It's getting a little crowded in there. I will go and get some lemonade, though."

Good thing since his mouth was dry as he scooted inside, settled with his legs crossed as Willow's were and reached for Harper.

"Your sister told me what you found out about Jace. I'm sorry about that."

He shook his head. "I'm just sorry you got caught up in the mess."

"It's okay. How are your arms?"

He glanced down at the bandages. "They're fine. Looks like we all are."

Luna was busy scooting her way over to him. When she climbed up on his leg, he lifted her to sit next to Harper and then ran his fingers through each girl's hair by turns.

"She liked you from the start." Willow pointed to her daughter.

"What can I say? You have a smart baby."

"She also was right about you."

He'd wanted to hear words like those from her, but now he found them unsettling. Had she come to him only because he'd rescued her child?

"I don't want you to feel beholden to me about Luna. In different circumstances, you would have done the same thing for Harper."

Willow shifted. This wasn't going the way she'd planned it at all. She needed to make him understand.

"I'm grateful to you, but if you think that's why I'm here, then you've got it all wrong. I came to you because—"

"Lemonade," Marlowe called out from outside the tent.

"Lousy timing."

At his whispered words, Willow grinned.

Instead of Asher's sister, Genevieve crouched outside

the tent entry. "We also thought two little girls might need diaper changes."

"Good idea," he said.

Genevieve reached in, and he handed Harper out to her. Marlowe set the tray with a pitcher of lemonade and two glasses on the cement outside the tent before her mother passed off the first baby to her. Then Asher shifted Luna into Genevieve's arms.

With a few chuckles, the two women were gone.

Asher shook his head. "I can't believe we were interrupted. *Again.*"

"I'm hoping we'll have the chance to get used to interruptions. Big ones. Tiny ones. Hundreds of funny, sometimes annoying disruptions."

"What are you saying?"

"That it's something the parents of two infants—nearly twins—would have to deal with regularly."

He cleared his throat. "Two?"

Willow nodded and gripped her hands together. She could do this. "So, before we're interrupted again, I want to tell you that I came because… I'm in love with you."

He opened his mouth to say something, but she couldn't give him the chance to reject her until she'd said everything in her heart.

"Maybe we never should have met. We wouldn't have, if not for a pair of grifters. You're a Colton, for goodness' sake." She chuckled, but tears filled her eyes. "I'm not sorry. And I won't be no matter what happens. Luna and I will be okay, but I did this for me. Loving you… It was worth it."

She stared down at her hands and waited, a lump forming in her throat. It was so quiet in the tent that the sound of her own tight breathing filled her ears. Her heart squeezed.

Well, at least she'd taken her shot. She'd had to know the truth.

"We were interrupted the night of the fire, too."

She swallowed. "Yeah, I guess we were."

"I told you I wanted you."

"I remember that." She recalled how much it hurt, too.

"Well, I was trying to say that I want *you*. All of you."

He leaned forward and took her clasped hands between his. "Willow, I'm in love with you, too."

She wasn't sure which one of them moved first, but suddenly his lips were on hers, and she was melting into him. Her fingers slid from between his hands, and they snaked up over his shoulders to nestle in the hair at his nape.

Gentle, warm kisses deepened, and she found herself trying to climb into him, both coming up on their knees. This was what she'd always been looking for. Him. She fit herself to him, wanting more, needing more and losing her ability to care that they were inside a play tent.

Finally, he sat back again. "I don't know about you, but my knees are killing me. And since I was about to peel your clothes off in a place where our daughters might one day have tea parties together…"

She chuckled as she sat back, this time stretching out her sore legs. "Yeah, me, too."

Again, he reached for her hands.

"I know I've asked you this before." He hesitated, clearing his throat. "Twice. And then I took the offer back when you said yes. But there's a question I'd like to ask."

"Go ahead." She wasn't sure how she'd even pushed the words past the lump clogging her throat. This was what she'd waited for, and it was finally here.

"Marry me, Willow. Not because it makes sense that we should be together to raise our beautiful girls, though it absolutely does. And not because we're so compatible in bed."

Asher paused to trace his gaze over her like a caress that began at her scalp and ended at her pointed toes. When she shivered, he grinned.

"Though that's true, too. We know the difference between real and fake now, and what we have is real. Be my wife because you love me as much as I love you." He licked his lips and stared into her eyes. "Well?"

"Yes. And don't you ever take that offer back."

She leaned in and kissed him again and again.

He gasped for breath. "I want to adopt Luna, too, and, if you're willing, I'd like you to adopt Harper."

"I want to do that, too. I'll love your daughter as if she's my own."

He started to kiss her again.

"Wait. I want you to know that I don't mind if you choose to keep your last name since I know you've had a problem with mine. Do whatever makes you happy."

"You make me happy, and I now associate that name with you, so I'll be happy to be a Colton."

A smile spread on his lips.

"Oh. One more thing. There were two more times when you were interrupted. After the fire and at the hospital. Both times, I think you were talking about me, and each time you said 'my' and stopped. What did you almost say?"

She smiled. "Oh, that's easy. Both times, it was the same, but I wasn't ready to say it yet. My *love*."

His eyes appeared extra shiny before they closed, so he could press his lips to hers once more.

Someone outside the tent cleared her throat.

"Speaking of interruptions."

He pulled away and then backed out of the tent. She followed him out.

Her cheeks burned as she found Genevieve and Marlowe sitting on the outdoor sofa, holding Asher's daughter and hers. The tray of lemonade had been relocated to the table next to where they sat. The two women tittered, possessors of an inside joke.

"It's good to see you both again."

Marlowe patted her own hair in a hint that Willow might need to check hers. She could only imagine what her mouth looked like when her lips tingled, having been thoroughly kissed.

"How long have you two been out here?" Asher wanted to know.

"Long enough to go to the safe and bring back this." Genevieve held out a tiny jewelry box.

Willow didn't even want to think about what else her future in-laws had overheard.

"Great-grandma Mays's ring?" He tilted his head to the side. "Wait. You never gave that to me when I asked…"

He didn't mention Nora's name, but his mother still shook her head.

"She wasn't *The One*."

Asher rolled his lips inward and nodded before crossing to his mother, leaning over to accept the box from her hand and kiss her cheek. Then he carried it back to Willow but didn't open it.

"My mother's parents weren't wealthy, but since I'm Mom's oldest son, the ring was supposed to come to me. You don't have to wear this if you don't want to, though. We can ride downtown and pick out a different stone for you. As big as you want." He made as if to put the box in his jeans pocket.

"Am I going to get to see it?"

"Oh. Right."

He held the box out to her and flipped it open. A small

solitaire diamond in a white-gold setting with tiny twin baguettes on either side stared up at her.

"It's perfect."

Asher grinned, his cheeks filling with color, as he withdrew the slim ring from the box. "If it doesn't fit or you don't like it when you have it on—"

"Asher, can we try it already?"

He nodded and held it to the tip of her finger. "Last chance. Still want to marry me?"

"Absolutely. Now put it on me before you try to take back your offer again."

He slid it over her knuckle, and both were surprised to find that it fit perfectly. She stared down at her hand.

"I love it."

Asher put his arm around her and faced his mother, sister and the two infants. "I would like to present my fiancée, Willow Merrill."

The two women clapped, and to everyone's surprise, Luna clapped twice, as well. Harper looked over at the infant who was soon to be her sister, and she mimicked her action, touching her hands together three times.

Asher and Willow stared at each other.

"Guess all that practice with patty-cake paid off," he said. "Those two will probably always be competing to see who reaches each milestone first."

Genevieve stood up from the sofa and carried Luna over to them. "That will be a lot of fun for the both of you when these beautiful girls of yours want to start dating."

Asher's hands immediately went to his head. "Oh. Don't tell me that."

The women on the porch got a laugh out of that one at his expense. The two babies, who'd just learned a new skill, laughed, too, and kept right on clapping. Their mom and dad were going to make them a family, after all.

Chapter 28

Asher couldn't stop smiling as he forked an ear of corn on the cob at his family's picnic beneath the retractable awning on the mansion's deck. He passed the tray to Willow. His *fiancée*. He liked the sound of that. Behind his left shoulder and behind Willow's right one at the long wood table, they'd parked high chairs where Luna and Harper sat pushing Os cereal around on the trays. Their *daughters*. He liked the sound of that, too.

Ainsley stood and lifted her wineglass. "Here's to these soon-to-be Coltons, Willow and Luna."

"Welcome, Willow and Luna," the others said in unison. They all clinked their glasses, some filled with wine, some with water or apple juice.

Willow lifted her glass again. "Thanks for the welcome."

The table was more crowded than usual, with all his siblings in attendance, plus brides- and grooms-to-be for all those who'd become engaged. Bowie was there with Marlowe, Kerry with Rafe and Savannah with Grayson. Hazel and little Evie were attending with Callum.

Payne's absence was still deeply felt and marked with his empty chair, despite a tight fit around the rest of the table, but Ace's absence hurt more that day, as well. How easily they'd all been willing to replace him with someone who possibly shared their DNA. Asher decided he would have to remember to call him.

"Do you guys always eat like this?" Willow asked as she added a small serving of potato salad next to her kabob and baked beans. "I've barely taken a bite, and I'm wishing I had an elastic waistband on my shorts."

"Are you picking on Dulcie's cooking?" Grayson said. "I'd definitely try it first."

Willow took a bite of the secret-recipe potato salad and then closed her eyes while she chewed. After she swallowed, she opened her eyes and wiped her mouth on a napkin.

Bowie pointed to her plate. "Well?"

Willow grinned. "Looks like I'd better buy some bigger pants because this stuff is worth every bite."

A phone rang at the table again, and this time Marlowe lifted her hands to announce her innocence. Finally, Asher pulled his cell from his pocket.

"Sorry, Mom, but I have to take this one. It's Spencer."

Ainsley leaned forward over the table. "He's calling *you* now. I thought he was supposed to come to me first."

He shrugged. "It's probably about the plan I told you all about. Just give me a minute. I'll let you know what he has to say."

Asher hurried down the deck steps and had a short conversation with his cousin. Then he returned to the table.

Callum was the first to speak up.

"All right. Give it to us. We're a family. We can handle it together."

"Yeah, tell us," Marlowe called out.

Asher held up his hands before they all chimed in. "The plan is a go. Spencer said the trail has gone cold, so he's given the go-ahead to flush the suspect out."

Rafe nodded. "Maybe this is the right thing to do. If the shooter thinks Payne is showing signs of recovery, he'll have to come after him."

"And then he's ours." Grayson held his hands wide. "I mean the decoy cop's."

Ainsley leaned on her elbows. "When does this thing go down?"

"The first week of June," Asher told them.

Willow cleared her throat. "Are you okay with all this, Genevieve?"

Immediately, they all glanced to the far end of the table, where Genevieve sat, hugging herself as if she was freezing.

"Are you, Mom?" Asher said. "We've already talked about this. You agreed."

Genevieve shook her head. "What if I was wrong? What if we all were?"

"He'll be safe, Mom," Callum assured her. "We promise. He won't even be there."

"Well, remember, he might be your father, but Payne is my life. If something happens to him…" She blew out a breath. "We can't let anything happen to him."

Genevieve excused herself, and the party fizzled soon after.

As the brothers, sisters and their significant others worked together to clear away the meal, Asher couldn't help watching them. This was his family, the people he loved. Someone was targeting all of them, not just their father. Until they figured out who was behind the shooting and all the mysteries, none of them would ever be safe. None would ever be able to live their lives without looking over their shoulders.

Was it the wrong time for him to invite Willow and Luna into the murky mix of their lives? Probably. But he could no more live his life without her than his mother could give up hope that his dad would awaken soon and come back to her.

His whole family was sick of living in fear. Whoever was coming after them would not be allowed to win. They were the Coltons, and they were ready to fight back.

* * * * *

WE HOPE YOU ENJOYED
THIS BOOK FROM

HARLEQUIN
ROMANTIC SUSPENSE

Danger. Passion. Drama.

These heart-racing page-turners will keep you guessing to the very end. Experience the thrill of unexpected plot twists and irresistible chemistry.

4 NEW BOOKS AVAILABLE EVERY MONTH!

#2083 COLTON'S DEADLY DISGUISE
The Coltons of Mustang Valley • by Geri Krotow

FBI agent Holden St. Clair and local reporter Isabella Colton distrust one another for good reason. But long days and hot nights searching for a serial killer prove they can share more than chemistry—if they survive.

#2084 COLTON COWBOY JEOPARDY
The Coltons of Mustang Valley • by Regan Black

Mia Graves and her child are under threat when Jarvis Colton finds them on his family's stolen ranch. They both need help—but their teaming up could risk more than just their physical safety.

#2085 SNOWBOUND TARGETS
by Karen Whiddon

When a mysterious woman with no memory and very good self-defense skills appears in his remote cabin, war correspondent Jason Sheffield tries to help her. But her mind holds the key to more than just her own past and uncovering what she knows could have deadly consequences.

#2086 BODYGUARD BOYFRIEND
Bachelor Bodyguards • by Lisa Childs

A street-smart bodyguard and a spoiled socialite have nothing in common. Until her father's position as a judge over a major drug lord's trial puts Bella Holmes in danger and Tyce Jackson is the bodyguard assigned to her case. He's only pretending to be her boyfriend, but as bullets fly, emotions run higher than ever!

"I'm sorry," he murmured, his voice gruff.

She furrowed her brow as she stared up at him. "Sorry
for what? I appreciate that you took me to look for the
jewelry."

"I'm sorry we didn't find it," he replied.

A wistful sigh slipped through her lips. She wished
they'd had, but Tyce had warned her that they might
never recover it.

"You didn't think we would," she reminded him.
"Why not?"

"Because I'm not sure that someone took it to make
money off it."

"Then why else would they have stolen it?"

"To hurt you."

Thinking of that, of someone wanting to hurt her, had
a twinge of pain hitting her heart. But she shook her head.

"Nobody wants to hurt me."

"Luther Mills."

"From what you and Daddy have said about him, stealing jewelry doesn't sound like something he would have someone do for him."

"No, it doesn't," he agreed.

"So you think someone else wants to hurt me?" She shivered at the horrific thought. She was careful to always be nice to everyone. Even Michael had not been that upset when she'd ended their arrangement.

Could someone want to hurt her, though?

Tyce stepped closer to her and touched her chin, tipping her face up to his. "I won't let anything happen to you," he said. "Don't worry."

She was worried about him hurting her—because she'd never been as attracted to anyone as she was to Tyce. She felt so incredibly drawn to him that she found herself rising up on tiptoe and leaning toward him.

When her breasts bumped into his massive chest, a jolt of heat and desire rushed through her. She wanted him so badly.

He tensed and stared down at her. His startling topaz eyes turned dark. With desire?

Did he feel it, too?

Don't miss
Bodyguard Boyfriend *by Lisa Childs*
available April 2020 wherever
Harlequin Romantic Suspense
books and ebooks are sold.

Harlequin.com

SPECIAL EXCERPT FROM

▶ mira

The town of Baywood is on edge after a series of bizarre murders. Detectives A.L. McKittridge and Rena Morgan will stop at nothing to catch this elusive killer before he strikes again...

Keep reading for a sneak peek at
Ten Days Gone *by Beverly Long.*

A.L. rode shotgun while Rena drove. He liked to look around, study the landscape. Jane Picus had lived within the city limits of Baywood. The fifty-thousand-person city bordered the third-largest lake in west-central Wisconsin, almost halfway between Madison and Eau Claire. While the town was generally peaceful, that many people in a square radius of thirteen miles could do some damage to one another. Add in the weekend boaters, who were regularly overserved, and the Baywood Police Department dealt with the usual assortment of crime. Burglary. Battery. Drugs. The occasional arson.

And murder. There had been two the previous year. One was a family dispute, and the killer had been quickly apprehended. The other was a workplace shooter who'd turned the gun on himself after killing his boss. Neither had been pleasant, but they hadn't shaken people's belief that Baywood was a good place to live and raise a family. People were happy when their biggest complaint was about the size of the mosquitoes.

Now for-sale signs were popping up in yards. There would likely be more by next week. Four unsolved murders in forty days was bad. Bad for tourism, bad for police morale and certainly bad for the poor women and their families.

In less than ten minutes, they were downtown. Brick sidewalks bordered both sides of Main Street for a full six blocks. Window boxes, courtesy of the garden club, were overflowing with petunias. The police department had moved to its new building in the three-hundreds block over ten years ago. Even then, it hadn't been new, but the good citizens of Baywood had voted to put some money into the sixty-year-old former department store. There was too much glass for A.L.'s comfort on the first floor and too little air-conditioning on the second and third. But it beat the hell out of working in the factory at the edge of town.

Which was where his father and his uncle Joe still worked. The McKittridge brothers. They'd been born and raised in Baywood, raised their own families there and had never left.

A.L. had sworn that wouldn't be his life. Yet here he was.

Because of Traci. His sixteen-year-old daughter.

Don't miss Ten Days Gone *by Beverly Long,*
available February 18, 2020 wherever
MIRA books and ebooks are sold.

MIRABooks.com